THE WIZARDS ON WALNUT STREET

Sam Swicegood

Dragon Street Press
-
Cincinnati, OH

Copyright © 2018 Sam Swicegood
All rights reserved.

All rights reserved. No part of this publication may be reproduced, distributed, or transmitted in any form or by any means, including photocopying, recording, or other electronic or mechanical methods, without the prior written permission of the publisher, except in the case of brief quotations embodied in critical reviews and certain other noncommercial uses permitted by copyright law. For permission requests, write to the publisher, addressed "Attention: Permissions Coordinator," at the address below.

Elsewhere Media Limited
PO Box 12106
Cincinnati, OH 45229

Ordering Information: Quantity sales. Special discounts are available on quantity purchases by corporations, associations, and others. For details, contact the publisher at the address above.

Orders by U.S. trade bookstores and wholesalers. Please contact Elsewhere Media Ltd at (607) 4-GAMES-4 or (607) 442 6374; or visit www.dragonstreet.press for further information.

This is a work of fiction. Names, characters, businesses, places, events, locales, and incidents are either the products of the author's imagination or used in a fictitious manner. Any resemblance to actual persons, living or dead, or actual events is purely coincidental. Also, wizards don't exist. At least that's what the Dragon of Cincinnati told me to print here.

Printed in the United States of America

First Edition
1 3 5 7 6 4 2

ISBN: 0692129669
ISBN-13: 978-0692129661

To Mom
who taught me that finishing a book is a journey
not a destination

EXIT INTERVIEW

Bolts of lightning, as it turned out, did not tickle.

Tom had wondered about that more than once throughout his career, watching them flash and flow freely out the tip of more than one aggravated wizard's wand. He had watched the bright flashes that stunned and elicited everything from a surprised yelp to a groan of defeat. Once, it had brought an embarrassed string of curse words, as the target fell, paralyzed, backwards into a portable toilet.

Lightning was, however, effective. It was one of the only offensive spells sanctioned for regular use in Cincinnati, due to its low potential for lethality. Tom had used it many times to stop would-be thieves thinking that a trip into a massive magic vault might garner them fame or fortune, only to find out that Tom was too brilliant and clever, and even if the massive assortments of sorcerous defenses failed, there was always a trusty lightning bolt to stop a bad guy in his tracks. From his perspective, though, the lightning bolt emitted only a mild buzzing sound and left his fingers tingly, with the hair standing on end. He wondered, sometimes, what it felt like to be hit with it, since his Employee Handbook described the effects as "mostly painless, I would wager." Had no one actually tested that theory?

Obviously not. The crackle of lightning felt like his back was being split open, and it took all of his strength and determination to wrench open the door to his condominium building and throw himself inside. There, he crashed to the ground in a sweat, shaking as the door clicked shut behind him. He was safe now—the protective wards across the threshold of the building would keep any intruder at bay…for a while at least. Just enough time to catch his breath and start to pack.

He would have to leave, now that he had been discovered.

How had it gotten this bad? Everything seemed to be working perfectly. No disruptions in his normal workday. No strange emails, no odd memos. There was utterly no sign anywhere of someone doing something devious. Had he missed a signal somewhere? Well, he had no time to reflect. He would have to get up and start a new plan to get out of the city before his pursuers could figure out a way to get past the wards. He had a little time, so long as none of them had gotten inside yet—

"Get up, Tom."

He snapped his eyes open to find himself face-to-face with a black, inky-looking canine with bared teeth. He did as he was told, rolling onto his stomach and slowly pushing himself up to a standing position. "What are you doing here? You aren't supposed to be here."

"Special assignment," it said gruffly, sitting back on its haunches and fixing the man with its glowing blue eyes. "You've got yerself in a bit o' a pickle, haven' ya."

"Yeah," He said, running his fingers through his hair. Had he lost his hat? Dammit, that was a nice hat. "But I can fix it. I know how to fix all this. I just need to go upstairs."

"Not goin' anywhere, for the moment," the dog said. "Unfortunately, they're already upstairs. So, here's how it's going to go."

"Wait, they're here already?" Tom choked out the words and stumbled backwards toward the door. "They're gonna kill—"

"Maybe, but that's not my business, now is it?" the dog snapped back. "I don' care what they've planned out, and I ain't here to get you out of it. I'm just here to observe, as usual."

Tom took a deep breath. "Can I get a last…request or something?"

"If it's something like a cigarette, then sure. If yer wanting a steak dinner, well…I've never been a good cook. Maybe I could whip up a bowl of cereal. Or a bag o' chips."

Tom chuckled and pulled out a stick of gum from his pocket and unwrapped it. "No, nothing like that. Just…a couple minutes to relax. I haven't really had that in years." Popping the gum in his mouth he took a seat behind the dog on one of the lobby benches.

"Can't stall too long. They're waitin'." The dog hopped up on the bench next to him and curled up with its head in his lap.

Tom petted the matted fur gently with his hand. "I had a good run. Did a lot of good things. Made some mistakes."

"Regrets don' help nobody when the end comes,

now do they? Regrets are just broken promises you made to yourself."

"Remember that time we chased trolls out of the fountain downtown? God…I smelled like bilge water for weeks. I regretted that."

"Never noticed. But maybe I was busy getting sick after biting one on the arse. Regretted that."

Tom grinned and leaned his head back. "Eh, you didn't notice because you smell far worse."

The dog let out a deep laugh. "Well, that's true."

They sat quietly for a short while, until the sugar in Tom's gum had begun to fade. "So, what now?"

"Well, I figure they'll come down those stairs any minute now. Might want to get tha' wand o' yours out and ready." The dog hopped off the bench and trotted over to a corner.

Tom stood up, brushing off his coat and pulling a dark wooden rod from his jacket. "Okay. They've got me outnumbered and outgunned. But," he added as the dog sat down and seemed to blend into the shadows, "I am probably the best Wizard this city has ever seen. Think I can take them?"

The dog shrugged and faded from sight. "Anything's possible."

Tom took a deep breath as the elevator door at the top of the stairs lit up and the doors began to open. "Yes," he said quietly as lightning crackled in his wand, "Anything is possible."

THE WIZARDS ON WALNUT STREET

CHAPTER 1

I first met them at Dad's funeral. Of course, I had no idea who, or what, they were at the time, but they arrived in droves. Crisp black suits and ties, without a single decoration or distinguishing feature to adorn them, they arrived all separately and did practically the same thing while I watched them with suspicion. Each one headed to the casket and seemed to analyze the still figure lying there as though looking for something. Whatever it was, they did not find it, for each of them turned and passed to the back of the room, to sit in the last few pews of the church like a black mass in the back that seemed to be of one single mind and body.

As the service started, I will admit, I didn't grieve. If I tried to pinpoint exactly why now, I wouldn't be able to; but I think that I simply didn't have the energy or the will to let myself grieve just yet. There was too much to take care of first. Too much paperwork to do, people to see, and things to pack away. There was a whole condominium in need of organization, and apparently, I had been left the two-bedroom property in Dad's will along with all its contents. All in all, I felt justified in my stoic existence, powering through the emotions in my stomach as the pastor read out words of comfort.

I have never liked funerals. Not just for the obvious reason of someone having died, but because no one seems to really know how to react. Sometimes funerals are a welcome relief from pain. Sometimes they are a massive burden on loved ones. Sometimes they are expected and sometimes they are sudden. But no one, in my opinion, really knows *how* to have a funeral. They just play it by ear and hope that someone, somewhere, gets closure and comfort in the face of mortality.

I recall that I took my turn at the podium, and the words that came from my mouth were carefully chosen and rehearsed; the last thing I needed was an anxiety attack to fall on top of everything else. But to be honest I don't remember exactly what it was that I said up there. I do remember that as I looked out and saw that black conglomeration of suits in the back of the room I was taken aback momentarily and had to swallow a lump in my throat before proceeding. They were a disturbing sight, like a void where people should be.

One of them took a turn at the podium as well. I hadn't expected this, but when one of them appeared in front of the microphone I was overcome with a strange sense of misplacement, as though the context for this man himself was not right. As though he, whoever he was, should truly be anywhere but here, and that the world was somehow wrong for his presence in this faded church.

"Tom was an asset," He began with a voice that seemed to fill and permeate the still air and demand attention. "He was the kind of man you could trust to have your back and keep you in line. Never erring from his principles, never deviating from his vision. There are places in this world that will be the less for his absence, and on behalf of all of *us*," he said, and his eyes swept the back of the room as though to lasso them all into a single conjoined entity, "I express my most heartfelt sympathies." He looked over at the casket.

He said something then that resonates with me to this day. It was soft, and his face was turned from the microphone. I don't know if anyone else in the room heard it, but from where I was I could make the words out quite clearly, and I could not get them out of my mind. "We'll get them back for what they did."

Few in the room would have understood the depth of those words had they been heard. Only a few people had known that Dad had been murdered, and so when I heard it I was stunned. I stared at the man as he got near me and reached out to stop him as he came into arm's reach. "Hey—"

He stopped and looked at me. "Hi. Andy, right?"

I nodded. "What did you—"

"Later." He gave me a very warm smile and walked off, leaving me frustrated and confused. I took my seat and returned my attention to the next speaker, but his words remained in the back of my mind and begged my curiosity to sate it. The moment the service was over I rose from my chair and walked toward the back, but the entire company of suits had slithered away while I wasn't looking and had disappeared. I asked mom who those people were. "Some of his work colleagues, I think."

I met them again when I went to check out my dad's condo. Well, it was my condo now, technically, but I hadn't really come to terms with that fact just yet.

I had never seen where Dad had lived. His visits to Washington had always been on my Mother's terms, and I never went to visit him in Cincinnati. Mom insisted that our visits were always supervised, and any attempts to convince her otherwise would lead to a long diatribe about how I clearly didn't love her and just wanted to run away and be with Dad. To be honest, a part of me would gladly agree with her, but that wasn't a fight I was planning on having anytime soon. Besides, Dad was a very busy man and I couldn't imagine that trying to live in a house with a mostly-absentee parent would be much healthier than living with a narcissistic one.

When I found the door open I wondered if my Mom had gotten a key of her own and decided to show up first. But the truth was far more disturbing—the people in suits were there, packing all my Dad's things up into tidy boxes. They were in every room, touching and moving everything. Even the furniture. In my head I imagined the walls and floor covered in fingerprints, and I had to shake the anxious feeling from where it was trying to lodge itself in the folds of my brain in an exceptionally unwelcome manner.

The one who spoke at the funeral was there and met me at the door. "Hello, Andy. Sorry, we weren't expecting you so soon. We're doing some cleanup here for you." He seemed sincere and I swallowed my reactive anger, resisting the urge to begin screaming at them all to get out.

"What kind of cleanup?"

"Your dad, you know, he worked really hard. Brought a lot of work home. We're collecting all those documents, so you don't have to sort through them."

"What about the furniture? And everything else?"

He shrugged. "There's not much else, really. Your dad lived pretty minimalist. But your…let me see." He checked his phone. "Your mom, right? She told us that it was her wishes as executor to have all of the furniture disposed of."

Oh, of course. Mom had taken control of the whole situation just as I knew she would. She just had to have her fingers in every pie, didn't she?

I sighed heavily, knowing it would be another fight if I talked to her about it, so I decided not to bother. "Right. Fine. Hey, while I've got you here…" I tried to formulate the words. "You seem to have known my dad pretty well. What…what can you tell me about him?"

The man opened his mouth to speak but then appeared to think better of his initial response. He considered me for a moment and then spoke in a way that seemed very deliberate. "Do you know what kind of work your dad did?"

I shook my head.

That seemed to satisfy him. "He worked for a consulting firm," the man said in such a practiced tone that I was pretty sure it was a go-to response of some kind. "If you want to learn some more, well...here." He handed over a business card, and I realized that the suited people had disappeared out the door behind me, leaving the condo entirely quiet and empty. He gave me a reassuring pat on the shoulder and then followed suit, leaving me standing, alone, in an unfamiliar city, with far more questions than I needed, and one less dad than I wanted.

Researching the firm had been relatively easy. The business card I'd been given included a web site, which I had spent an afternoon perusing and making notes. It seemed to be entirely above-board, its fancy serif writing at the top spelling out "50 Thousand Consulting" in gold letters bordered by a black tessellated box. "Committed to Success and Lasting Results," the headline read. Beneath that, in purple, the company touted itself as "one of the world's largest alternative consulting firms" with "a global team that aligns our interests with those of our clients."

The pictures didn't give much clue either to the mystery of what exactly this company did. A group of men and women in suits applauding under a shower of confetti, a picture of the Cincinnati skyline at night, a shot of a busy street filled with people...all high-quality stock footage that proved to be utterly useless in deciphering the code.

Speaking of code, the site's HTML was similarly unhelpful. A basic, out-of-the-box stylesheet and not a single commented line, the best I could decipher was that the person making the site was far too addicted to JavaScript and that there was probably some poor technical support guy who was getting java error calls all day because of how poorly it was built.

In the end, I almost dropped the whole thing until I spotted a tiny "Careers" button near the bottom that caught my attention. A few clicks later I saw that the company was going through a hiring rotation for co-ops.

"Potential hires must have the following," it read, "(a) an Associate Degree or higher, (b) three or more years of experience in an office environment, (c) a strong desire to learn and a devotion to making people's lives better." It went on to include that such an esteemed person should be able to lift 60 pounds and communicate well by email, because why would someone be good at helping others and yet lack basic computer skills?

After considering that I met nearly all the requirements, I briefly considered my life back in D.C. A life full of guilt trips and narcissistic family members…and I don't think I need to explain the plight of a poor college-age kid in America to get the point across that leaving it behind wouldn't be the worst idea in the world.

I booted up my resume and started the application process.

I had gotten my call a few days after sending in my application, and a notice of my scheduled interview with the company followed in the mail. I was directed to show up with a pencil, paper, and several copies of my resume. I was also directed to bring "Nothing made of silver, or silver alloy, including jewelry.[1]" Armed with my best business-casual outfit and having succeeded in finding a parking space that cost less than $4 a day, I made my way to Downtown Cincinnati in search of the address in the email.

The Queen City, I had to admit, had a certain charm about it, in the semi-Germanic architecture and the way that the homeless people seemed to space themselves out so that you could catch your breath after dealing with one before the next one came along. I was particularly impressed with the Gothic architecture of many of the older buildings, and I mused to myself how much Cincinnati's town hall looked like a vampire's castle from a horror movie.

Finally, on Eighth Street, I found the address, and I double-checked the email on my phone to be sure. The place was a coffee shop, and a small and dingy one at that; I furrowed my eyebrows together and started toward the door, terribly confused. A multi-billion-dollar firm, and it was holding its interviews here? Something was amiss for sure.

Inside, the warm smell of coffee and cinnamon hit my nose and I couldn't help but stop and breathe it in. The mild chill outside had been unexpected

---

[1] "Potential employees who have silver as part of a medical bone prosthesis, orthopedic reconstructive surgery, or cardiac device should inform the recruiter ahead of time. Potential employees who imbibe colloidal silver as part of a homeopathic remedy should stay home and rethink their lives." - 50 Thousand recruitment interview letter, Page 2

(And, having not been warned of Ohio weather, I didn't realize that the daily forecast could simply be summed up as "subject to change") but within this shop it was a cozy and inviting bubble of quiet contemplation. A few people dotted the small tables and I intentionally paid them no mind—because the last thing I needed was to be caught ogling some hipster with his decaf soy vegan no-foam skinny latte—and confidently strode up to the counter with a smile on my face.

Behind the bar was a single barista, finishing a single pull of an espresso shot for another patron. His skin was the color of the coffee he pulled, and his hair, hanging around his face in loose dreadlocks, swayed slightly as he practically danced to the groove of the coffee-brewing experience. I must admit that my romantic preference has always swayed towards women, but at the moment I found myself entranced as if under a spell, and I couldn't help but get caught up in the moment of the sculpted man's grace and elegance as he served the coffee and returned to the register. Now, he was saying something, and his voice was deep and rich, and his eyebrows were furrowed slightly. It took me a moment to realize he had just asked me for my order and I was standing there like a fool.

"Oh. Um." I dismissed my smoldering thoughts and composed myself. "I have an appointment for an interview, and I thought it was here—"

He held up a hand to stop me with a smile. "Of course," he said. "Have a seat over there while you wait. Can I get you a water or a coffee on the house?" I shook myself mentally—the spell had appeared to have worn off.

"Yes please." I seemed to have rediscovered my voice. "I guess they do a lot of interviews here?"

"All of them. Nice, relaxing place. Good for morale." He picked up a coffee cup. "What's the name I'm putting on here?"

"Andy." I looked around and didn't feel compelled to stare anymore, as though a spell had been lifted; I focused again on my interview which was due to start in—I checked the clock on my phone—fifteen minutes. I took the coffee and glanced at the barista's name badge. "Thanks, Apollo."

"Don't be a stranger," he said with a wink, and then turned his attention to the next person in line. I turned and considered the size and shape of the coffee shop, wondering if I needed to sit somewhere specifically. A few of the spots offered better light, or a slightly more open spot that probably would be more comfortable to interview in. I looked back and forth between a few before selecting my seat and waiting patiently.

My wait was not long; a few minutes went by before I was joined at the table by a short, scornful-looking woman with long grey curls, one of which draped lazily down her face. Her expression gave the immediate impression of someone who had been denied coffee this morning and possible had needed to cover up a murder or two.[2]

---

[2] "At 50 Thousand Consulting, we recognize the important role coffee plays in most of your daily lives. With that in mind, we highly encourage you to take advantage of our Caffeine Assistance Program, which is a company-funded spend account usable at any of the many coffee shops in Cincinnati.

"Andy...LaFayette." The woman leered down at her leather-bound notepad and spend an agonizing moment reviewing her notes. I tried my best to put forward an appearance of patience and complete presence of mind, but underneath I was roiling with massive amounts of nervousness that I couldn't shake off. I still had no idea what this firm did, what my job would be, or even if I would be able to do the work. I only kept hoping, relying on my strong façade of confidence.

It was impossible to know if it worked. The woman, whose name I don't think I ever even asked, and who only more sour as the moments wore on, started down the lists on my resume. The Maryland schools I had gone to and the college where I got my associate degree. The classes I had taken at a four-year college that, ultimately, I had not completed. My first jobs, my more recent jobs...nothing particularly notable. This was far from my first job interview but something about the way the questions were asked unnerved me beyond measure; as though the woman was peering into my very soul and trying to pry deep, real answers from beneath the surface.

Furthermore, we should iterate that coffee is very important, and anyone attempting to deliberately prevent an employee from obtaining it should expect to receive disciplinary action. This is especially true for the hard-working Human Resources employees, such as the one who wrote this. You hear me, Carol? If I haven't gotten my coffee yet, then leave me the hell alone. And if you do it again, I will pull you into my office and fire you myself and when you sob and ask why, I will point at THIS paragraph and laugh in your stupid face, okay Carol? DON'T SCREW WITH ME, CAROL." - 50 Thousand Employee Handbook, page 130

"Given who your father was," the woman said with no amount of softness in her voice, and I momentarily tried to decipher if she had added unnecessary emphasis to the word *was*, "I assume you understand the kind of work you'll be doing."

I slowly shook my head, my cheeks burning. "The job posting was very vague," I admitted, "but since I met or exceeded most of the qualifications I felt it would be a good fit." Oh man, more job-interview pseudospeak was pouring out of my mouth and this woman could see right through it. The logical part of my brain was telling me that this whole scheme would never work. I would never find the answers to Dad's death and I would spend a life wondering. I was such an idiot for even thinking—

She closed her notebook. "Do you know what kind of firm your dad worked for?" She lifted a finger and twirled it in the air, like she was writing on an invisible chalkboard. She blinked in surprise. "Hmmm…Oh dear. Alright, tell me this: how exactly did you hear about this job?"

I produced the business card I had been given and, with a shaking hand, passed it over to her. She examined it with narrowed eyes and then put it into her notebook. "I need to make a call. Don't go anywhere." She got up and walked out of the coffee shop with her notebook, leaving me with the most awful anxious knot welling up in my chest, my breaths coming in shallow gasps as I tried to retain my composure. I waited there, my fingers curled into fists under the table, not sure if I should just stand up and leave. Had they figured out why I was here? Had I already crossed a line?

She returned and resumed her seat, her face

aggravatingly masking whatever was going on inside her sour-faced head. "There's been a small mistake, and unfortunately we won't be able to continue the interview process."

My heart felt like it had been hit with an icicle. Inside I was utterly deflated, but outside I tried to retain my composure. "I...um..."

I was about to wish her a good day and leave, but at that moment I heard a deep voice in my ear, as though coming from directly behind me. It was soft, and dark, and sent a chill down my spine. "*Say no.*"

I straightened and resisted the urge to look behind me. "I...I don't..."

"*Tell her you wanna continue the interview.*"

My heart began to beat fast in my chest. I didn't know what was happening, but the voice was so soothing and silky that it filled me with a wild, illogical courage. "I would like to continue the interview, please. Even if I am not qualified for the job."

The woman narrowed her eyes, analyzing me for a long moment. I had just said something really...odd, to be honest, and I didn't know how she would react. I cannot explain, even now, how I continued to keep her gaze, but she leaned forward, intrigued. "You want to continue the interview for a job you don't know anything about, that I am telling you you're not qualified for?"

I swallowed hard, and I felt a bead of sweat dripping down my face. "Yes."

"Why?"

Before I could even think of a proper response, I heard the voice again. "*Tell 'er you agreed to come here in return for an interview, and you 'spect that promise to be kept.*"

What a ridiculous thing to say. And yet, the words spilled from my mouth before I could even consider their meaning. "I agreed to come here for an interview. I expect that promise to be kept."

The woman nodded and opened her notebook again as my mind record-scratched to a halt. This made absolutely no sense. This had to be some kind of psychological trick, or a test to catch me off guard. Maybe I was simply in a stress-induced hallucination. Was I even at this coffee shop at all? Was there even a coffee shop?

"I see, you do have proclivities for the science. Either that or your silencer's whispering good counsel in your ear. Either way…It's odd that you're so uninstructed, but not entirely unheard of." She checked off something in her notebook and removed a piece of gold-lined paper. "Sign this non-disclosure agreement and we'll begin."

I took it and scanned it briefly. Despite the fancy writing and the expensive paper, it was a rather ordinary agreement, and I tentatively picked up my pen.

In that moment, with my pen poised above the paper, I had a sudden and overwhelming feeling that is hard, even now, to describe. It was the stirring feeling of watching a stack of dominos fall, or spinning top begin to slow; that anxious, expectant feeling that builds up right before a satisfying conclusion to something that is already in motion; the instants before a storm breaks. But more than that, I felt like I was one of those falling dominoes or raindrops, and that by signing this paper I would be pushing forward toward that inevitable, unavoidable fate. I shuddered and looked up at the woman in front of me, and something glittered in her eyes—a look of anticipation and something slightly more disturbing—almost like a hunger for me to sign this paper. All these feelings together began to tie up my stomach, and even my breathing, which had suddenly, I noticed, become quite rapid.

Clearly, I was about to have another massive anxiety attack, and I simply could not afford to do that right now. Trying to keep my fingers as stable as possible, I signed the paper and handed it back quickly. As if on cue, a rumble of thunder sounded outside, and a torrent of rain began to slam down on the roof of the shop.

I suddenly became aware that the other people in the shop were all staring at our table, and I immediately wanted nothing more than to melt into the chair and slither off in a puddle.

"Now," the woman said, rolling the paper up, "Let us discuss what you've just done." She tied the paper with a white ribbon and slid it into her bag. "You have sworn never to reveal the mysteries of *The Secret*. You're lucky, you know—" She twiddled her fingers together menacingly, and I froze in my seat, unable to look away from her deep, cold eyes. Her face, no longer sour, now seemed to be nearly inhuman with its wicked smile full of teeth...so many teeth. "—not everyone has the proclivity for it. But the blood of the parent courses through the veins of the child. Now...give me your hand."

I trembled, sweat beading down my face. I extended my hand out obediently, my mind feeling foggy to the point where I don't know if I could have resisted the suggestion. But she took my hand softly, delicately, and traced the folds of my palm with a long pink fingernail. When she spoke, her voice seemed deeper and bolder than it had any moment before, and I could tell that they were more than words...there was power behind them. *"In the name of the Ancient and Cryptic Societies, I bind you to the Great Treatise, never to reveal this Secret so long as you live."*

She let go of my hand and I pulled it back quickly, feeling dazed, confused, and nauseous. I tried to bring words to my lips but my whole throat was dry. The room was spinning around me, and I desperately held onto my senses to keep from passing out...

I yelped as my arm suddenly blazed with pain. I looked down and watched, in horror, as a black series of lines, like a bar code, burned its way across my forearm, making a stripe of clear markings over my skin and forming the shape of a strange cryptograph I had never seen before. I gasped out words and could feel warm bile rising in my throat.

I felt an arm touch me gently on the shoulder and I heard a familiar, smooth voice in my ear. Apollo? "Breathe, Andy. Just breathe."

I sucked in some air into my lungs and felt a cooling sensation filling my chest, dampening down the fire that had suddenly welled up. I couldn't fight the encroaching darkness any longer, though, and the last thing I saw was the woman's mouth full of far-too-many teeth before the whole room went dark.

CHAPTER 2

I awoke to the sound of light jazz music and found my face buried deeply in a plush pillow. My head felt like it was utterly full of rocks or possibly soft cheese, and I moved only with the greatest reluctance, so that I could breathe slightly better.

With my head turned to the side, I could see that I was still in the coffee shop, and by the looks of the window outside it was still rather dark. I was stretched out on a long sofa along the far wall, and the entire room was empty except for Apollo, back behind the counter with a cleaning rag, humming to himself as he finished his barista duties.

I took in a few long breaths, my brain still struggling to move properly. The events with Madame Sour-face seemed like a far-of dream and in the fog of my head I couldn't quite put it all together as events that actually occurred. Maybe I had showed up, fallen asleep on the couch, and dreamed it? That would mean I had missed the interview...right? Things weren't making sense just yet.

Apollo spotted me moving and picked up a nearby cup to bring it over. "Hey there, sunshine," he said, sitting down and putting the steaming mug before me. "You took that a little harder than some folks I've seen, I'm not gonna lie. I thought you were a goner for sure."

"I...I'm sorry I fell asleep on your couch. I'm so embarrassed." I yawned and clumsily made myself twist into a sitting position, the inside of my head still tumbling around like a stack of books toppling over. I went to say something else, but I spotted the marks on my forearm, which had lightened into a muted red, and I stopped, a gasp of air rushing into my lungs and my eyes snapping open wide. I grabbed my forearm defensively as though to cover the lines in my skin. "Oh god. It happened. It really happened. What...what *was* that?"

Apollo scooted the tea closer. "Tea first, take a sip, calm your butt. Come on." I took the tea obediently and gulped down some of the hot liquid. I didn't even care that it scalded my mouth. "You," Apollo continued after I had set the cup back down, "have just been granted entrance into a very exclusive society. From the looks of how completely confused you are you've got no clue about any of it, so I'll be your welcoming party and give you the Readers Digest version."

I held up a hand. "One second." I focused on maintaining my breathing, closing my eyes until I could feel my heartbeat starting to relax.

I could almost envision him tilting his head. "Anxiety?"

I nodded. "Yeah. I take meds for it, but it's been a…" I breathed in and out again. "…tough couple of days."

Apollo said nothing until I had again opened my eyes and nodded my assent for him to continue. "So…where do I start…Okay, many myths and fantasies you've ever read or heard about have some kind of basis in truth. Not complete truth—and there's far more fake stereotypes than real ones—but enough truth. Monsters, wizards, magic, the works. All of it. I'll give you a second to take that in. Feel free to pass out again."

Andy.exe had encountered a problem and needed to close. I opened my mouth and some noises came out, but it was probably an embarrassingly long couple of minutes before they converted into actual words. "And….m-my—"

"Your Dad was a wizard." Apollo was very matter-of-fact about the ridiculous words coming out of his mouth. "Bit of a reputation, too…He did a lot of work for the city. I never met him myself, but I recognize the name. Of course, from what I've heard some people weren't very sorry to hear he's gone. Which I assume is why you're trying to get a job at 50 Thousand, too."

I nodded slowly, my head starting to clear up and the cogs moving forward again. "We were told it was a random killing. Some gang-related thing. But no one told us how, or why, or where…I just think it was something more than that. I think it was targeted."

"What makes you think that?" he said in what sounded like a purposely neutral tone.

I opened my mouth to respond but didn't really have an answer.

"Just a feeling?" Apollo raised an eyebrow. "Yeah. You're not the only one. But nobody's looking into it yet because they're waiting to see what the Dragon does."

"Dragon?" I took another gulp of tea and tried to not choke on it.

"Yeah. Every city has one…every city that's got magic in it anyway.[3] They set the rules for how all of us act and operate in the area."

I stared at Apollo for a long moment. "Us? You're a wizard?"

He laughed. "No, no, not at all. I'm an Incubus, which means I don't fall into the same society as wizards do. I follow slightly different rules. See," He leaned forward. "There's six big societies. We can cover them all later, but the one you're in is called *Sorcera* and it's made up of normal humans like you who learn magic. You all," he gestured vaguely in my direction, "Have to get licensed to operate. Speaking of which…" He pulled some papers out of his pocket. "These are for you. The Baga Yaga you were interviewing with left them behind for you."

I took the papers and looked them over. The first

---

[3] "**Q**: Why is travel to Chicago prohibited by employees of 50 Thousand Consulting? **A**: It is a matter of record that Chicago had Society governance under a Dragon until 1871, when the Dragon of Chicago became quite intoxicated and started a massive fire commonly known as the "Great Chicago Fire" while sleeping in the barn of local Irish immigrant Catherine O'Leary. The fire, and the following attempt to cover it up by the aforementioned Dragon, led the *Dracontos* society to remove the dragon from the city and brand Chicago as a city where magic does not live. Go Bears." - 50 Thousand Employee Handbook, Page 530 (Travel FAQs)

was an invitation from *The Societas Sorcera* informing me of the date and time of my licensure examination. The second was a welcome letter from 50 Thousand Consulting, congratulating me on the beginning of my employment as a "Casting Technical Intern (CTA) I".

I had done it. Somehow, I had done it and gotten the job.

"I…you…" I spat out question-sounding words. "I…the Job. You…Incubus? Baba Yaga? License exam? What?!?"

Apollo gave me deep look, and I suddenly found myself able to look at nothing but his dark, caramel-colored eyes. "Breathe. Calm down." And I did, instantly—my heart suddenly became calm and my breathing slowed, and he looked away.

He continued to talk, while I blinked, shaking myself mentally from whatever had just happened. Did Apollo just use…*mind control* on me? I felt a little violated.

"One thing at a time," he said, standing up suddenly. "First: I'm an incubus. You know what a succubus is, right? Well, I'm the dude version. Incubi and Succubi—a race called Lilin—we feed off pleasure. Not just physical pleasure, mind you, which is why I work here: people love coffee in a way that's almost inappropriate. And I feed off that every time they take a sip. Plus, with 50 Thousand just down the street, I get a lot of repeat customers that generally feel pretty safe here. You follow so far?"

I nodded and offered him my empty teacup. He took it and went behind the bar to refill while he continued his explanations. "The woman who interviewed you is a Baba Yaga—contract dealers. Things they write down and contracts they make have magic powers, which is why you'd imagine a corporate firm wants them in Human Resources. That contract you signed was magically binding, and that magical binding is marked there on your arm." He returned with a cup of tea and took my arm gently. My skin tingled under his touch and I felt my cheeks burn. "This mark says you're *Sorcera*. This one means you're human. This one means you're employed by 50 Thousand. The marks are a *Sorcera* thing, don't worry about it. Your whole group's got 'em. It's a really old tradition. I think you guys should just have IDs, but that's just me…"

I swallowed and took the second cup of tea, inhaling the herbal scent deeply. "What about the licensing?"

Apollo took his seat again, and I noticed his forearms didn't bear any marks at all. I pushed my question to the back of my mind as he spoke. "Yeah. *Sorcera*, since you guys aren't born with magic, you all have to be licensed. So you go, take a basic knowledge exam, and get a learner's permit. Like a car," he added sheepishly. "And I think you might have to buy insurance. I dunno. *Sorcera* is way too much paperwork in my opinion."

"What do I even need to know on the exam?"

"Basic history. Names of the people, places, things, some basic rules. I think it's even multiple-choice."

A long silence fell between us as I sipped my tea and he watched me, curiously, as though analyzing my reaction. I wondered if he had this conversation with people often. Finally, he stood up. "You should probably head home and get some sleep, by the way. And then, just…relax? I can even call you a lift." I shook my head and stood up; the condo was only a few blocks' walk. "Okay then. Read over your Handbook. See ya. Stay out of trouble." I didn't get a chance to ask any other questions before he disappeared into the back of the shop to turn off lights. Shaking, and with most of the tea finished, I gathered my things and went to the door. It had stopped raining but the dark wetness outside was not a fun sight.

The walk back to the condo was long and very quiet. Cincinnati at night was beautiful and bright colored for sure but the people were cold and self-interested. It was as if someone had switched the whole city into scary-mode.

Not a single glance in my direction met me as I walked a whole three blocks to the building which, this late at night, was eerily quiet and dim. My shoes clicked on the marble of the entrance lobby and up the stairs to the elevator, and the echoes down the hall made my ears tingle.

I couldn't help but feel entirely, utterly alone as I rode the elevator toward the top floors and mulled over the ridiculous, unbelievable nonsense I had just experienced. But for the marks on my arm and the monstrous form of the Baba Yaga's mouth full of teeth seared into my memory, I might have not believed it, but I had long passed the point where doubt was an option. Unless I had simply gone insane. I wasn't ruling that out quite yet.

I arrived at the door of the condo and stopped, taking a moment to recompose myself completely. My dad was a wizard…and I never knew. Did mom or my brother know? Maybe she never noticed? Or she never thought it was important? I was tempted to call her and get more answers from her but the thought of more guilt-trips and "why don't you love me"s and "when are you coming home"s made my stomach churn.

I pushed the door open and felt it hit something on the floor on the other side. Cautiously, I looked around and saw a brown package just inside the door, with a single label: "To: Andy LaFayette". Groaning at what was sure to be yet another surprise today that I really didn't need, I closed the door before heading to the bathroom. One anxiety pill and a glass of water later, I was ready to open the package and find out what awful thing was inside. Taking a seat in the middle of the empty living room floor, and by the light of my cell phone's flashlight, I pulled apart the packaging.

Inside was a thick, spiral-bound tome which bore the words "50 Thousand Employee Handbook"[4] accompanied by the 50 Thousand logo. I opened it and thumbed through a few of the sections, a little taken aback by the style and the nonchalance with which things like "Company Policy on Time Travel" and "Potion Addiction Resources" that filled the many numerous corporate policies. It seemed so

---

[4] "The 50 Thousand Employee Handbook is the culmination of many studies of corporate culture, countless focus groups, committee meetings, emails, committee meetings that could have been emails, emails that would have been avoided if people read their emails, conflicts that should have been passive-aggressive emails, committee meetings that were canceled in lieu of passive-aggressive emails, and third-party business consultant reports whose suggestions were ignored." - 50 Thousand Employee Handbook, Page 17 (History of the 50 Thousand Employee Handbook, Part 1)

amazing and yet so utterly boring at the same time, and as I felt another anxiety attack rising in my stomach I closed the handbook and laid back on the carpet, closing my eyes and feeling the warm fuzziness against the back of my neck.

Work would start on Monday.

CHAPTER 3

My orientation leader, Lisa, handed me the next of the many brochures I had been presented with since the day had started. This one, bearing the blazing words *Your Healthcare is Simple: We Promise!* got tucked under the others inside my folder haphazardly as I continued to listen. She handed out the other brochures to the other three people who accompanied me, most of whom had a lost, deer-in-the-headlights look. I wondered if I might have that same expression and not realize it; to compensate I tried to rearrange my face and hoped it would be read as attentive, professional interest. I didn't want them to think I was scared or anything. I wasn't scared. Not at all.

In fact, I was pretty excited.

Of course, we still hadn't gotten to the office building and I didn't know what to expect. We were told to meet at Fountain Square over on Vine Street, and we had spent the last half hour walking from the heart of downtown several blocks to our destination. I couldn't figure out why they had decided to start the day this way; the only explanation I could think of was that they wanted to give us a sense of normalcy before dropping us on our heads in insanity.

I did notice that one of the guys didn't look apprehensive at all; in fact, he looked downright bored. Tall and lean, wearing his suit jacket collar turned up and his dark, thick-rimmed sunglasses hiding whatever douchebag expression was hidden in his eyes behind them, he gave the immediate impression of a complete slimeball. He seemed to hang to the back of our orientation group as though he had no interest in what was going on. At the moment, he was looking over into the reflective glass of a nearby window, cataloging his appearance in detail as if he was the protagonist in the first chapter of a badly-written novel. I glanced at his nametag, spotting the name "Devin" for a second before we rounded the corner onto 9th Street. All at once, the building came into view.

We all stopped simultaneously and stared at the glistening tower, its face a smooth sea of green glass glittering in the morning sunlight. It positively dwarfed the older, historic buildings on Walnut Street, and surely the rest of Cincinnati as well. Frantically I shook myself mentally, trying to recall why I had never noticed this building before, either in the few weeks I had lived in Cincinnati nor in the many images of the Cincinnati skyline that were plastered on windows and on placards in stores aimed at tourists. In the way it glittered, it almost appeared to be a single huge chunk of green crystal, but as we crossed the street and moved closer, I could make out the brass trim around the frame of the doors and windows. People bustled in and out of the single revolving door at the base of the tower, which was planted firmly where I was sure the 9th and Walnut parking lot used to be.

We followed Lisa through the revolving door and into a warm, glossy lobby that was a nice respite from the end-of-summer heat. The walls, the pillars, the desk, the ceiling—all of it was a green or white marble, and the richness—and surely the cost—of this room alone staggered my mind.

"So, let's get started with a brief tour of the parts of the facility you may visit in the near future, as well as the place you're going to be working after your training is done. You'll be given a swipe-badge like this one which you'll need to get access to…"

I looked over to a small segregated area that looked kind of like a café in the lobby about twenty feet away. A man in a wrinkled suit sat in one of the padded chairs reading from a tablet device. Was he one? I eyed a girl sitting near him, unwrapping a granola bar. Maybe she was one. Nobody particularly stood out to me or gave me the impression of having some dark secrets. How would I know one when I saw them?

"…So don't ever do that and you'll be perfectly safe," Lisa was saying. Crap, was she saying something really important and I missed it? *Okay,* I reminded myself, *pay attention. Stop ogling.*

As we stepped onto the company elevator, I tried to keep myself from looking like a kid in an amusement park. I briefly noted the dozens of buttons on both sides of the elevator door and then tried to busy myself by looking through my first-day folder. *The Keys to Your Benefits Packages* one brochure read. *Security: More than Just Passwords!* read another. *Keeping Your Mind Safe from Intruders* read a third. Wait—what? I went to take a second look at that third one but was interrupted as the elevator door slid open and I was forced to stash the brochures back away.

Beyond the glass doors ahead the corridor spilled out ahead of us. On either side, I could see winding rows of open-air desks, each adorned with a pair of monitors and peripherals. At the far end, doors to offices ran from one wall to the other. "We don't believe in cubicle farms here," Lisa said, gesturing as we passed the rows of desks. "Open air communication leads to open minds and open ideas!" I resisted rolling my eyes. Lisa stopped and reconsidered what she had just said. "By the way, related to 'open ideas', be careful about your thoughts, you don't want them to get overheard, especially if they're inappropriate. Some of your coworkers can read minds." I took in a deep breath, as my mind at that moment decided to think some very loud swear words. *Why would you do this to me, brain?* "So keep your mind nice and closed. But also…keep it open." She seemed momentarily flustered, and I could almost hear the sound of a hamster rapidly running on its wheel as Lisa untangled the conflict between her own uncannily cheery demeanor in the crossfire of corporate policy.[5]

---

[5] "If you find yourself caught in a conflict between your own thoughts and feelings and those of the company policies, please take a moment to breathe and remember who signs your

"Anyway, moving on!"

∗∗∗

Finally, we were led to a small lobby where Lisa instructed us to take a seat and cool off. The white and blue vinyl chairs weren't particularly comfortable, but after walking for an hour and a half it was at least some form of welcome respite. I took a seat and listened to my new coworkers chatting; maybe I could try and take my mind off my nerves.

Carma was a curvy, loudly-dressed young woman with a bright smile that could melt ice. Her hair, in dark curls around her eyes, bobbed erratically as she talked, and her voice was poignantly accented by the sharp jingle of several metal bracelets around her wrists, which she was at this moment complaining about—she had been told never to wear silver ones.

"...and so, I tried to explain to Lisa that they're family heirlooms and that I've worn them ever since I was a little girl, but she said *no* and told me that it was something to do with magical flow. Now my *grandmami*, she was a *bruja* and I've never heard her say anything like that before, so I don't know if it's one of those real safety things or some kind of weird corporate policy that doesn't have any real reasoning, but it really messed me up, man."

"Mhm." Jake, on the other hand, was the complete opposite of Carma. Quiet, bearded and painfully blonde, he seemed to just be an observer on the ride around him, listening quite actively and

---

paychecks." – 50 Thousand Employee Handbook, Page 2 (Introduction)

occasionally indulging in a brief word or vocalization from the back of his throat to indicate assent or dissent.

Elmer kind of kept to himself, his eyes focused on his phone and always appearing to only half-listen to anything. He almost didn't seem interested in his first day here at all, and I admit I made some pretty harsh initial judgments about his work ethic in the first few minutes we had met. Now, however, he looked up and tuned into the conversation.

Then there was Devin, the slimy-looking young man I had noticed earlier. He seemed completely uninterested in doing anything but looking smug and correcting everyone around him as if he had invented the word 'actually'. "*Actually,* it's because it's *silver*. It rejects magic. Too much of it and it's a *liability*. There's a reason these decisions get made, you know. But I wouldn't expect you to understand. This is your first day after all."

"Yours too!" Carma retorted in indignation.

Devin shrugged. "Yeah, but I've been coming here since I was little. I know most of the people here already just through…you know. Networking." Oh, how I instantly disliked this child. I say child because, despite being an adult, his mannerisms were far too reminiscent of a spoiled man-child who desperately would have benefited from a smack across the forehead with a glass bottle.

Carma opened her mouth to argue buck but Lisa chose that moment to reappear at the doorway. "Alrighty folks. It's getting to be close to noon and your testing is scheduled at 12:30 at the *Sorcera* offices down the street. Let's get going!"

We departed the 50 Thousand building and headed toward Vine Street, to the entrance to a dirty Fountain Square parking lot. Passing a beaten sign which denoted the fees for parking (to which I utterly balked at the idea of parking for $18 a day), we entered a side door and went through an underground corridor to arrive at a set of glass doors which read in lasered lettering "*Sorcera* Society, Cincinnati Office". Lisa bid us good bye and we went inside.

Beyond the glass doors was an utterly pristine lobby, in an impeccably white decor. It was as if the whole room was designed and maintained by a person who feared the slightest speck of dust would tarnish a perfect reputation. A secretary with greyish-blue hair gestured to a sign nearby which directed us toward a testing room.

"What is this place, anyhow? The magical BMV?" Carma was asking no one in particular.

"*Actually,* it's the Society satellite office," Devin interrupted in his ever-increasingly slimy fashion. "The headquarters is in Tampa but every city with a Dragon has an office. All the societies have an office, if you know where to go. Of course, I know where *all* the offices are located…" He continued on, but I ignored him, instead focusing on calming my heart rate that had suddenly shot up into a massive tizzy.

I know, looking back, that I shouldn't have freaked out about the test. The way Apollo had described it was pretty accurate: a basic knowledge check of basic things that had simple answers. And they did mostly happen to be multiple choice.

The man handing out the tests was dressed in a dark suit and deep purple tie, and his lapel bore a shining gold pin that I got to glance at as I passed him at the doorway. I recognized it instantly and looked down at my forearm—as I suspected, the same symbol was there, etched into my skin like a scar. I rubbed the tattoo gently with a finger and felt very awkward.

"Hello," he said in a tone of utter indifference, "I work with the *Sorcera* Society Regional Licensing Director for the State of Ohio. This is an open-book test. You have forty-five minutes to complete your test and your results will be sent to you within the week. When you're done simply leave your paper up here and you are free to leave for lunch. Begin."

I took a deep breath, thanked myself for remembering to take my anxiety medication, and started down the list of questions, frantically perusing the 50 Thousand Employee Handbook for the answers.

Janice has been bitten by a werewolf. Should she (A) turn in her resignation and tell no one; (B) resign herself to a life as a werewolf; (C) scrub it with a silver-infused antibacterial soap and then inform HR; or (D) Nothing. Werewolves don't exist.

C, maybe? Or D. I scanned the Employee Index and found a whole three pages on werewolves, and confirmed it was in fact C. OK, one down, about fifty to go.

Some of them were particularly easy to find the answers to and I was beginning to feel a bit more confident by the time I was fifteen questions in, but others confused me quite a bit.

Your supervisor recently got back from a hiking trip in Massachusetts. Which of the following is a sign that your supervisor might be possessed by a Pukwudgie? (A) He forgets your birthday; (B) He invites you over to his house after work; (C) He spends the afternoon eating lots of berries, or (D) He seems to have lost the ability to speak anything but puns.

The Handbook didn't have anything that would indicate anything like this. I searched through it twice, and for a moment I could have sworn that the book was different each time I looked through it. I was starting to get confused so I skipped the question and moved on.

Halfway through our allotted time, Devin stood up and strutted over to the desk, slammed his paper down, and walked out. I wondered, vaguely, whether it was his real intention to have such a desperate lack of redeeming features, or if it was innate to his personality.

But the time was over half done and I was under half finished with the test. Redoubling my searching efforts, I answered a few other ones that seemed relatively easy, such as one that asked what weapon would be likely to be wielded by a Goatman if traveling in Maryland (Which I, like any Chesapeake Bay native, would know was an axe). There were also a few short answer questions that I had neither the time nor energy to try and compose decent answers for, such as *Explain, briefly, why particleboard is not a useful substitute for wood when using a wooden stake to neutralize a vampire.*

"Because particleboard isn't a useful substitute for wood in any context," I wrote, and moved onto the next question.

Carma finished after me, and then Jake, leaving me alone as the last few minutes of the test wound down. I had answered every question I could find the answer to outright, and I realized, to my horror, that most of the multiple-choice questions were still unanswered. In desperation, I randomly filled bubbles down the sheet, marking the last questions just as the clock buzzed.

"Time's up," the director said, and I looked up to find him standing at my desk already, picking up my test. "You're Tom LaFayette's kid, right?"

I gulped hard. "Yessir. I'm Andy," I said tentatively, offering a hand. He didn't shake it but instead nodded sagely. "Your dad was a good guy. Glad to see you're following in his footsteps." He turned and headed back to his desk, so I rose, thanked him, and headed out the door.

EXCEPT FROM A BRIEF HISTORY OF SORCERY (1943) BY RAMFORT YUNG, ESQ.[6]

As a result of the changes that came with exploration, and the mixing of cultures which resulted from the exploitative and intrusive cultures of the

---

[6] "The 1943 Edition by Yung was considered the definitive edition until 1977, when a competitor released *Magic: An Annotated History* by Nigel Backhorn. The new book was wildly successful due to both its readability and comparatively low price. As a result, in 1983 Yung struck a deal with a Djinn to travel back to 1943 and rewrite his book. Yung succeeded in arriving in 1943 but changed his mind and instead courted Backhorn's mother before his father would have the chance. Since then, no competitors have put out other major versions of the Cryptic history for fear of Yung suddenly becoming their new father. *A Brief History* remains as dry as ever." 50 Thousand Employee Handbook, Page 895 (Additional and Suggested Reading)

Spanish upon the New World, it became clear that the rules by which sorcery were governed were incompatible. As an example, Mayan magicians were well-known to control and subjugate cultures, demanding sacrifices and other atonement actions in return for more wealth and power (which would, quite obviously, break many magical laws today regarding the impersonation of Deity). Similarly, the Greek and Roman style enumerated many different interactions of magical beings and the Mundane world which, today, would be met with grievous action against the magician involved, if not the ultimate penalties.

At this time, it was a dragon by the name of Azu who took the prerogative to combine the cultures and set regulations. Major cultural differences and lack of governance was leading to significant conflict among the magic users of the new and old worlds, who often saw each other as threats to their own existence. Azu collected as many different types of creatures as he could and met in Santo Domingo's *Fortaleza Ozama* (This event is commonly referred to as "The Spanish Conclave") At this time, most different types of creatures were fragmented but fell into different major societies. Azu led the proceedings in merging many of these fraternities into collective groups:

- The *Kobolda*, for creatures monstrous or otherworldly in appearance with no way to innately disguise themselves, such as goblins or trolls;
- The *Empyrean*, for intelligent ethereal, spiritual, or otherwise deified creatures like ghosts or demigods;

- The *Vulnerabl,* creatures who innately could appear as mundane, and could hide among the masses, such as shapeshifters or werewolves;
- The *Sorcera,* otherwise mundane creatures who had gained magical skills or knowledge, such as sorcerers or Hedge Magicians;
- The *Luprican,* tiny creatures who either lacked self-governance or were incapable of being governed, such as pixies or pech;
- And *Dracontos,* the Dragons.

This categorization initially led to some further conflict, as some creatures resisted being categorized or governed separately from those whom they had previously been associated. One example of this conflict arose among the Unicorns and the Pegasi, who were very close and commonly intermingled in European settlements. Pegasi, with the innate ability to hide their wings and appear as simple horses were labeled *Vulnerabl* and given rights and privileges not afforded to the Unicorns, whose unearthly appearance branded them *Kobolda*. Being grouped in with all manner of monstrous beasts the Unicorns fought vehemently against this division, but without innate abilities to hide, no change could be made. Unicorns and Pegasi later engaged in a brief violent conflict in central Europe before withdrawing from many of their shared communes and leaving a rift between the two species that continues to this day.

This consortium of societies governed independently until the mid-17th century, when the close of the Renaissance period and shifts in European powers made it difficult to manage interactions between the mundane and magical beings. Despite the obvious division between the two worlds, the complexities of cultures were rapidly becoming incompatible. The heads of the 6 Ancient and Cryptic societies met again in 1662 in Oxford. Much like the First Oxford Conclave three hundred years prior, The Second Oxford Conclave was riled with conflict and lasted many days. Records indicate that for almost three months the Societies' representatives argued about the movement forward and, somewhere in that time, finally agreed that a withdrawal from the world of the Mundane was the best option.

The next thirty days were filled by massive research functions and communications, building a spell powerful enough to massively alter the entire planet. Such magic had only been theorized, but with the investment of energies from the thirty-two dragons in attendance, the idea was finalized. The final incantation was cast on August 12, 1662.

The result of this spell was far-reaching and particularly effective: evidence of the presence of all magical and ethereal creatures was wiped from the face of the earth, leaving behind only stories, myths, and legends. The Societies at the time justified this as a matter for protecting the particularly weak and helpless mundane beings from harm. A cursory glance at mundane human history indicates that mundane people are perfectly capable of harming themselves and each other without magical influence.

CHAPTER 4

There is something to be said about the productiveness of Tuesday in an office environment. For one, the end of weekend blues have vanished by the time Tuesday rolls around, and the coffee is flowing hard enough to kickstart anyone's life into gear. I remember reading a business article that Tuesday is the most productive day of the week, and I can understand, tangibly, why that is the case.

I also understand that I am an outlier and Tuesdays are just as bad for me as any other day.

I got my cubicle on Day 2, along with a large stack of even more brochures and flyer to go along with my huge handbook. All of these got stuffed into my desk drawer the moment Lisa was out of sight. Speaking of Lisa, hadn't she said they didn't believe in cubicle farms? Mine was a decently-sized cubicle, to be sure, about 5x5 with a desk and a set of drawers on the side. Looking around the office and its winding cubicle farm, I honestly couldn't bring myself to believe that anything special happened here at all and I must admit I was mildly disappointed; for all of the wonder that some kind of magical world might be, so far my experience had just been oodles of paperwork. I was working for a firm that hired *wizards*, and here I was in a cubie, with a computer and a desk and a chair. I was surprised to find the chair was rather comfortable, and I lazily kicked back in it as I waited to find out what exactly I was supposed to do as a "Casting Technical Analyst" anyhow.

I didn't have to wait long. "Andy LaFayette." I looked up and leaned back into a more professional-looking stance as a short, older lady with long amber curls appeared next to the cubicle with—of course—more papers in her hand. "I'm Carrie and I'm your supervisor. I know you have a lot of questions and I'm going to honest I only have a few of the answers right now but I'll do what I can, okay?" She looked at me with a hint of desperation that made me think she hadn't worked under 65 hours a week for years. "Come on." I followed without a word and we were out of the cubicle far, down a hallway where dozens of offices lined the far wall, each with its own etched glass door. Rows of names were on those doors, and I read a few as I went past. *Jon Kilwinning - Junior Associate Wizard. Leon Caliburn - Junior Associate Wizard. Esther McMakin - Senior Associate Wizard.* Even though I couldn't see the people behind the frosted glass, it gave me chills to think that behind each of these doors was a person who likely had unimaginable power. I wondered if they wore suits or patterned wizard robes.

"Your job is really, really simple once you get the

hang of it," Carrie was saying. "As a CTA you're basically at the beck and call of any of the Wizards on this floor. They'll give you things to do, things to research, files to sort…your basic office tasks. Once your permit comes through, later this week, you'll start on actually assembling things, maybe observing some light casting…but that might take a while. Depends on how quickly you catch on."

We continued to wind through the offices and cubicle farms a bit and stopped at a big grey door. "This is the archive room and is a huge project we're trying to sort through. See, every client we have has a file, and sometimes people forget to file things in the right place, and they just sorta pile files everywhere. We've been dealing with that for a while and need to reorganize."

I nodded but furrowed my brow. Something rather…important occurred to me. "Um, Carrie, this is going to sound really dumb, but what does this company *do?*"

Carrie stared at me as though I had just called her mother ten different awful names. "You—-I…wait. No one even—? GAH!" She threw her hands up in the air and pushed the grey door open, pulling me inside.

"I really appreciate you meeting me here on such short notice."

Rajesh nodded without a word, his smile plastered almost coldly on his face as he took a sip of the cappuccino in front of him. A plate of biscotti crumbs sat next to his coffee cup, and he gestured for the server to bring more.

The server nodded and offered Henry a lunch menu, which he politely declined before taking his seat. Rajesh hadn't told him to bring anything in particular, so he had printed some quarterly sales figures and put them in his portfolio, which he held to his chest like a breastplate whole waiting for the man opposite him to say something to open the encounter. He found himself wondering what it was about Rajesh which so intimidated him, but he couldn't put his finger on it.

"You have had some financial troubles in your company," Rajesh said slowly, as though his words were very calculated. "Corporate leaks, bad investments, PR disasters. Many would chalk it up to bad luck."

"Well—yes." Henry nervously set the portfolio down and opened it. "I was told you are a specialist in this kind of situation? Some kind of consultant?"

Rajesh nodded as the server set down a tray of fresh biscotti. His long, twiggy fingers gingerly picked one piece up, dipped it into the swirling mist of coffee, and raised it to his lips for a bite. Henry began to feel increasingly uncomfortable; the way this man seemed so completely unruffled by the situation might have been a comfort except that the circumstance was so dire. He was right, however—at the moment, the company was chalking it up to 'bad luck' but that would only last so long before the company's shareholders started looking for a place to put the blame. And blame, as it happens, would probably start at the top of the food chain.

Henry anxiously tapped his fingers on the table. Rajesh hadn't made the slightest move to look at the papers he'd brought. "So...what kind of services...I mean how can I take steps toward—?"

"The misfortune your company has experienced is of no fault of your own," Rajesh assured, taking an impeccably careful bite of biscotti. "What you're experiencing is a form of corporate sabotage by a competitor."

Some of the color drained from Henry's face, his mouth frozen half-open. He quietly suppressed the panic firing up behind his eyes. He adjusted the open portfolio in front of him, perhaps as some way to take a bite of control in this environment where he was feeling so helpless, trying to avoid Rajesh's gaze. "What...what kind of sabotage? Our systems are secured with some of the most intricate—"

Rajesh stopped him by waving the biscotti dismissively. "No, no, Henry. It's far subtler than that. This kind of sabotage is untraceable. Fortune itself is working against you. Fate is being thrown around. It's a relatively common mid-level enchantment."

Henry blinked, and his eyebrows furrowed as he tried to parse Rajesh's sentence. "A mid-level...what?"

Rajesh stopped in the middle of his next bite and fixed the man opposite with a curious stare. "Come now, Henry, surely someone explained these processes to you. Or...hmmm." He chewed and swallowed. "Maybe not, since you don't have any protections currently set up."

"What are you talking about?"

Rajesh completed his bit of biscotti and leaned intently forward. "Offensive enchantments, Henry. A consulting firm similar to the one which employs me has deployed offensive magic against your company."

The sentence hung in the air for a moment and Henry's eyes slowly began to crinkle into slits. "What…kind of scam are you pulling here? Just who do you think I am?"

"You," Rajesh said pointedly, "Are the CEO of a company that has taken a hit to nearly every part of your company's influence. Despite your best efforts, only thing you can find is that it's a bad bit of luck, but it's all happening so fast. How much have your stocks dropped in the last, oh, 48 hours?" Henry didn't answer; he looked like he was ready to stand up and walk out at the sheer ridiculousness of it all. "Most people in your position are already aware of the kind of services my company offers. And the woman who referred you to me holds our services in the highest esteem. We protect companies like yours from the exact kind of attacks you have been the victim of recently. And if you don't employ my services—and soon—you will see your company's misfortune grow. You will lose key employees. You will have workplace accidents. You will have scandals. And they will come seemingly from nowhere, as if…conjured."

Rajesh's eyes were steely and intense. Henry couldn't seem to look away from their gaze. A knot had welled up in his throat. A single thought kept poking the back of his mind. Was he desperate enough to entertain this idea? Linda was his mentor and had never led him astray. She'd given him some strange advice in the past, but it had always worked out well. But it had never been quite this strange.

Henry leaned forward. "Ok, be straight with me. Is this a protection racket? Are you extorting me? I really need to know, because—"

Rajesh leaned back. "One hour, Henry. Give me one hour to get a reasonable counter-enchantment going. Your luck will change within the hour. And if it doesn't, then you can write me off as the strangest business proposal you've ever received. But if you don't…" Rajesh let his words trail off and glanced down to the leather portfolio Henry was now gripping in either frustration or fear. The consequences didn't need to be stated aloud, but Rajesh did anyway. "If you don't, your company will be done for, and soon. Someone really doesn't like you, Henry. And they've paid someone a lot of money to take you down. You can either stand up to them or you can fight them."

Henry sat there a long time. His head turned, and he watched the people across the street over at Fountain Square going about their hustle and bustle. His mind seemed slightly fogged, and the idea of potentially losing his company for any reason—magical or otherwise—was simply not one to trifle with. And if he ended up with egg on his face, he could chalk it up to desperation.

Rajesh straightened his tie. "Also, our services are often tax-deductible."

Henry nodded. "One hour."

Rajesh took out his phone. "I thought you'd say yes, so I took the liberty of getting a head start. Our best technicians have been working diligently since the moment you walked in. You'll start getting some very encouraging emails probably by…oh…" He gestured to the server. "…by the end of another cappuccino, I think. In the meantime, let's talk business." He gestured to the leather portfolio still gripped tightly in Henry's hands. Slightly shaking, he laid it on the table and opened it. He took a sharp intake of air as he saw that his sales figure paperwork had all been replaced by gold-trimmed letterhead bearing the embossed name 50 THOUSAND CONSULTING and a client welcome letter.

Rajesh smiled as the server set down his next cup of coffee. "So, Henry, our basic retainers begin at a very reasonable monthly price…"

CHAPTER 5

Carrie shut the door. "So in short," she finished, "we are a really big firm that practices protective and beneficial magic. Wealthy and influential companies hire us to either help boost their profits with basic enchantments and spells, or protect them from Dark Magic."

"Dark—?"

"Shh, I'm explaining. See, most Dragons don't allow Dark Magic casting in their jurisdictions. Cincinnati doesn't, for example…but some Dragons do, and in those cities an unethical wizard can make a killing by using Dark Magic against a company or a person. So those folks hire us to imbue their companies, assets, and even themselves with protective spells. We're the top people in the country for this so we have a lot of the highest-class clients.

"Also, because like I said the Dragon of Cincinnati doesn't like Dark Magic, we have a large commissioned security force that polices the city for people doing unlawful spell casting, and we have a contract with the Dragon of Cincinnati to keep and maintain his laws. So *you*—" She pointed at me irritably, "are here to enable the wizards out there to keep their wealthy and powerful clients happy which is why your job is very, *very* important. Those guys don't have time to assemble spell ingredients or brew options. They're the lawyers, you're the paralegal. They're the doctors, you're the nurse. Do you understand?"

"I do all the work and they get the credit?" Carrie ignored my quip and went on to explain her "system" of filing that seemed to be shuffling files into groups like "March thru something", "Misc" and "Other".

My dad was a wizard. He was one of those people. He had an office and he did important things. I can't explain why this lightened my heart so much, but after 20 years of knowing the man only by the occasional birthday card, it was an indescribably amazing feeling to realize that not only was he a real, tangible person, but that he did good things and protected people.

And then, I realized as I felt my heart deflate, someone had killed him.

"…so if they catch fire the whole room's going to go up. So don't do that." *Dammit, I did it again.*

I nodded again as though I had been listening. "When do you want me to start on this?"

"Pretty much right now. Good luck." She gave me a pitiful smile and then headed out the door, leaving me alone in the dusty archive.

⁂

What she had called a need to "reorganize" was quite possibly the worst-organized file room I had seen in my life. Files, folders everywhere, strewn all over the floor. Photographs, reports, and pieces of notebook paper scrawled with handwritten notes as far as the eye could see. It also made me slightly queasy because this room appeared far deeper that should be possible given the route we had taken around the floor of the building, and I had to tell myself "It's magic, that why it doesn't make sense."

The files themselves were immensely interesting. Each file was a single client—Blue for businesses, red for individuals, and purple for other things. From what it looked like, nearly every major company in the United States had a contract with 50 Thousand Consulting, with a variety of different plans and services. One company, a tech startup in California, had paid a handsome sum to protect its lead employees from "Curses, Hexes and Vexes", while a large New York City investment firm had a yearly retainer covering all its major employees with protective enchantments of the highest quality. The number amounts paid were mind-boggling, and the sheer amount of wealth being poured into this business was staggering.

By noon I had done little more than some light reading, not caring too much about the whole task of organizing at all and headed to the break room for my lunch break. It was a quiet place, dotted with a few people here and there eating food from the many different places to eat in Cincinnati. I had noticed that on my last jaunt downtown: there was just a huge plethora of places to get food from and it boggled my mind. Food of all kinds, from Indian to Korean to Vietnamese…Cincinnati's dining scene was rocking.

Right now, though, all I wanted was a cup of coffee, and I headed through the tables and chairs to the large, industrial coffee machine. An espresso pour spout stuck out of the sheet of metal, below a button that read "Push for Coffee." I grabbed a nearby foam cup and put it in position before hitting the button. Nothing happened. I waited a few moments to be sure it wasn't a delayed response of some kind and hit the button again. Nothing.

"Stupid thing," I muttered, and started to look around to see if there was another switch.

"Excuse me?" I heard a voice say, and I looked around. No one was looking at me and I shook it off. "Who exactly are you calling stupid?"

I blinked. The espresso machine was *talking* to me.

"I…I…" I tried to form a sentence. "I didn't mean to, I'm s—"

"I will have you *know*," the coffee machine said, its insides audibly boiling with rage, "That I have a Ph.D. in Classical Literature *and* Germanic Languages. I have written *two* books on the legal delineation of identity and its implications for individuation and migration as manifest in German exile literature of the period 1933-1945. *Who is stupid now, human!?!*" The espresso machine screeched, and I turned to see that half the break room was now looking at me. A man in a suit nearby pointed at a sign on the wall; I read it and turned a deep crimson shade in my cheeks. *Please do not insult the espresso machine. It is sensitive about its useless graduate degrees.*

I picked up my coffee mug and decided to get

some air.

⁂

The coffee shop where Apollo worked was only down the street from the 50 Thousand building, and I was thankful it was so close. Even despite the mid-Tuesday rush I was able to grab a seat at the bar and get a cup of coffee relatively quickly.

I took a few minutes to look at some of the people dropping in and out of the shop. How many of them were some breed of supernatural…thing? More than once I spotted a red mark on someone's arm that indicated their membership in *Sorcera*, but beyond that I had no idea. I didn't even understand what that meant, for me or for anyone else.

"It's rude to stare at people, ya know." Apollo's voice was a welcome distraction from the crowd-watching that was beginning to well up my anxiety.

"Sorry, I was just thinking about—"

"—Who is what and how would you know?" He chuckled and continued pulling someone's espresso shot. "You'll mostly see *Sorcera* and *Vulnerabl* here. At least, coming in the front door."

I gestured to my arms. "But you all don't have…you know…"

Apollo nodded and snapped the lid on a cup, handing it across the bar to a frumpy-looking old woman, before relaxing in the moment of a lull between customers. "No, we don't do the whole 'branding' thing that you folks do. Instead, we wear these." He stepped back and gestured to a gold chain around his ankle. "Gold jewelry," he explained, "Traditional and supposedly boosts your capabilities.

Plus, it's way classier than magic bar code tattoos, let's be honest. So—" he leaned over the counter, flashing a brilliant smile. "How's your second day on the job? Make any new friends?"

I thought for a moment about Carrie, Carma, Jake, the espresso machine—none of them particularly friend-like. Acquaintances, maybe, but certainly not friends. "I'm sorta…in the process?" I gave Apollo a sheepish look and took a gulp of my mocha-caramel-whatever latte. "I sorta don't fit in very well. I got in a fight with an espresso machine, for Pete's sake."

Apollo pulled a double-shot of espresso into a small coffee cup. "Yeah? That's nothing. One time I spilled a cup of tea on a customer's shoes and she ended up hexing me. I spent seven days completely unable to pick up anything breakable or I would immediately drop it. You just get used to this stuff I guess."

I nodded and took another sip. "You grew up knowing about all this…stuff?"

Apollo downed the double-shot of espresso without adding anything to it. "Yeah. So I don't have the whole context of somebody's 'first day' in a world filled with wizards and dragons. But I've seen enough new employees around to get an idea of what you're going through and to tell you the truth, you're taking it pretty well. You're not curled up on the sofa crying or bugging people to teach you magic spells or asking around about magical drugs. So there's that at least. What do they have you doing, anyhow?"

"Paperwork and filing. I've been here two days and it's already a little soul-crushing."

"That's *Sorcera* for you, hon. All the paperwork

and bureaucracy of the most micromanaging governmental entities of the world, all coiled around the ability to cast basic spells; but think of it this way—all the other societies have innate weaknesses and limitations on what we can and can't do. So, unless *Sorcera* shows, consistently, that it can govern and manage the nearly-limitless powers of its members, the other societies will see it as a threat. When you think about it, *Sorcera* has the potential to cause the most pain, chaos, and destruction on one of the largest scales, so it puts all kinds of roadblocks do even the simplest tasks because the alternative is a slippery slope toward massive chaos. In fact," Apollo downed another double-shot of espresso, "in some cities, *Sorcera* are banned completely because the Dragon in charge, and the societies living in that city, think it's too dangerous to have a human walking around who can blast holes in buildings or dry up a lake."

I drained the rest of my latte from the cup. "I guess that's reasonable. It just sucks that it means someone's got to do all the paperwork in the meantime."

Another customer approached the bar and Apollo reached out and patted me on the head lightly. "Aww. Poor Andy has to do work. You'll be fine, just keep doing your thing and you'll get your permit soon. Then you'll start doing fun stuff. Maybe."

Tuesday having wrapped up without much further event, I headed back home. I lugged a folding chair up and sat in my empty living room, my phone propped up against a fast food bag and lazily marathoning something on my phone.

Bzz. A notification drifted across the top of my phone screen. *Mom: Hey love, can you call or txt me as soon...* I popped another curly fry into my mouth.

Mom: Haven't heard from you in a... I took a sip of my soda.

Mom: Are you avoiding my calls? Ple...

I sighed and leaned my head back against the wall. Yes, I was avoiding her calls. I didn't need another guilt trip or another victim complex right now. "Why did you drop out of school?" "Why aren't you applying yourself?" "Why don't you ever call? I'm a widow now, I need support from you." No, do not want. In fact, the only thing I wanted was a bit of extra sleep and another season of this show to get released to streaming video.

The video stopped on its own. *Incoming call: Hank.*

My brother. Dammit. I couldn't avoid it, could I? I considered just muting my entire family, but with the strange happenings from the last week I honestly had a lot of questions I wanted answers to. I hit the handset icon. "Hey Hank."

"Andy. How's Cincinnati treating you?"

"About as good as it can." I tried to keep my tone as neutral as possible and not open myself to further criticism I'm sure was powered by Mom's nagging. She might even be on the other line, just listening in.

"Mom's been trying to reach ya. Are you avoiding her?"

Too late. "I'm uh...I'm just doing a lot. Not trying to be, like, specifically *avoiding* her..." Lies, Andy! You're a liar. All the lies.

"Yeah, sure...but Mom's getting pretty upset.

You don't want Mom upset, do you? She's already going through *so* much."

"Wait, *she's* going through so much?" I couldn't help the rising anger in my voice and I took another big gulp of soda while I mentally bit my tongue.

"Well, yeah. She just lost a husband, Andy."

"Well, she's also been keeping some major secrets, Hank. Wait till I tell you what I've found out since moving out here—"

The phone made a squealy noise and the call disconnected. I picked it up as my TV show restarted on its own, and I swiped to close it and call Hank back. Had I lost reception? Weird.

I pressed "Call" on my contact list. The call immediately disconnected without even going to voicemail.

"Did you...*block me*?" I said to no one, frustratedly launching my video streaming app again. Dammit, Hank. As the video resumed, I stuffed another fry into my mouth to stifle the curse words coming up my throat.

Don't do that again.

I choked as I heard the deep voice in my ear, jumping nearly to my feet. It was that same dark, cranky voice that had been in my ear during my interview. "H-h-hello?" I said through bits of potato.

Yer brother don' know. Yeh aren' allowed to tell him. Understood?

I stood there a long moment, shaking as I looked at the darkness of the walls and corners of the condo, trying to discern the voice's source. It seemed to be coming from everywhere. "I—I—"

Understood? It was far more threatening this time.

I coughed out a "Yes" and picked up my drink to

wash it down. When I finished hacking up whatever was in the back of my throat, I had the feeling that the source of the voice was gone.

Gone, but not forgotten.

CHAPTER 6

One thing I can never stand about the 9-5 grind is Thursday. It exists, and we as people recognize its existence, but I have yet to find a person who works the standard corporate schedule who enjoys Thursdays. Wednesday gets lots of flak for being "hump day" and the middle of the week, but when you break Thursday down, you find that it's the epitome of end-of-the-week exhaustion. Fridays, even, end up being a better day because of the morale boost of the oncoming weekend, and the fact that no one really delves deep into hard work on Friday. Mondays get a lot of hate too, but on Mondays at least you're rested enough to be half-conscious after a cup of coffee or two. So you're left with Thursday, the worst possible day of the week, which by all rights should be taken out back and shot.

Wednesday, to its credit, had been long but bearable. The entire day had been spent in the file room, putting things into piles mostly absent-mindedly. I didn't really care much about the job itself, or any of the perks that came with it. The idea of wizardry and sorcery, while really cool, were also a level of ridiculousness that I didn't particularly need in my life. And, to be fair, all signs of cool things were under heavy paperwork to uncover, none of which I felt particularly compelled to complete.

This Thursday, however, was truly a credit to its species.

The folder hit my desk with a sharp slap, and I jolted upright, tearing my eyes away from the company email I had been trying to decipher (*Re: Fire Safety and Evacuation - Sorcerous Fires and You! (Part 2)*[7]) and gave my best impression of a raptly-attentive employee while gazing up at the button-nosed Wizard in front of me. I had started to recognize them on sight. Why did they all have to look so similar? The same pinstripe suits, the same blue-and purple paisley ties, the same obnoxiously smug look plastered over their stupid faces. I could already see Devin fitting in with them someday.

He glanced at my nameplate. "Alright…*Andy*," he said as though my name was a foreign word he was attempting to pronounce correctly for the first time, "Since you're the only co-op free right now due to the maintenance outage, I suppose you'll have to do."

---

[7] "Corporate policy mandates that any sorcerous fire that cannot be put out by normal fire-extinguishing means be documented and filed with the Audit department for review. If said fire happens to currently be on you or someone else's person, then it is suggested this paperwork be completed with all haste." - 50 Thousand Employee Handbook, Page 172

I smiled and nodded politely, holding back an eye twitch. I did not like this man. *I'll have to do, will I?* I began to mentally drop profanity.

"I wouldn't finish that thought if I were you," he snapped. *Dammit, Lisa was right.* "Now if you're quite finished with being a contemptuous new hire, you might actually learn something."

"Yessir."

He scowled at me over his horn-rimmed glasses. "Now, you'll find that I have a list of items that need purchasing. Go down to the 14th floor, and you'll find the security office. Borrow a bodyguard and get these things from the market. I expect them to be delivered to my office by 2. Give your receipt to accounting."

Without another word he turned on his heel and was gone down the hallway.

Deep breaths, Andy. Shaking myself mentally, I opened the folder to find a small list of items—Gold foil, wooden skewers, a crystal cup, and something called "Calfnot"—and it didn't seem too difficult. But where I would buy these things I had no idea. I glanced at my watch: it was already almost noon. I leapt up and grabbed my hoodie from the hook and took off toward the elevators. A minute later I emerged on the 14th floor, greeted with the same matte gold walls and white marble tile floors as my own floor. The sign directed me around the corner to the security office and I entered, my heart beating in my chest. What kind of security would be employed at a company that employs powerful wizards?

The office, however, was empty save for a security desk and a single door. I glanced around to be sure I was in the right place and spotted a "Press here for assistance" button on the desk. I pressed it, my finger shaking from the trepidation.

The door opened, and a tall, stern-faced woman stepped through to meet me. She was dressed in a form-fitting business casual outfit, and I might have doubted she was any kind of security guard whatsoever if not for the sword that hung, sheathed, from her belt. Auburn-red, wavy hair hung loosely around her freckled, stern face, which currently fixed me with a cold stare. "What can I do for you?"

"I—" I stumbled over my words and tried to sew them together into a cohesive sentence. I bought time by opening the folder and shuffling the pages inside briefly. "I was told to get a—a bodyguard—"

"Great, let's go." She slipped past me toward the door and held it open. "Where are headed?"

Dammit, why were these easy questions so friggin' difficult? "I don't…some kind of market—I have to get—"

"Are you new?" She stopped, and that icy glare was on me again. An awkward silence thick enough to frost a cake settled between us for a long moment before I nodded.

She gestured out the door with her head impatiently. "That's fine, I'll fill you in while we go." I followed her down the hall, to the elevators.

My eyes were stuck forward as the elevator made it swiftly down to the ground floor. The folder clutched protectively to my chest like a +1 shield of organization, I willed myself to not say a word and risk sounding utterly stupid. And then, of course, was this woman, who was apparently a security guard at a firm that, again, hired powerful wizards. Was she a wizard herself? What kinds of weapons did she have at her disposal besides the sword? No way to be sure. Clearly, I didn't want to piss her off.

"Okay," She said as the elevator began to slow, "You seriously need to chill out. I can, like, feel your tension." She glanced sideways at me. "You're going to give yourself indigestion or something if you keep that up."

I opened my mouth to apologize, or argue, or something, but at that moment the door to the lobby opened and she was off again, slipping past the front desk and out the doors onto Walnut Street. I followed as closely behind as I could. "Um…Hey…security…person—"

"Killian." She stopped and rounded on me impatiently.

"Right. Killian. I don't know where we're going. I'm not trying to bother or anything, but I really could use some context here. If you can fill me in it would really help me toward the whole 'chilling out' thing."

Killian gave me an analytical gaze, as though trying to determine whether giving me context would be worth her time. The alternative, it appeared, would be to drag a huge ball of over-wound nerves behind her like a wounded puppy. The payoff was worth it, apparently, so she took a deep breath. "So, Wizards need spell components to do the stuff they do. Of course, going out and buying those components is, like, beneath them or something, so they have co-ops like you doing it. You, however, have absolutely no way to defend yourself if someone tries to screw with you, so I'm here to keep you from getting killed.[8] It's

---

[8] "Avoiding death or serious injury in the workplace is

company policy if a co-op is headed to the Market."

I took a gulp. Why would something try to screw with me? I still had no idea what kind of dangerous things I might meet at any given time. "The Market?"

Killian gestured down the street. "Walk. I'll explain." I took off, feeling slightly less anxious as I kept up with Killian's long stride. "The Goblin market," she explained, "is pretty much the only place to get anything you need for spell components. Stuff has to have levels of purity to meet corporate standards, and your standard department store doesn't meet those. Goblins, however, refuse to do business by mail-order, so we have to go to them; it's a *Kobolda* thing about upselling and doing business face-to-face."

"Kobolda are one of the Societies, right?"

She nodded. "Anything that is innately supernatural and can't blend into society without a disguise or some other magic is in *Kobolda* by default. And they govern on a strict meritocracy with archaic codes of conduct. So their word is their bond, and their currency is the art of the deal. It's called the Promise Code."

We crossed another street, ending up on Central, where we stopped to wait for the light to change. I looked at Killian and noticed that her sword seemed to have disappeared. I must have been rather obvious about my gaze as the light changed, because she

---

everyone's responsibility. Especially your own! The best and most efficient way to avoid death or dismemberment while on the time clock is to make sure you clock out promptly before being dismembered or killed. " - 50 Thousand Employee Handbook, Page 57

raised an eyebrow at me. "Either you're wondering about my sword or you're checking out my backside, neither of which are your business."

"No, I—" I started to protest.

She rolled her eyes. "You're fine, it was a joke. Remember what I said about chilling out?" As we reached the far corner, she looked down at my name-card handling from my jacket as she held out a hand to stop me. "Andy. Alright Andy, you need to breathe. I'm not taking you any further until you take a deep breath."

She locked eyes with me and gave me a look of impatient, but understanding, concern—like an Aunt who always makes sure you've eaten enough and only gives cash for birthdays. I felt the rush of air in my lungs as I did as I was told, and then nodded. "Alright. I feel better."

"Good, here we go." She reached for a nearby bronze-edged door into the corner building but then stopped, pulling her hand away as another thought seemed to occur to her. "Do you know the rules of the Market?" I shook my head. "OK. Rule 1: Never put anything on store credit. Rule 2: Never take anything that's offered for discount or for free. If they try, always insist to pay. Never pay less than the posted price. Rule 3: If anyone asks if you work *for* 50 Thousand, you don't. You work *at* 50 thousand. That is immensely important. Understand?"

I nodded again, more confidently this time. Understanding at least a little of the rules was comforting to my anxiety-tangled mind. Killian pushed the door open and led me down a dim hallway to a staircase. She took them two at a time, with me following behind her as we went down a few flights. Finally, at the bottom, we emerged into the Market.

Situated inside a spacious area much like a convention hall, the Market appeared to be row after row of booths and shop fronts. The corridors between these shop fronts were filled with people of many shapes and sizes. I couldn't help but stare for a moment, as a large rock-skinned man strode past, gingerly carrying a soft rabbit in his massive hands. Behind him, an old woman was begging him to let her pet it. Several smaller people in black hats swept past me down the stairs and into the crowd. Nearby I overheard an argument between a shopkeeper and customer about whether a gem was a particular shade of blue.

Each and every shop in the Market was manned by a goblin—tiny, greenish-grey creatures with multiple eyes and many more digits on their hands than seemed completely necessary. One of them spotted me and waved, gesturing for me to come join him at his booth. I politely shook my head and looked desperately toward Killian.

She held out her hand for the folder, which I passed to her; I felt somewhat more *Vulnerable* without it, however, and sidled a little closer to her side.

"Hmmmm…Seems pretty easy. I think I know where you could get the foil…the others would be there too probably… But Calfnot…I'm not sure on that one. You may have to ask someone for that information. Come on." She handed me the folder back and started off into the crowd. I quickly followed, not wanting to lose my bodyguard in the mess of the Market.

In a moment we had parted the crowd and ducked into a small dingy booth with a hanging cloth sign that read *Dingo's Din*. Inside, I found myself in front of dozens of overflowing shelves carrying all manner of items from toilet seats to jewelry to rubber ducks with demon horns. Before I had more than a moment to take it all in, however, Killian cleared her throat and gestured to the shop's Goblin, the eponymous Dingo, who sat nearby on an upturned bureau with a sparkly "My name is" nametag. His three eyes all pointed at me while he twiddled his disturbing number of fingers impatiently.

I took another steadying breath and stepped forward. "Hello, I need to…buy…a few things." I hoped I sounded more confident than I felt.

The goblin regarded me for a second and one of his eyes looked from me to Killian and back. "Right, right. What do you need?" He spied my folder. "Got a list?"

I had barely taken the page from the file folder when it was snatched from my grasp by a hand that had what seemed like eleven fingers. One eye read the list while the other two made darting motions from shelf to shelf. I gave a sidelong glance toward Killian who had leaned against a shelf and was now watching me with crossed arms and a bemused expression.

The goblin handed the list back and grabbed a bucket before springing into the shelves and digging around, knocking things to the floor as he did so. He seemed to know exactly what he was looking for, however, because he soon returned, the bucket now containing a pack of wooden skewers, gold foil, and a crystal cup. He sat them on the counter.

"How much?" I asked, unable to contain my

smile. This was a lot easier than I had expected.

The goblin pulled out a large ledger and checked an index. "Let's see…Crystal cup is fifty…skewers are twenty…and the gold foil…that's a doozy. Almost a hundred on its own. But I tell ya what," He looked up with a very sincere smile. "I'll save you trouble and give you the whole thing for a hundred and fifty bucks."

I shook my head. "I'll pay full posted price, please."

The goblin frowned and looked back down at the book. "Aw, you're no fun. Fine, fine. Full price is one sixty-five."

I glanced over at Killian for approval and she gave me a shrug. I furrowed my eyebrows and counted out the money, trying to keep my fingers from shaking. I reached out to hand over the money before I stopped as I watched the goblin gingerly putting the items into a plastic bag. "Wait," I added. The goblin looked up innocently. "How much is the posted price for the plastic bag?"

The goblin gritted his teeth, knowing he'd been caught again. I heard a snort behind me and looked to see Killian chuckling under her breath. I wondered vaguely if, had I neglected to pay for the bag, she would have stepped in to correct me or let me get caught in whatever trap had apparently been set.

The goblin pointed at the book with a finger. "One dollar."

I handed over the money and took the bag, feeling a sort of warm confidence building up in my stomach. I thanked the goblin, and we left the shop. "OK," I said as soon as we were out, "What was that all about?"

Killian broke into a smug grin. "Goblins look for any opportunity to have you indebted to them. Discounts, free services, all these things are sort of an implied type of transaction, and they take that really seriously. Oh, they might call on that favor ten years from now, or twenty, but that favor is valid enough that they can make you do something later that you don't want to do."

I frowned loudly. "So I might have some kind of debt I owe and not even realize it?"

She pointed down the row toward a sort of banker's cage a few rows down. "The tellers have all the records of every debt, so it's never a bad idea to go check and make sure every once in a while. Then, you can go to whoever you owe the debt to and offer to repay it on your terms. Honestly, I'm not sure why they haven't covered this in training yet for you. Did you even read your Handbook—hey, wait!" But I was already gone, heading toward the banker's cage. I thought had stuck me and any thought of completing my list was gone for the moment.

Debts…maybe they were a key to finding out what had happened to Dad. Maybe he had been killed over them, and there would be a record…if I was even allowed to find out.

I reached the teller and put my hands on the counter. The three goblins behind the cage all wore the same gold-flecked, marble-patterned jacket and were shuffling massive amounts of papers back and forth between each other. The one in front of me stopped and peered at me quizzically through its four—no, five—eyes. "LaFayette, A."

"Y-yes, that's me," I said, suddenly realizing that in my impulse I hadn't bothered to think about how this teller desk works.

"No debts recorded."

I let out a breath. "Can you look up someone else's records?"

It narrowed three of its eyes. "Depends. For a price."

I opened my wallet and took out all of my remaining cash. "Is forty…forty-five dollars enough?"

The goblin gestured to the porthole in the cage and I passed the bills through. After counting it twice, the bills flicking through its fingers—ok, really, that many fingers are just *not necessary*—it put them away. "What's the name?"

"LaFayette, Thomas."

The goblin scanned his book and flipped through it, his eyes scanning multiple pages at once. Finding the entry, he looked up at me with a single eye. "Deceased?"

I nodded.

"This record is sealed," he said slowly, "under orders of a Dragon."

"What does that mean?" I said, putting my hands up on the cage desperately.

"It means," came Killian's voice behind me, "That a member of the ruling society wanted that record sealed, and only another Dragon can undo it. And *please*," she added with a very stern glare, "Don't run off like that. I am literally here to keep you safe and I can't do that if you do things like that, alright? Next time you're going on a leash."[9]

---

[9] "50 Thousand Consulting is often known to have 'fun' and 'interesting' company events, such as Seventies Week and various holiday celebrations. It is worth noting that the formerly

"Sorry...I'm just trying to make sense of everything, that's all."

Killian looked like she was ready to unleash a string of profanity at me, but the goblin cut her off. "Fletcher, K," the goblin said, flipping through his book, "Perpetual debt owed to her by the Gnome Nation—"

"Oh, shut up," Killian snapped before turning on her heel.

I followed, taking out the folder and checking off everything but one. We were still making good time; it was only a quarter to one. "So what's this 'Calfnot'?"

"It's a plant," she replied over her shoulder as we rounded a corner past an old goblin woman selling enchanted soaps (with such attractive scents as "Dandelions and Bacon" and "Fresh Corpse"), "We'll go to the greenhouse. It's where most magical plants are." We made another turn and then ended up against one of the side walls of the exhibit area in front of an elevator. We stepped on and Killian pressed the "ROOF" button.

The doors closed, and I let out a deep breath. "I...I appreciate you helping me out. I'd be really screwed right now otherwise."

Killian shrugged and didn't look at me. "It's fine. We were all new once. You just really need to relax,

---

annual 'Take your Pet to Work day' was cancelled permanently a few years ago due to wide misunderstandings regarding what constitutes a 'pet'. At this time, pets of any kind are not allowed on company premises, no matter how cute they are, or how much they beg, or how much you swear they are really a dog and not your neighbor in a dog suit under an enchantment. Looking at you, Brian." - 50 Thousand Employee Handbook, page 312

listen, and be more cautious. But if nothing else, you're hella entertaining." I couldn't think of a response and just stayed quiet as the doors opened up, and we found ourselves on a rooftop.

Sprawled out to my right was part of the Cincinnati skyline: Carew tower rising up above the other buildings like a golden middle finger facing the Kentucky border situated just across the Ohio River. The roof we were standing on was paved, and covered with several rows of glass, steamed-up shelters. I could see the shaped of trees and bushes inside, and I looked around for a goblin attendant. I didn't need to wait long.

"Hello, hello!" came a voice from inside one of the greenhouses. A smiling, wrinkled old goblin woman came trotting out to meet me. She actually appeared quite pleasant, with a wreath of honeysuckle resting between her gnarled ears. "Don't you two just look lovely today? What can I do for ya?"

Killian again stepped back to let me work and I wondered if she was just enjoying watching me be awkward and nervous. "I'm looking for Calfnot."

The goblin stroked her chin. "Calfnot, Calfnot…Follow me, I think I've got what you need." She trotted into the nearest greenhouse through a glass sliding door, and the two of us followed.

"Calfnot…Wizards should learn to use the proper names for things. Calfnot is also called Calves' snout," the goblin said in a musically informative tone, "Commonly known as 'snapdragons'. But snapdragons are actually a whole genus called *Antirrhinum*, and there's 19 species there this could refer to. But out of those, seven are nonmagical, and of the remaining 12 three are only used in minor enchantments. I'm guessing since you work for 50 Thousand that it's some kind of curse repellant, which means that only three of those species makes any sense."

Killian nudged my ribs from behind; I looked back and she mouthed the words "At 50 Thousand".

I cleared my throat. "I work *at* 50 Thousand," I corrected.

The goblin waved a hand dismissively and started picking through rows of pastel-colored flowers of all shapes and sized in a bed of flowering plants sever rows into the greenhouse. "Yes, yes, of course you do. Now of those three species, the first one, *Antirrhinum nuttallianum*, is native only to California and doesn't travel well. On the other hand, *Antirrhinum vexillo-calyculatum* does travel well but doesn't produce as much consistency in the spells in the summer time, so that leaves us with…" She pulled out a string of purple flowers on a stem, each petal tinged with a yellowish tip, and offered it. "*Antirrhum Majora*. Should do your Wizard pretty well."

I gratefully took the flower. "How much?"

"Twenty dollars."

I reached into my pocket, coming to the sudden realization that I had just impulsively dumped all of my money downstairs on a dead-end chance at information on Dad. How could I be so stupid? My heart immediately started to race and I stumbled over what I would say next. The goblin woman grinned and opened her mouth—almost certainly to offer me store credit.

But she didn't have to. Killian reached past me and handed the goblin a twenty-dollar bill. "Come on, you're going to be late, Andy. You owe me lunch or something." I gave Killian a grateful look and turned to leave.

"Andy...not Andy LaFayette, by any chance?"

I stopped and turned. "Yes?"

The goblin scratched her chin. "Now that's interesting, isn't it? Someone was just here a few minutes ago asking about you. They said you'd probably come by. They wanted me to tell you something." she gestured for me to come close. I took a step forward and leaned down, the goblin putting her lips up to my ear.

"Stop searching," she whispered, "Or you're next." I barely had a moment to register the words before a searing pain split my head as the goblin dug one of its fangs into the upper cartilage of my ear.

What happened next was just a blur, as I was nearly thrown aside by Killian as she placed herself between the two of us, her sword gleaming in her hand and pointed at the goblin's wicked grinning face. Grasping my ear in one hand and my bag of spell components in the other, I stumbled out of the humid greenhouse with Killian backing me up, cursing under her breath.

As soon as the elevator doors closed behind us she pulled a small pouch from her pocket and took out a tiny jar, from which she drew a cotton ball soaked in some kind of amber liquid. "Put this on your ear." I did so and tried to calm my rapid breathing as the burning in my ear began to subside. She looked me over, as though checking for other injuries. "Are you OK?"

I gulped hard to swallow the knot in my throat. "I-I think so. More...surprised, than anything, I think." I looked at the cotton ball. "I don't think I'm even bleeding."

Killian shook her head as the elevator doors opened to the market ground floor again. "Goblin bites are mostly an intimidation tactic; it probably didn't even break the skin. Sorry that happened to you…I don't know what could have provoked that kind of response. What did she say, anyway?"

I shrugged again. My detective work was getting noticed and I didn't want to drag someone else into it just yet. As we left the market I took one last look behind me at the people milled about in the vendor hall, going about their business. Was I looking in the wrong place? It was hard to tell.

Killian barely said a word on our brisk walk back to the office. I asked if she wanted to join me for a cup of coffee before going in, but she declined and told me she was more of a tea person anyhow before slipping past the jade and bronze doors to return to the security desk.

I dropped the components off with the wizard's assistant, an older lady with many pictures of cats in frames around her cubicle, before taking a break for lunch. With no one else to go see, I decided to take a walk and find someone to help me make sense of it all.

CHAPTER 7

"So you think the Goblins have something to do with it? Like…all of them?" Apollo took another bite of his vegetarian sushi and chewed thoughtfully.

Fountain square, situated in Downtown, was definitely a good spot to try and calm one's nerves, to be sure. The 43-foot fountain splashed water loudly over the bronze statues decorating the massive piece near the center of the square, while high office buildings rose up all around to give the whole plaza almost the sense of being in a clearing among the massive forest of city blocks. Apollo, coming off another morning shift, seemed mildly distracted by the people passing by but tried to listen attentively as I told the tale of my experiences in the Goblin market.

"I don't know," I replied. "The teller seemed to know something, and if Dad's records are sealed then that usually means something important, right? I mean…I'm looking for any leads at all, and I'm so desperate to just find something."

Apollo nodded, his eyes following a handsome young man in a suit crossing from the bank building past us. "The problem is that you don't know what kind of stuff your dad was into. If dragons are involved, it's probably big enough that Employee-who-started-on-Monday might not want to stick their cute little nose into it."

I shrugged. "That's fair. Maybe I'm pushing too hard. I need to stop being so impulsive. Also, don't call me cute, please." I watched Apollo's attention span shift again. "Are you alright? You're like…literally everywhere else today."

Apollo snapped back to attention. "Sorry. I'm just…" He took a deep sigh. "I haven't…*fed*…recently. The coffee shop helps stave off the hunger, but a man's gotta eat."

I raised my eyebrows. "Ah. Right." I contemplated it for a moment. "How often do you have to…?"

"Every couple weeks at the least. But I'm picky, I guess…I try to avoid people I might run into again later. It gets all kinds of awkward."

Holding back an amused snort, I gave him a sympathetic gaze. "Poor Apollo. Constantly combating his worst enemy of all: awkwardness."

"Alright, alright, enough of that." He took a steadying breath and focused back on our conversation. "So, what do you know so far? Your dad worked for 50 Thousand for, oh, ten years or so."

"*At* 50 Thousand."

"Right. Also, he had a debt record and it's sealed. Some goblins know about it. What else?"

I shook my head. "That's literally it. I lived with the man for most of my life and I never knew about any of this. I seriously just thought my dad worked for a bank." Frustrated, I dug my fork into my Caesar salad, which hadn't really seemed that appetizing to begin with and so had gone mostly untouched.

"From what *I* know, he was a well-respected guy, but I don't know much more than that. But you got his condo, right? There's no papers or anything...no notes or pictures anywhere at his house?"

"50 Thousand confiscated pretty much everything including the furniture. They were scouring pretty hard." I put the lid back on my salad and bagged it again. "I'm wondering if he might have hidden something that they missed, but I can't imagine that a team of wizards would be able to miss much."

Apollo stroked his dark goatee. "You never know...and if you wanted to *misbehave* slightly..."

I raised an eyebrow. Was he suggesting what I thought he was suggesting? "What about awkwardness?"

He cleared his throat. "No, no, not that kind of misbehave! No, no," He adjusted his shoulders as if he was pushing dirty thoughts away. "I have a few books that might be useful, and I have a few tricks up my sleeve as well. If you felt like doing some...I dunno, divining or scrying or something. We could give it a try. It's an old house, right? Those are usually really resonant for scrying spells. They're not hard to set up either."

I felt some of the color drain from my face. "Me? Casting a spell? I don't know. I've been a co-op for, like, a week. I haven't been allowed to even see any of the Standard Casting Manuals the wizards use, let alone actually do any magic myself."

"Sure, sure…" He raised his eyebrows and lidded his own lunch. "But once you get your Permit, then any spell book you get your hands on is fair game, in theory. Call it…independent research."

"Right." I felt my phone buzz and I checked it. "Huh. I just got an invite to a meeting with someone called a…'Silencer'. What's that?"

Apollo's eyes went wide. "Oh. You're meeting your silencer today. Well…you have fun with that." He got up to leave.

I grabbed his hand. "What's a silencer? Don't do that, you'll freak me out even more."

He sat back down. "Sorry, sorry…I didn't mean to scare you. It's just…ok. Let me explain. Everybody who's in on the Secret gets assigned a watcher. See, they don't want wizards and goblins and werewolves going rogue and causing problems in society—"

"—werewolves?!"

"—yes, now listen. Imagine having your own guardian angel. Except that instead of protecting you, they're protecting the world *from* you. Silencers keep The Secret…well…secret. They'll follow you around and keep you from doing anything stupid."

A long silence hung in the air. "You're saying I…I'm meeting someone who's going to be watching me forever?"

Apollo nodded grimly. "Pretty much. Sometimes, if someone's done something great or immensely beneficial for the Societies at large, a Dragon can call off their Silencer and declare them *'Pro Veritate'*. It's a pretty big honor."

I looked around. "Do you have one?"

"Yeah. But I've had mine since the day I was

born, and I don't see him very much. They tend to stay invisible unless they want to be seen." He looked at his phone to check the time. "But you'll be fine. Just be polite."

⁂

After leaving Fountain square I felt a distinct sense of dread looming over my head as I headed back toward Walnut Street, trying to contain the growing ball of tension welling up in my stomach. At this rate I was going to end the week with a stomach ulcer. What kind of creature would fit the bill for the enforcers of all magic-kind? At the same time, Killian seemed to be relatively normal and I'd had similar concerns, so it reasoned that I shouldn't need to worry now. Not to mention the fact that if this was the first time I'd heard about the Silencers at all, it probably wasn't quite as intimidating as it seemed. Maybe mine would stay invisible all the time. I could only hope…my mind kept envisioning a large, slimy creature watching me in the bathroom or while I slept.

When I arrived at the location specified in the email, I found a lot of the new hires already there in a waiting room situated outside of several meeting rooms. I spotted Jake and Carma in a corner and headed over. "Hey guys, how's your week been treating you?"

"Andy!" Carma leapt up and threw her arms around me. "Been wondering how you were. Everything's been fine over here what with Jake and I in the same department, but we were wondering what happened to you, especially after Elmer." Jake nodded solemnly.

"Wait," I said, taking a seat, "What happened to Elmer?" I almost forgot about the phone-addicted young kid from my first day.

Jake looked down at the floor and Carma glances surreptitiously around before leaning in to whisper. "I heard that he tried to steal something really valuable and got caught. And we haven't seen him since."

I swallowed another lump in my throat. "And Devin?"

"Got promoted already," Jake spat. "Some kind of fast-lane for potential Wizard Partners. Must be nice to have friends in high places."

The wait for these one-on-one silencer meetings was excruciating. As each name was called, the room became emptier, and the people coming back from their meetings all looked quite flustered or terrified. At least three didn't come back at all.

Jake was called before me, and when he returned, his stone-faced demeanor was faltering a bit. He was sweating, and his eyes were watery. Carma badgered him with questions but he dismissed her with a wave before saying simply, "Be truthful...that's all they want." He then headed out the door toward the elevators.

We continued to wait.

"LaFayette." Lisa called my name. Carma gave me an encouraging smile and two heavily-jeweled thumbs-up as I picked up my phone and headed back toward one of the offices. Lisa ushered me inside and closed me inside.

The room was empty of furniture except for a white table with chairs on either side. There wasn't any decor of any kind—including the muted-tone paintings that adorned the rest of 50 Thousand. It seemed almost clinical, and it was hard to tell if the chill in the room was from the room itself or emanating from the ice-cold glare of the creature on the other side of the desk.

Its light blue eyes seemed to pierce me as they gazed down the creature's long snout. Its ears twitched and the scraggled fur trembled slightly. It was a very strange sight, as the form of the creature seemed to be an old and sickly black dog with many scars and matted fur, but I could almost sense that it was more massive and unquestionably powerful than it appeared.

"Sit," The dog said, and I obeyed.

The dog looked down at an open folder in front of it and nosed through the paperwork. "Just checkin' a few things here, Andy. Jus' sit tight, and we'll get started." It spoke with a tired, west London gruffness but it didn't seem angry. I was almost relieved; I had the distinct feeling that I didn't want this…thing…mad at me. "How's yer week been so far, eh? Not too rough?"

I trembled. "N-not too rough, I guess. No."

He didn't seem at all fazed by my nervousness as he continued to ruffle through paperwork. "Get inta any trouble yet?"

I blinked. What exactly constituted trouble? I considered a cordial and vague "Not really," but Jake's admonition about being truthful rang softly in the back of my mind. The dog looked up and I could feel it eyes piercing my skin, and my heart started to race; not wanting to have a panic attack I did my best to steady myself with a few breaths. I probably looked very silly in my attempts to not hyperventilate, but the mangy dog didn't give any indication that it minded the extra moments of reflection. "I don't know if it's trouble, but a goblin bit me on the ear earlier today."

It nodded. "Eh, we'll get into that. First let's make ourselves acquainted, eh?" It dropped from the chair and trotted around the desk to sit on its haunches in front of me. With a twisted grin it offered me its paw. "I am the Moddey Dhoo." I took the paw in my hand and shook it lightly, the pads of the dog's foot leaving a tingling sensation on my fingers as it returned to its chair behind the desk.

"Ya been told how this Silencer stuff works, right?"

I nodded slowly. "You prevent me from spreading The Secret and from killing people, violating laws.... something like that, right?"

"More or less. There's only one big law that my kind care about, ya see. That's the one ya already know: The Silence. *Sorcera* calls in the Non-Disclosure. If ya start blabbing on to someone who's not in on the Secret, then that's where I step in. So don't do that and you and I ain't got problems."

I thought back to my phone call with Hank. "Did you disable my phone?"

"Yep."

"So that was your voice."

"Yep."

"And at the interview. That was you."

"Yep yep. And I'll turn yer phone back on, now that we've had this chat, but ya need to realize that ya can't go doing that anymore. Clear?"

"That's all fine," I replied, "but what happens if I make a mistake?"

"Mistakes happen. Do it at work you might get

written up or somethin'. Do it outside of work, and you and I have a talk."

I nodded again.

"Now on the other thing," He added as he closed the folder with his nose, "Is this stuff ya been doin'. This investigatin'." My heart dropped into my stomach with the realization that the Moddey Dhoo had probably seen my failed attempt to wrestle information about my Dad from the goblin teller's desk. Had he seen the goblin on the roof attack me too? "I know why yer doin' it," he continued, "and I'm not saying *not* to do it. I'm jus' saying that ya gotta be more careful who yer talkin' to about it. I know of yer Dad and I know he worked in some pretty messy business. Probably 'ad more enemies than friends, ya see. So if yer doing something and yer pokin' yer nose into what happened to him, make sure ya know who yer talkin' to and make sure ya have a plan of escape. Got it?"

A long moment hung in the air between us as I took in this bit of information. I sat there, my eyes gazing down at my shoes, while I waited for the Moddey Dhoo to say or do something else, anything else, that could move our interview along and get me out of this room. I felt my cheeks starting to burn and I realized how utterly foolish I must have appeared simply by my actions in the last few hours.

It finally spoke up. "Why are ya working here, kid? Ya don' seem like yer here to make a livin' or even get involved in this Secret business. I know ya spent yer whole life not knowin' and most of the time folks like that don't jump into working at a place like this. It's raised a few eyebrows 'round here, fer sure, and if there's anybody should know what yer reasoning is, it's gonna be me."

I looked up slowly, composing my thoughts and calming my breaths. "I came here to find out what happened to dad. I mean, magic and stuff? It's cool. It's overwhelming. But it's secondary to that, okay? I just want to know. It's not right and I want to know. I don't really have anything to lose."

It narrowed its eyes. "You'd think that, not knowin' what ya don't know. Fer certain, you've got a lot to lose, in fact…Not everybody's capable of being part of The Secret. Don' have the mind fer it, or the patience, or the willpower…in fact, I'd say that it's a safe bet that mos' people are just your usual mundane. So you've got a whole world in front of ya that you have chance to grab by the tail and make somethin' with. Ya gonna do it? If not, better let folks know now." It hunched backward in the chair. "Say ya do find out what happened to yer dad. What then, eh? You gonna stick around or you gonna bugger off? That's not a choice you can put off. You gotta make that decision now. An' it's a big one."

I tried to reply but I couldn't formulate my exact words. It occurred to me that everything I had seen so far—the wizardry, the magic creatures, and even the Moddey Dhoo, had been distinctly brushed off in my pursuit of information. I had just accepted it, apathetically, without even considering the surreality of my surroundings or the possibilities of them. It was very clear that I had started off this adventure on the wrong foot, and even now, on reflection, it felt like I was stumbling. I had been over-impulsive and avoided looking at the big picture—a chance to leave behind a mild, mundane existence in lieu of something more. Even if that 'more' was a cubicle farm. It would be a *magical* cubicle farm. And if I wasn't careful then I would probably end up losing my job and with it any chance of continuing my search.

These thoughts continuing to bounce around, the Moddey Dhoo seemed to understand that a bit of reorganization was going inside my head. "I'm not normally one to give ya some advice, now, kid," it said in a mildly gruff tone that certainly indicated impatience, "But you need to focus right now. People fight for jobs like yours day in and day out, and ya might not even realize it, but ya didn't get this job by accident. An' after that, you've got a stack of handbooks and pamphlets at your desk stuffed in a drawer like ya don't even care. But if ya do," it said, leaning across the table menacingly, which caused me to cower backwards in my chair, "If ya really do care than ya need to sit down and ya need to read 'em and give yerself some foundation. Otherwise yer not gonna be as strong when the storm hits. Ya understand?"

I did, or at least I thought I did, and I nodded my assent. The Moddey Dhoo gestured to the door dismissively. "Good. Now keep outta trouble and take this weekend to catch up on what ya should have been doing in the first place. Now git." The last word was barked through gritted teeth that left no doubt that I needed to vacate the room immediately.

I got up and hurried from the room, breezing past the others in the waiting room and not allowing myself to relax until I was safely back in my little cubicle. I put my head in my hands and sat there for a few minutes that seemed to pass unfathomably slowly. It wasn't an accident I was here…people who were raised knowing the Secret were probably far more qualified than I was to be sitting in this chair and yet here I was, risking it all…without a safety net.

I opened the drawer and looked down at the pamphlets I had so casually discarded. They stared up and me like orphaned children, and I gently picked them up to put them in my bag. I had reading to do. I had a foundation to build.

DEAD END

I couldn't think of what I was going to say first. My mind kept racing with worry and possibility, a tumult of words and actions spinning around in my head and barely dented with the sound of the little digital doorbell as I stepped out of the sunlight and into the dim coffee shop.

I didn't spot him at first, half-leaned over a corner table with some kind of iced drink on the table next to him. The ice had long melted, leaving the sweet concoction strangely separated: clear on top and cloudy on bottom. He, meanwhile, sat as if frozen to the seat, his eyes lazily staring at the coffee-themed painting on the wall. Some modern take on espresso-themed art, with curly words and fancy swirls.

I took a long moment to catch my own breath. All day I'd been dreading this moment. The hunt had been long to find him, and yet here he was, as plain as day. A lifetime of work seemed to be all for nothing. I felt like he should be running, and I should be chasing. And yet, here, in this cinnamon-scented air, the chase seemed to be entirely at an end.

Then again, I reminded myself, *there's no reason for him to run anymore.*

I headed for the bar first. "What can I do for ya?" The attractive black barista asked me, and I clearly stated my order while glancing periodically to make sure the corner table was still occupied. He didn't move. It was strange; as I turned my back he might have fled out the door—but something deep in my stomach gave me the distinct feeling that he knew I was here before I even walked in. If he had wanted to run, he'd have done it by now. Besides, it didn't hurt to leave the guy on edge for a few extra minutes while I paid for my cinnamon latte and a small pack of cookies. A drop of guilt hit my stomach momentarily, as though by postponing the inevitable I was causing him undue distress. Wasn't I, though? He knew why I was here. Perhaps I'd let him savor his last few moments before declaring victory. I tried not to let my smug feelings make their way onto my face as I turned and made my way to his corner table. The chair squeaked lightly as I pulled it out of position and, setting my coffee down on the stained hardwood, took a seat.

The sunlight was quickly fading, A splash of orange-yellow light creeping across the wall behind him, glistening on the expensive French presses and glass tumblers that sat perfectly perched in their places on the shelf. This place was well-kept, surely a side-effect of being a corporate franchise in the suburbs: close enough to town for there to be customers to service daily and just far enough from the city to demand perfection or risk losing customers. Customers were valuable here, so every detail had been inspected and double-inspected to be certain that nothing could possibly be seen as wrong or out of order. I had to respect that, in my line of work. Small mistakes could turn into disaster particularly fast.

I took a sip of the latte. My line of work...what would happen now that I had finally caught my prey? The Order of St. Hubert had a very specific task with specific skills, so now that her task was finished she would probably have to take up a new line of pursuit. Werewolves, maybe.

As I sat my cup down his eyes finally came back into focus and he seemed to recognize that I was there. His face was younger than I had expected; I was almost taken aback by the fact that he could have easily been a younger brother I had never had. Clearly this was meant to put me on edge, or maybe make me feel bad for arresting someone so young. I wouldn't fall for that trick again. His face couldn't hide what I knew about him, and how long he had really been running from justice.

He cleared his throat and took a deep, ragged breath. "I'm not going to run."

"I know." Wait, was that...was that compassion in my voice? *Dammit, get it together. You've won.*

"What's your name?" He asked, meeting my eyes with distinct curiosity. "I'd like to know who it is that's come all this way and chased me for so long."

I paused, suddenly feeling uncomfortable as I looked him in the eyes. Something was wrong there, as though his eyes were ages older than the rest of his body. "Lynette."

He nodded like I had just spilled my soul in a single word. It looked like he was pitying me. Was he? "You've been at this a long time. You and your—" He choked on a word. "—organization. I've never understood any of you, or why you do what you do."

"The Order of St. Hubert is noble and good," I said with more than a hint of edge in my voice.

"Is it? Is it noble and good to hunt something defenseless?"

I rolled my eyes. "You say that now, but it's hard to push that argument when you're moving in the blink of eye and nothing but claws and teeth. *We*—" I pointedly tapped my index finger on the table, "—protect people from *you*."

He shook his head slowly. "Back in the 15th century, perhaps, when my kind had rogues and criminals—much like yours. We hunted them with you. We took them down together and saved countless lives with our actions. But then there were fewer of those, and then none, because all of us that remained swore oaths of nobility, to protect mankind." He winced at the thought. "And you took our oath…and used it against us." He shifted his gaze down to the swirling clouds of creamer floating in my latte. "The Guild of Hunters became like caged birds and taught only fear."

I raised an eyebrow. "What?"

He didn't look up. "Caged birds. Put something shiny in a cage with birds. They'll all want it. But then, whenever one of them goes for it, you shake the cage and scare them. You do this for some time, and after a while the birds learn not to touch the shiny thing. Then…then you take one of the birds out and put in a new bird. Do you follow so far?"

He looked up at me. I nodded, very slowly.

"The new bird goes for the shiny thing, but the other birds know that leads to a shaken cage. So, they attack the new bird and keep him away from it because they are afraid of the consequences. And the new bird—he learns that touching the shiny thing is something he should be afraid of. You do this again—replacing the birds one after the other in slow progression…and they all learn not to touch the shiny thing, but none of them know why. Even if you never shake the cage again."

I pursed my lips. "But they're fearing a real threat. You could still shake the cage."

"No, they're not. The danger is passed, but the fear remains. This is what my kind is to yours. A baseless fear."

"You're acting like you were the victims."

"We were."

Dammit, my smug smile had finally broken through. "So why didn't you ever fight back then, if you were feeling so…persecuted?"

"Because we swore not to!" he snapped. "We should never have taken that oath. We did it as a show of good faith…as a truce, for peace between my people and your ancestors. And your ancestors knew when we made that oath that we could not break it from then until eternity."

"What are you talking ab—"

He cut me off with a snarl. "'*By the grace of God, we swear our blood and souls into these words.*' A binding magic the likes of which shall never be seen again was cast that dreadful day—and because we swore to never harm mankind again on pain of death, we could never fight the Guild of Hunters when you decided to betray us."

I gritted my teeth but made my best to look calm as I took another sip of the latte. "I don't believe you."

He sighed deeply. "You don't have to. But haven't you ever wondered why we never fought back? Why we always ran from you when you came for us? It's not because we feared your skills as hunters. It's because we feared harming you by accident. Were we to strike even one of you…all of us would die a slow, and painful death. Each and every one would suffer for the sins of a single vampire who would dare harm a single human life." He sighed. "We were fools."

A stinging silence descended between us, broken only by the light jazz music playing from the speaker in the ceiling. The last dregs of sunlight slipped below the horizon across the parking lot, and the coffee shop was cast into a gloomy atmosphere that gave the room an unearthly feel.

He finally spoke again, softly. "She was pregnant."

"Who?" I sat the cup down again.

"Elissandra. She was with child…we had tried for centuries. We believed—we believed that if we could bring one more of our kind into this world, that perhaps *that one* wouldn't be bound by his ancestors' oath, and that he could fight back and save our race. A savior. It was an impossible dream—a hopeless chance. A doomed idea. And…however small the possibility…" He swallowed hard. There were tears in his eyes. I didn't know his race could even cry. "It died when you killed her four days ago."

My hand shook. I put it under the table to hide it. "I didn't…I didn't know. I'm sorry."

He shook his head from side to side. "My race is dead. I am the last."

I nodded grimly and looked down at my phone to read the time. I wasn't in a particular rush, but the conversation was beginning to weigh on me in a way I couldn't understand. "Well...it's time to go."

He didn't move. "'*If we should strike any sons or daughters of mankind, verily we shall all perish.*' Those are the words I swore eleven centuries ago. We were noble and strong and wished only for peace. But now we are gone."

"Come on, quit stalling." I stood up.

"You don't understand," He said, his breathing beginning to rise in sharp breaths. "If I strike any of mankind, there are no more of my kind to fear for their lives. I am...I am the last. No more would their deaths weigh on me if I were to break my oath."

I blinked incredulously. "But you would die."

I took a step back as he looked up and met my eyes one last time. "Yes, I would. Eventually. But you would die first."

I ran for the door. I ran as fast as my legs could carry me.

CHAPTER 8

Friday began with a far more pleasing note than Thursday had ended. I was already one indulgent dark chocolate mocha into the day ("As dark and sweet as the barista himself," Apollo said with his stupid irresistible smile as he handed me the cup) and the caffeine had begun to work its magic greasing the gears of my mind.

The previous night had been spent in Dad's still-empty condo, where by candlelight I had spread out all of the new employee materials before me and sorted them into the levels of importance. More mundane ones like *The Best Places to park in the Queen City* and *Social Ostracism from Being a Fan of the Wrong Chili Restaurant* were pushed aside in lieu of more potentially important ones like *7 Signs You're Secretly Possessed by an Evil Spirit* and *Understanding Your*

Relationship with Your City's Dragon (A Guide).[10] Those, plus the ever-important Employee Handbook, became my nighttime study material.

I instantly regretted not going through some of these pamphlets on the first day. Had I actually take the time to read through them, or even just the hot tips, the past week would probably have been an immensely more enjoyable experience. In the back of *Keeping Your Mind Safe from Intruders*, which I had noticed but not actually read on Monday, one of the tips was to carry a piece of onyx in my pocket to prevent from passive thought-reading. Very useful, especially with how awful the Wizard Partners at the firm seemed to treat co-ops. Toning down my frustrated thoughts in their direction would have been a chore unto itself.

"Andy." I looked up and saw one of the Wizard Partners at my desk. It was the man who had sent me into the market yesterday.

"Yessir." I felt my heart start to pound again.

"So, I had the opportunity to check the components you procured. If I'm honest, the task wasn't very high on my priorities and I figured if you didn't get it right, then I'd have time to find someone else more competent to take care of it."

I nodded with as much of a polite smile as I could muster. The Wizard waited for a moment and the edge of his lips twitched amusedly. "Huh. Finally started blocking your thoughts, huh? Well that's a good sign." He seemed to relax a little bit and picked

---

[10] "Do what they say or The Dragon will eat you." The rest of the pamphlet is blank.

at his middle fingernail with his thumb. "In any case, I didn't have to find that more-competent person because you pulled it off. Good job. Keep it up." Without another word, or the opportunity to respond, he had turned on his heel and was gone.

I felt completely elated, like a balloon of happiness was bubbling in my chest. I returned to my reports and inventory lists with a newfound sense of purpose—that of keeping my job. Once that was secure, I'd be able to work on my other goals. But until then, I would completely put all investigation out of my mind while—

An envelope hitting my desk brought me back from my moment of joy and I looked up to see Killian. "Hey you."

I grinned. "Hey Killian, what's brings you all the way up here?"

She gestured to the envelope. "Exam results are in for Co-op licensure. Security's handing them out because…well, not everybody passed. And those people get escorted out."

My heart sank. I had completely forgotten about the exam results that I had been told would determine if I was being hired on fully. All of my elated feelings quickly deflated, and, with trembling fingers, I picked up the envelope, and momentarily considered the simple manila item.

"Why would they even hire someone who hasn't passed the test yet?"

"Because working here looks good on a resume, even if it's for a week. I think they do it as a courtesy."

"What happens if I get denied? I need to know."

She leaned up against my desk and crossed her

arms. "It's not so terrible. You could opt to have your memory wiped and go back to whatever your life was like before—"

"Next."

"—or you can look for work elsewhere. As long as you're in on the Secret there's places that hire, but if I'm honest they don't pay well and normal humans without licenses don't have good job prospects. Unless you hedge."

"Hedge?"

"Yeah, Hedge Magic," she said, pushing a lock of her hair out of her face, "It's when you do freelance wizardry. Stock up on potions, scrolls, other one-time-use items…Basically folks who either don't want to keep up with renewing their license or would rather not deal with quite as much paperwork. If you're good at it, resourceful, and quick on your feet you can get some good money and even get contracts for stuff. Like being a security guard." She raised her eyebrows in apparent snark.

"Oh!" My eyes went wide with realization. "You're a hedge…wizard?"

"Hedge Magician," she corrected. "which is basically the wizard equivalent of a freelancer. I have been for quite a few years. I can go toe-to-toe with some of the top dogs around these days, and it's all experience. But quit stalling and open your envelope."

I nodded, and then took a few steadying breaths and opened flap of the manila parcel. Inside, a small folded piece of paper fell out and onto the desk. I picked it up and, saying silent hopes and prayers, opened it to read:

The Office of
The Most Venerable Sir
THE DRAGON OF CINCINNATI, OHIO

Having been satisfied that one ANDY LAFAYETTE has met the requirements specified by the *Sorcera* Society, and furthermore that proper notice and application has been made by 50 THOUSAND CONSULTING on behalf of said person, and furthermore reposing our confidence in both of the preceding that they shall conform to the Codes and Regulations of this city, and by the power invested upon us by Ancient Society of *Dracontos*, we do hereby approve a PERMIT for the practice of APPRENTICE LEVEL SORCERY by said person for the duration of ONE YEAR from the issuance of this Document, and enclose said permit with this letter.

> In witness whereof
> Under my own righteous claws signed
> At the Lair of My City
>
> Todd
>
> The Dragon of Cincinnati

I read the letter over several times before looking up. "Todd? The Dragon of Cincinnati is named *Todd*?"

Killian nodded solemnly as though the name carried great weight.

I shrugged and checked the envelope. Enclosed with it was a small, silver disc engraved with the *Sorcera* Society's sigil, accompanied by my name and a permit number. I sat, I am sure, for more than a few moments when Killian tapped my shoulder. "Congratulations. I don't have to escort you out." With a wry smile she got up to leave.

I stopped her. "Hey…thanks."

She waved dismissively behind her and disappeared down the hall. I instantly pulled out my phone to text Apollo[11]. *Got my permit!*

Apollo replied a few minutes later. *congrats. does this mean partying? or misbehaving?*

I thought about it for a few minutes before hitting send. I now had the ability to start a little external

---

[11] "50 Thousand, like many corporate firms, employs electronic device policies when in the workplace. Occasional and incidental use is permitted so long as it does not interfere with work. Furthermore, use of any company-provided PCs to do online shopping, blogging, social media-ing, or other things ending in -ing besides 'working', will cause your supervisors to hassle you to no end despite the fact that they, too, are answering some quiz about which Beverly Hills Cop character they are or sharing a meme about their favorite TV show. Why are you people so easily distracted? What is wrong with you? Why can't I understand kids these days? Why am I so out of touch? No, don't write that, Carol." - 50 Thousand Employee Handbook, page 584

investigating, and it would be on my own time and not the Company's. *What do you suggest?*

scrying he replied. *whats your address?*

The rest of the morning seemed to pass as slowly as I could remember. Friday, I was told, was "Casting day", where all of the preparation for wizard spells from the week before culminated in some kind of large conference where all of the Wizards of the company cast the spells. People kept shuffling in and out of the office, mostly to get coffee since the Espresso Machine was having a crisis and refused to work until it had "found inspiration".

I tried to keep myself as busy as I could. I redoubled my file room efforts, sorting things into date and then by the file's color, and despite ending up a sweaty mess I was pleased by the time my lunch break rolled around to say that a sizeable dent in the organization had been made.

I had also picked up some more information about what the firm did. Every spell cast by 50 Thousand was guaranteed for a certain amount of time: most of them lasted months, but some were as long as decades and a few were short-term ones that lasted less than a week. Each spell could be expected to last a certain amount of time in most cases, so the Firm guaranteed those spells for an amount of time that was about 60-70% of what the spell would be expected to last. That way, the client would never be in danger of risking a spell expiring, and the company could make a little extra money by recasting a spell that wasn't near actually expiring at all. It seemed to be good business practice, even if it was a little slimy. And the customers, of course, didn't seem to mind in the slightest.

Especially given the alternative. In each of the files I saw "response reports"—strangely ominous documents that listed cities and the names of other wizarding firms who were casting some kind of offensive enchantments. Each "event", which were days, weeks, and even months apart, was cataloged in great detail with the type of magical offensive effect has been aimed at the person or company. Common ones included spells to cause PR disasters, spells to cause financial problems, and spells to reduce efficiency in the workplace. Others, however, were a bit more sinister, including causing workplace accidents, causing sickness, and in a few cases even, spells intended to kill.

All in all, 50 Thousand appeared to be very good at its job. Each of these events was tagged with the phrase "Effects nullified" at the bottom of the page indicating that the magical effect, at least, had been stopped.[12]

"Most cities don't allow offensive enchantments," Apollo had explained, "but a few Dragons allow them in their cities because they can be very lucrative.

---

[12] "50 Thousand offers many products that can stop the effects of enchantments, hexes, vexes, jinxes, and curses. 50 Thousand does not offer mind-altering substances (such as love potions), magical weapon enhancements, quest advice, lost items found, portals to fictional universes, resurrections, waistline alterations, timeline alterations, hairline alterations, or continuations of your favorite TV show that was canceled. Private party entertainment is considered on a case-by-case basis." - 50 Thousand Employee Handbook, Page 119 (Services)

Companies that do it make a killing doing this stuff. Pun intended."

"And 50 Thousand?" I had inquired with more than a tinge of anxious edge to my voice.

"50 Thousand has a reputation—they've never dabbled in Dark Magic as long as they've been around—and they've been around for easily two thousand years or more. That's part of the reason 50 Thousand is so prestigious."

The idea that wizards, somewhere, were specifically targeting people with deadly spells, and that our firm was their defense, strengthened my resolve in the matter of my employment. The company I now worked for was doing a good service, and I needed to be on top of my game or people's lives might be in danger.

Of course, I reminded myself, working in a dusty file room was unlikely to have any effect on anyone's health, unless one counted the risk of Chronic Obstructive Pulmonary Disease from the dust.

"Hey," a voice came from the door, and I turned to see Carrie, flush-faced, gesturing me to follow. "Come on, you're supposed to go to Casting."

I rubbed one of my eyes with a free hand while I laid another folder down which was showing the aftereffects of a fire that had broken out in a client's basement. The fire control system had nearly malfunctioned, the report read, but had clicked on at the last minute. To the mundane eye, it was simply an averted accident and a lucky break, but to the wizards of 50 Thousand it was a jinx that had been unjinxed just in time.

I followed, stretching my arms above my head to relax the joints. Regardless of my aching desire to do better at the job I had already spent a week slacking off at, the aching in my muscles from sitting bent over a dusty file box for hours at a time was undeniable. "Do I need to actually *do* anything at Casting?"

Carrie shook her head as I followed her past the now-empty rows of cubicles toward the elevator. "No, you being there is mostly just a formality. Though if you screw something up it's easier to point fingers if they can physically point at you."

I took in a deep breath, thankful that the wizard, whatever-his-name-was, had already told me that my ingredient procurement had met with his satisfaction. It occurred to me that I was slowly uncovering a long plethora of things in this company that, if they were not done with the utmost care, would lead to disaster.

Carrie, for her part, was a strange component in the 50 Thousand machine. While I knew she was my supervisor, and I knew she was constantly in a state of heavy breathing and reddened face, but the exact specifications of her job remained a mystery to me. Did I have coworkers who also reported to her? And when would I end up meeting them? I briefly considered vocalizing these thoughts to Carrie as we boarded the hallway elevator, but she seemed to be stretched so thin with whatever tasks she was currently completing that I figured any further burden of inquiry might have caused the poor woman to snap like a rubber band.

We boarded the elevator and there was a beep as Carrie waved her card against the electronic pad that gave access to the upper floors of the building. I looked down at my feet and tried to appear perfectly engaged in examining my shoelaces as Carrie took out her phone and began texting at breakneck speed. The small patter of key-presses did not stop until we reached the 73rd floor, at which point the phone again vanished into her pocket and elevator doors slid open.

The decor of this floor was completely unlike the muted grey and beige of my own cubicle farm. The floor was a deep, swirly green and appeared to be made of single, massive sheets of marble interfitted with such exactness that I could not see where the edges connected. The walls, covered in a deep walnut paneling, were lit every few feet by silver and gold lamps that were both timeless and modern in their appearance. The ceilings were more marble—a light, glossy white canopy dotted with mini-chandeliers. I must have been standing with a look of awe, as Carrie tapped my shoulder and ushered me down the hall. We passed a few unmarked walnut doors and then arrived at a larger, double door labeled with a single brass plate: *Casting Room Two*.

The inside of this room was like a miniature arena. Audience chairs filled the upper level where I was now standing, many of them already filled with the many casting techs and other employees of 50 Thousand. The whole upper level could easily hold several hundred people, it appeared, and I glanced at Carrie to see where I was supposed to go. She was back on her phone again, however. "Find somewhere to sit. See you later," she said without looking up, and disappeared into the crowd.

I walked toward the front rows to get a better look at the main area. There, a long wooden conference table was laid out in view, the center of which was elevated and covered in an assortment of different items. Buckets, cups, sticks, bags of herbs, musical instruments—no two things were alike that were laid out upon the surface of the table, each tagged meticulously with printed labels. Around the raised part of the table, dozens of chairs were lined up, each with a placemat and a small folder bearing the 50 Thousand logo.

"Andy!" I turned to see Killian in a nearby seat, waving me over. Thankful that I wouldn't have to make new friends, I gratefully took a seat next to her. "This is your first Casting, right?" I nodded. "Well, it's a lot of pomp and circumstance but otherwise pretty routine. But educational. All of the different casting reagents that were collected throughout the week are all lined up near the Wizards whose responsibility it is to cast those spells. See right there?" I followed her gaze to a part of the table near the end, where the calfnot and other items I had collected on Tuesday were arranged in an aesthetic manner.

Before I could comment, the lights in the upper floor dimmed and the room became very quiet. The sound of a door opening echoed throughout the chamber, and a line of Wizards in impeccable suits spilled out around the conference table, quickly taking assigned seats. When they had finished, only four seats remained empty: one near the door, and three near the far end.

Another door across the room opened, and three Wizards entered slowly. Two of the three were quite pale and frail-looking—one had a long and quite wizardly beard that flowed down his chest. The second was an old woman with a snow-white perm atop her head and lips that stretched tightly over her teeth in such a way as to leave a contour of the gaps in between. The third was younger than the other two but still an older man; his hair still retained some of its color and his beard was slightly more kempt.

I glanced at Killian. "The managing partners," she explained in a whisper, "Hemlock, Willin and Blake. Hemlock is the older man: most senior Wizard at the firm. Then there's Willin. She's older than dirt and hates everyone but she knows more about countermagic than anyone in the world. And Blake is the younger guy. Appointed last year. Those three are some of the only people who work *for* 50 Thousand."

I wanted to ask more about that, but she stopped me. Down below, the three partners having taken their seats, Blake raised a wooden gavel and rapped it. It was apparent that despite his junior status among the managers, he was in charge of the proceeding for one reason or another. "Lord Wizard Chamberlain. Are you satisfied that those present are only those under the strict and bonded employ of this circle of sorcery?"

One Wizard at the end rose and made a point to gaze around the room searchingly. Whether it was for show or for actual reason was not clear, but he gave a curt nod to the Managing wizards. "I am satisfied." He resumed his seat.

Blake rapped the gavel again. "Lord Wizard Ritekeeper," he addressed another at the table, and I realized that he was referring to each of these people by titles and not by names, "Are you certain that the rites and reagents of the spells ascribed for this Casting are complete and correct?"

The Ritekeeper stood. "I am certain," she said simply, before taking her seat again.

The gavel came down a third time. "Lord Wizard Archivist," he addressed an older man near him, "Are you assured that all who receive the benefits of our Magic today are entitled to do so, and have paid this circle of sorcery a due sum for those benefits?"

The Wizard arose and nodded. "I am assured."

Hemlock nodded approvingly as the wizard took their seat. Blake continued on, in a deep and authoritative voice that pierced the hall. "Before we proceed with the ceremony, I would like to bring your attention to the empty chair at the end of the table. For many years, this chair was occupied by a Wizard of distinction. A man who was known for his devotion to the firm, to this city, and to our Society."

I froze. The empty chair at the end of the table had been my Dad's.

"His life was ended too soon, and in the service of our firm no less. While his body is lost to us today, I know that his personal integrity and loyalty will live on in our hearts and in the exercise of our ancient and revered tasks. *Video et taceo*," He said in conclusion, and all of the Wizards at the table responded with the Latin phrase in unison.

I took a deep steadying breath, but it could not stifle the anxious shiver that had crept up my skin, making me feel cold and tingly. The deep, soulful proceeding and the unexpected tribute to my father had made me feel thoroughly uncomfortable. How many people here knew my Dad? How many knew I was his child?

Killian seemed to sense my discomfort. "You ok?"

I nodded and gave Killian a half-smile, half-grimace as Blake resumed the ritual. "With no further preparations to make, let us proceed to cast." He rapped the gavel twice, and all of the wizards around the table stood. "Let us begin. Lord Wizard Hemlock will lead us today." He nodded to Hemlock and they exchanged places.

"Assembled Wizards," Hemlock said in a frail, but magnetic voice that still seemed to fill the room as he spoke, "we are present here this 12th day of October to invoke…" he glanced at the notes in front of him, "…seventy-four spells for the benefit of our clients who have reposed their trust in us. Let us repel the darkness in these times of trouble." He reached into his pocket. "Wands, please."

Each of the wizards drew a slender rod from their jackets or bags and held it out in front of them. I was glued to the sight, with the several-dozen wizards standing as still as statues awaiting their next instruction from the head Mage.

"Prepare to cast on my command," he said, and the hair on the back of my neck began to stand up. I glanced around the room to see that most of the audience was thoroughly unimpressed by this proceeding—they had probably seen it hundreds of times by now—but to me, I was lost in the sheer power of the moment. "Three, two, one…" All of the wizards then spoke in unison, and I strained my ears to try and understand what was being said, but it sounded like pseudo-Latin gibberish. When they were done, there was no flash of lighting or loud noise, and for a moment I wasn't sure that anything had transpired at all. The lights then flickered, and I felt a sort of a hum, like the deep hum of a motor or an electronic device, that lingered a moment before dissipating. As the wizards all lowered their wands, there was a sort of static feeling in the air that wasn't there before, and I became acutely aware that I had been holding my breath. I tried to gulp down some air without attracting attention from anyone around me.

The wizards began to file out of the room and I turned to Killian. "That's it?"

She nodded. "That's it."

I turned my gaze back to the empty chair at the end of the table where my dad had once sat. Killian followed my gaze and seemed to understand. "Hey. Your Dad did a lot of good work around here. He'd probably be proud that you're following in his footsteps."

I wasn't so sure. If he'd wanted me here, why hadn't he told me about The Secret in the first place? Did he think I couldn't handle it, or that I would somehow screw it up? Did he think I didn't have the fortitude or the willpower? Worse that the reasons he didn't tell me are the reasons why someone so respected by the people of 50 Thousand would have met such a terrible fate. "In the service of our firm," Blake had said. Dad had been doing something for this firm, and he had been killed. The unanswered questions bothered me immensely. It occurred to me, as I surreptitiously scanned the room that his murderer might be in this room somewhere.

I thanked Killian for the support and headed back toward the elevators, following the throng of departing employees. Despite my assurances to the Moddey Dhoo, I still wanted to find answers…and I had found myself with another piece of the puzzle that, like the others, didn't seem to fit in anywhere.

CHAPTER 9

A sense of relief washed over me as I pushed out of the glass doors at the base of the glassy green tower. I had survived a week here and was no worse for wear, unless you counted the occasional twinge on my ear where the goblin had bitten me.

And the storeroom! It had a sort of sense of organization now, and I was pretty sure that I had gotten the hang of sorting things into places. While the whole thing was sort of soul-crushing when I considered it as a work prospect, the fact that I had made some kind of progress was still satisfying enough to give me an accomplished feeling.

"So what's the plan?" I asked Apollo as we started down the block toward my condo. He had been nice enough to meet me at the door to 50 Thousand, and the plan to do some scrying was finally going to come to fruition.

"Well, we need a few ingredients are you familiar

with the Goblin Market?"

"Unfortunately," I replied, rubbing my ear.

We started off toward the Market as Apollo dug in his pockets, finally pulling out what looked like an old page torn from a book. "Here you go." He handed it over.

The page was definitely torn from a book; and an old one, if the hand-lettered text was any indication. It was written like a recipe, with ingredients and instructions that seemed relatively simple to follow. "Is this a spell from a spell book?"

He nodded. "Yeah. Most of them look like that. I dunno if it was so they could hide them inside cookbooks in the event of snooping, or if it's honestly just easier to write them like that. When you think about it, though, you're basically cooking up a result using ingredients and actions. So it's not completely unusual."

This spell seemed to be relatively simple as far as ingredients went: A rose quartz, some local dirt, and a crow's feather. Having already made my first foray into the Market over the week, I was pretty confident I could do this in under an hour.

The Market was a lot calmer this time, perhaps because it was the end of the week, and I made a beeline for the store where I had bought stuff before. Dingo was sitting on the counter—at least, a goblin wearing his nametag was. It was clearly not the same goblin, however, and I thought to ask why this might be the case but stopped myself. It didn't really matter, and the answer was probably something stupid anyway.

Having bought the quartz, feather and even a baggie of local dirt, we headed out of the Market and back onto the Cincinnati street. Apollo seemed concerned that I was eager to get out of there so quick, but if he had questions about it he at least didn't vocalize them which I told myself was a good excuse to explain it later. Instead, he turned the topic of conversation to my meeting with my Silencer. I explained about my meeting with the mangy dog, the Moddey Dhoo.

"Moddey Dhoo?" He sounded genuinely surprised. "That's an English Black Dog legend. Not very common, if I remember correctly. Glad he seems like a nice enough guy though."

"Nice enough," I supposed with a shrug, "But still creeped me the hell out. What are these Silencer things, anyway? I mean...like, *what* exactly are they?"

"They're part of a society called *Empyrean*," he explained. "At least most of them are. Empyrean includes ghosts, myths, legends, spirits, and other ethereal things. They're difficult to contain but they govern themselves with a strange hierarchy that seems to work for them. As long as they're under control, right? That's sorta the point."

I furrowed my brows. "I don't follow."

"Control and governance. I was talking about that before, right? Like *Sorcera*'s paperwork to prove to the other societies that they can govern themselves without intervention. They're proving that despite being one of the more powerful groups, they can manage to keep themselves so tightly under control that none of the other societies feel threatened. Compare that to, say the *Vulnerabl*, where our whole thing is a sort of a, uh, class system thing. We have local leaders in sort of a royal family who keep us all from going too crazy."

It did make sense. I considered the idea that Wizards were among the most powerful creatures in the Secret World, and it seemed a little crazy given the fact that Dragons still sat at the top of the food chain. But wizards had spells that were flexible enough to do all sorts of things, and from so far away, too…a single curse could cross thousands of miles and without firms like 50 Thousand they could wreak massive damage.

We lugged the bag of spell reagents upstairs and to the condo. I was happy to see that some of the furniture I had ordered online had arrived, and Apollo helped me drag the big boxes inside and unpack them. In a few minutes I had unfolded a small table and chairs, which made the otherwise creepy-empty condo seem just a slight bit more livable.

"Don't you have a TV? Or a bed?" Apollo seemed appalled, particularly at a lack of the latter.

"Not yet. I've been wrapping myself in a blanket and snoozing on the floor."

Apollo gave me a concerned mom-look. "Okay, darling, we're going to need to fix that soon, alright? People don't live like this. You have yourself a nice little condo here in the middle of Downtown Cincinnati and the least you can do it put something in it."

I dismissed his concerns with a hand wave. "I will, I will…but for now let's do this scrying thing." I opened the bag and started sorting through it.

Suddenly, there was a knock on the condo door. Apollo and I looked at each other and then stuffed the reagents back away; he tossed them in a closet as I opened the door.

"Nice place," Killian observed. "Good location.

Your dad's?"

I blinked. "Yeah…it was. Killian, what are you *doing* here?"

She smirked. "Company sent me a message that you might be doing irresponsible things tonight. Now I'm not here to stop you, mind you," she added as I opened my mouth to argue, "I'm just here to be a responsible adult for the apprentice who has had a magical learner's permit for all of six hours." She raised an eyebrow with what I hoped was bemusement rather than scorn. "But if you go buying spell ingredients after hours at the goblin market, someone might just notice. In this case it was one of your coworkers. Some guy named Devin."

"*Devin?!*" I was disgusted again. "Why is he bothering in my business? And how would he have seen me unless he was at the market too? I should just—"

Killian put up a hand. "It's fine, I'm on your side, I'm just here to keep you company." She nearly pushed past me into the apartment and then stopped as her eyes landed on Apollo. Her demeanor darkened. "Unless you already *have* company."

Apollo took a deep breath. "It's not like that, Killian. I'm just—"

Killian shook her head. "It's fine, you do you, Apollo. I'm not judging."

I looked between the two of them. "You guys, uh…friends?"

"Sorta," They replied in near-unison.

I felt immediately quite awkward and kept myself out of it while I closed the door and turned on the rest of the interior lights. "So what are you two doing, anyway?" She asked Apollo.

"Scrying. Andy thinks that they might have missed something when they were scrubbing this place clean of magic stuff."

"They?"

"Yeah. You folks, 50 Thousand. Or maybe just the *Sorcera* Society. Either way, Andy's doing some snooping. And I had some useful spells."

Killian nodded in something that seemed like approval. "Let me see what you've got."

Apollo handed over the scrying spell and Killian looked it over. "Wow, this is an older one. Did you steal it from an old lady or did you find it in someone's attic?"

"It was my *grandfather's*, if you must ask," Apollo replied acidly. "He was really big into *Sorcera* magic but never really had a knack for it, so he studied it academically. I have some of his notes, that's all." For some reason, the tone of Apollo's voice suggested that he might not be telling the complete truth, but I had no intention of pressing him on the subject. I ignored the two as they continued to bicker in the background and distracted myself by running a hand up the wallpaper of the kitchen. This had all been Dad's at one time, and I don't think I had ever seen it until now. I was once again taken in with a feeling of loss—not just for my Dad himself but for a lifetime of silence that could have been an adventure shared. I guiltily thought about calling Mom, but the idea also chilled me given our bad relationship. Plus, if she ended up being ignorant of the whole thing, then the Moddey Dhoo would just shut my phone off again and probably berate me over it.

I was torn from my thoughts by a loud, sarcastic laugh from the living room. I peeked in the door and saw Apollo looking particularly disgruntled. "Maybe I wouldn't *have* to if you weren't such a—"

"Everything ok?" I asked innocently.

They both looked at me and nodded almost in unison. The third-wheel awkwardness was starting to get to me. "Well if you want I can just screw off somewhere if you two want to keep bickering like a married old couple."

Killian turned a deep red and opened her mouth with a look that could kill, and Apollo snorted loudly as he busied himself with filling a saucepan with ingredients. I dodged back into the kitchen as Killian tried to throw something at me—a shoe maybe— and cackled as I went to retrieve some water from the tap.

"Are you sure tap water's going to be okay?" I called into the living room.

"It should be. If it's from this apartment that's best because it's, like, connected or something."

"'Or something?'" Killian repeated with an incredulous tone.

"Hey, do I look like a wizard to you? I'm entirely theoretical over here."

I returned to the living room and knelt on the floor. Apollo had set up the saucepan over a portable burner and filled it with the dirt and other ingredients he had in his own bag. Killian was watching with a critical look.

"An induction burner?" She inquired. "That's a new one to me."

Apollo glared. "I figured Andy might not want a hole burned in the hardwood. Besides, the source of the heat doesn't really matter, does it?"

Killian shrugged and kicked off her remaining shoe. "What are you expecting to find, anyway?"

I was quiet for a moment as I formulated a response. Once again, I realized I was so caught up in the investigating part that I hadn't considered what I was actually looking for. "An answer, maybe. Not only was my dad murdered but now I know it happened while he was working. And someone's trying to cover it up and discourage me from investigating. And that's…that's worth looking into."

"So you think the *safest* course of action is to meddle in something where someone was murdered? In a world you don't even really understand? I mean, let's be honest. You're a week into this stuff." Killian raised her eyebrows at me.

I gave a sheepish look. "At least I'm not doing it alone?" I gestured to Apollo.

Killian rolled her eyes. "That makes it better. Now the bad guys have three targets instead of two."

Apollo looked up. "Three?"

Killian stopped, her mouth hanging open as if she was considering backtracking. "Yes. Three. Because I'm going to be honest, there isn't a lot of excitement in my department, and I'm interested, too."

I smiled and looked down at the pot of brown gloop. "So what now? Do I need a wand or something?"

"Oh, right." Killian dug in her bag and pulled out a padded envelope. "I was supposed to hand these out Monday, but I snagged yours." She handed it over and I eagerly unwrapped it. Inside, in a small cardboard carton, was a wand. But it was the most plain, uninteresting cylinder of wood I had probably laid my eyes upon. Painted a corporate grey, it was a single, thin dowel rod about a foot long, with a serial number near the side I assumed was the handle. "This is it?" I looked incredulously at Killian as I tapped the wand with my fingers. "Is this *particleboard?*"

She nodded. "If you want better, you have to buy your own. This is a standard-issue corporate wand. No bells or whistles."

I tried to hide my growing disappointment about how boring the world of sorcery was turning out to be, and focused my attention back at the sizzling pot and Apollo's recipe for the spell. "'Extinguish heat and place the quartz crystal in the mixture,'" I read out loud, "'and circumvolve thrice along the solar rotational axis.' What…?"

"It means to swirl your wand around it clockwise 3 times," Apollo translated.

"So why don't they just say that?"

Killian snorted. "Because wizards love paperwork. Haven't you figured that out yet?"

I rolled my eyes and kept reading. "'After allowing the crystal to soak for 60 minutes, retrieve it before submerging in an ice bath.' That part seems pretty easy. But that's where it ends. What am I supposed to do after that?"

Apollo took the recipe and flipped the page over to look at both sides. "Huh. I dunno. Maybe at that point it's self-explanatory? I've never actually done this."

"Great. Well, here goes…" I picked up the crystal and dropped it into the pot of mud with a *plop*. The mixture bubbled but nothing else particularly interesting happened. "OK…so we have an hour. Anybody for pizza?"

Thirty-five minutes (or it's free) later, the three of us had gotten pizza and beers, and were sitting in wait around the no-longer-bubbling pot of mud which had begun to solidify into a dirty mess at the bottom of the saucepot.

"And your dad never told you anything about this at all?" Apollo was asking. "No bedtime stories or prophetic, foreshadowing ominous statements?"

I shook my head. "I barely knew anything about him except that he lived in Cincinnati." I took a bite of the pizza and turned to Killian. "Did you ever meet him?"

"LaFayette? Not really. I saw him every week in Casting, but I don't really remember seeing him around the office or even at office parties. He really kept to himself."

"What did he do? I know he was a Wizard but what was his job, exactly?" It occurred to me that I probably sounded slightly desperate. But to be honest, I was. Any dreg of information was like a drop of water in the desert now, and my inborn impatience was not helping me handle this situation with any level of grace.

Killian considered the question for a minute as she took a swig of beer. "If I remember right, he mostly worked in Reclaim—basically, recovering stolen magical property and turning it into the authorities—the Dragon or one of his deputies. 50 Thousand does some work with helping magical things get transported, because we can be trusted to have major defenses in place. Now if stuff went missing, on the other hand, like reagents or artifacts or something, your dad and his team would be the ones handling it. In fact," She added thoughtfully, "I think he was the head of that department. It's called the Vaultkeeper."

"So why might somebody want 50 Thousand's Vaultkeeper dead?"

"Any number of reasons. Maybe he crossed somebody that was doing some kind of black market artifact deal. Maybe someone double-crossed him over some kind of transportation. I honestly don't know. I wish I had a better answer." She stirred the put of mud, where a better answer was still soaking.

"What about you?" I asked. "Didn't that goblin say something about a huge debt you were owed? I don't mean to pry, it just caught my attention."

Killian rolled her eyes. "Oh, don't even get me started. Gnomes...following me everywhere, giving me things, telling me I'm so awesome..." She seemed genuinely irritated.

Apollo stifled a chuckle. "Killian's a *chosen one*," he whispered.

"Oh shut up, you," Killian snapped, shoving Apollo with her foot. She saw my inquiring look and sighed. "So sometimes people are born with some kind of destiny thing, right? Something that's big and important enough that it gets 'foretold'" —Killian made the most sarcastic-looking air quotes I had ever seen— "and the person's a *chosen one*. It's really common. Common enough, in fact, that I got sent to a school for *chosen ones* which sounds cool except that everyone shows up with some kinds of powers manifested and don't follow school rules. Half of them have this whole worldview that they're *the* chosen one and the world revolves around them, while the staff are all clueless, and something attacks the school like once or twice a year and the students get instructed to leave it alone. But of course a handful go and investigate and there's a big fight and if the staff had just listened in the first place it would've—" Killian stopped herself and took a deep breath to dismiss her tangent. "—but I'm getting off track. So I was born with this whole destiny thing that I was going to defeat some dark lord who was subjugating the Gnome nation. So off I go to Chosen One School where I learned to fight and got a lot of practice hedging. I got assigned an old man mentor like everyone else and after what was probably a very amusing training montage I was totally ready to go fight this dark lord guy." She swigged her beer again and became very quiet.

I pressed. "So did you? Defeat the dark lord and free the gnomes?"

She grimaced down at her beer. "No. He had a brain aneurysm while I was at school and I never got to defeat him. But the leaders of the gnome nation thought I did it, so they offered me life debts and I got all kinds of fame and fortune…which isn't really as cool as it sounds. So I ditched the gig and moved to Cincinnati, where nothing ever happens."

I looked over at Apollo who was busying himself with a set of copper tongs to pull out the quartz crystal. He glanced at me and mouthed the words *she's super sensitive about it*.

While Killian downed the rest of her beer and cracked open another, Apollo handed me the copper tongs. I checked the recipe once more and picked up the wand with my other hand. "Okay. How do I even pronounce these magic words?"

Killian and Apollo looked over my shoulder. "That one's 'oss-ten-dee' I think," Killian offered.

"Yeah, that one's 'soo-pell-ectil-um.'" Apollo put emphasis on the syllable "pell".

Killian shook her head. "No, it's 'supil-ECK-till-um'."

"No," Apollo corrected. "The stressed syllable needs to come in the first two. Su *pell* ectil um."

"Where did you hear that stupid rule? It doesn't even sound right. It's—"

I interrupted both of them with a glare to each one. "Do not make me turn this spellcasting around." They both went quiet. I took a deep breath, pointed at the pot of dry mud, and tried to pronounce the best something-that-sounded-vaguely-like-latin that I could. "*Ostende mihi facium supellectlum.*"

The room went very quiet and I felt that motor-like hum deep inside my ears. I wasn't sure if it had worked at all. I glanced over at Apollo, who shrugged. Gripping the copper tongs tightly in my fingers, I pulled the quartz crystal from its mud covering.

The crystal was glowing softly with a light blue color. I stared at it in awe, admiring the fluorescent facets under the surface. "I did it," I whispered. "I…I cast a spell."

Apollo reached out with his fingers and gently pulled the stone from the tongs. "Nice job," he remarked, brushing some of the dirt off. "This looks like it'll last a while. But let get started, huh?" He handed the stone back to me. It felt slightly cold, like it had been sitting in an icebox for a few minutes. I stood up and held the stone out.

As I continued to brush dirt from the crystal, the light from the stone bathed the walls and the ceiling with an unearthly glow. "So…what now? What are we looking for?"

Apollo and Killian both shrugged and I started to move around the mostly-empty condo with the crystal held out like a lantern. In the light of the stone, tiny sparkles darted here and there though the air, but I had no idea what it meant. From the living room to the kitchen I walked, sweeping the light back and forth, and as I entered one of the back rooms of the condo, I took in a deep breath.

Some of the sparkles were congregating in the corner of the room, pulled there by some unseen force. As I watched and moved closer, the sparkles began to form a cohesive shape—first an outline, and then slowly filling in details. As I crept ever closer, thankful to hear Apollo and Killian behind me, I realized that the shape was of a person, sitting in a chair and hunched over a desk. "D-dad?"

Apollo put a hand gently on my shoulder. "It's an impression left over from him living here. He must have spent a lot of time at this desk and it's left a kind of a…shadow. But that's all it is."

I shrugged Apollo's hand off and stepped closer. The face was slowly becoming more detailed as the sparkles drifted into place, and when my heart could take it no more I turned and walked out, holding the stone as the sparkles dissipated behind me. I caught a glimpse of Apollo's concerned face and what looked like Killian glaring at the glowing shadow of my absent father as I passed out of the room into the next one. Neither said anything but I think that they realized there wasn't much consolation to be had at the moment. My angry and distraught thoughts were shaken away, in any case, as I walked into the bathroom.

Clean and spotless, I was about to turn and move on when I spotted something on the floor. I bent to look, and it definitely looked like some of the sparkles in the air were slowing as they passed a spot on the floor, which looked kind of like it was reflecting the quartz's light. "Hey guys..." the other two crowded into the bathroom behind me. "Is it me or—"

"Something's under the floor," Apollo confirmed, reaching out to touch the vinyl tile floor with his fingers. "It might have been missed if they thought it was a reflection or something. We just need something to—"

He was interrupted by a *snikt* sound as Killian flipped open a knife. "May I?"

Apollo and I stepped back to let the redhead with a knife take point on the situation. Killian felt around the floor for a moment with a finger and then dug the blade into the vinyl flooring, which carved away with ease. Beneath the surface, resting on the floorboards underneath, was a single silver coin. In the light, I could barely make out the shape of a wheel carved into one side. Killian stared at it for a moment, and I caught what looked like a greedy look shadowed across her face, before she composed herself and spoke up. "It's a Greek Drachma," she said softly.

I tentatively reached out and picked it up. "What does it mean?"

Killian stood up and put her knife away, her eyes watching me carefully as if to gauge my response. "Might have to do something with the company's history. Maybe this is some kind of souvenir given to wizards of the firm? But I'm not a wizard. I don't know."

I ran my thumb along the design on the face of the coin. In the light of the glowing quartz crystal, I could see the speckles of energy in the air lingering near the coin, but I had no idea what, exactly, it meant. I pocketed it and moved on to the next room.

The condo wasn't large, when it came down to it. A few bedrooms and a bathroom, a kitchen and a living room—basically a small apartment, even if the placement in downtown Cincinnati made it prime real estate. The remaining rooms in the condo heralded neither secret objects nor glowing shadows of my father, and as we returned back to the living room I felt a profound sense of having missed something nagging at the back of my head.

The three of us went back to eating pizza and drinking beers. I stayed relatively quiet and listened to Killian and Apollo bickering over the best way to dispose of the pot of mud, and whether the pot should be used for cooking afterward (The answer, they finally agreed, was probably not).

Killian looked at her watch. "It's getting late. I should probably…" She gestured to the door.

Apollo raised an eyebrow. "It's Friday. You don't stay out late on Fridays?"

Killian opened her mouth to respond, looking mildly irritated. "It is late. It's like…ten."

Apollo checked his phone. "I mean, yeah, which is way too early."

I stood up, my head feeling mildly groggy. "Nah, Killian's right. It's kinda late. I'm tired after a week of…all this nonsense."

Apollo looked mildly disgusted at the both of us for bailing out so early. "Fine, fine, you both do your thing. I guess I'll catch up with y'all later." He headed for the door and stopped. "Anyone up for getting a bite tomorrow? You're new to Cincy, Andy, and could use some of the local cuisine."

I shrugged. "I dunno. I'm trying not to burn too

hard into my savings before my first paycheck comes."

"My treat. You too, Killian." He elbowed her playfully and she glared in response.

"Sure, sure. Maybe Sunday. And hey, thanks for coming, Killian. I appreciate the…uh…support."

Killian nodded and headed out the door without another word. Apollo walked over and grabbed me in a sudden hug that lasted only a moment. "You take care of yourself, kid, alright? Get some sleep and stuff." I couldn't think of a good response and so I just nodded with a smile and started to clean up the pot of dirt as he left.

As soon as I heard Apollo's footsteps disappear down the stairs, I put the pot down and picked the quartz stone back up. In a moment I had crossed through the kitchen into the second room, getting another look at the shadow of my father.

I studied the shape of him as it slowly came into view again, trying to discern a facial expression or some other detail, but the image was too fuzzy. I followed the shape of his arm with my eyes down to the shadow of the desk, where he appeared to be writing something. I looked closer, but the speckles of light refused to stay still long enough to make out anything being written.

I stayed there for a long time, the room bathed in blue light from the crystal. I was feeling so very conflicted about the figure before me, and even after I had grabbed a chair from the other room to it near the shadow, I couldn't reconcile the twisted feeling in my stomach.

People had known this man and respected him for work he had never told me about, and the sheer fact that this swarm of glowing particles was here, led to an impression from where he presumably spent a lot of his time, made me irrationally angry. All that time at this desk, and not a single phone call my way? Not a moment or two to even recognize the child that was several states away and wondering where the man had been?

Finally, I could take it no more, and I picked up the chair and walked out, once again with more questions and not enough answers.

CHAPTER 10

The feeling of not having to get up early was very welcome, especially given that a dinner of pizza and beer had not been the healthiest choice the night before. I untangled myself from the blankets on the floor and groped for my phone, grabbing it and pulling it under the covers with me. After dismissing about 20 notifications and spending an embarrassing amount of time browsing memes, I groaned and pulled out of the blankets and into the real world.

What was the real world, even, I asked myself as I dragged myself to the bathroom. What was particularly *real* about the world had become particularly vague as of recent, what with the recent addition of a hundred or more things I hadn't thought were real in the first place. Werewolves. Wizards. *Dragons.* The thought of it jumbled around my head like a kid in a bouncy castle and made me wonder what treasure troves of secrets I had yet to uncover in my week and a half of being in on the Secret.

I glanced at the hole in the vinyl floor, the back of my mind making a note to get it replaced—or maybe to cover it with a bathmat—as I turned the water on. The hot water brought me back to my senses a little, and by the time I had dried off and changed into something decent to wear out of the apartment I had resolved myself to take the 50 Thousand Employee Handbook, some pamphlets, and do some exploring.

The target of my adventure would have to be the Goblin market, since it was the only place—besides 50 Thousand—where I knew there was a great congregation of Society people. From there, maybe, I might get a better perspective on where else to go. I wondered briefly if there was some kind of secret library with instruction manuals. Or maybe, I considered, I could just explore the city which had now, rather suddenly, become my home.

My first stop was, inexplicably, the Library. Cincinnati's downtown office was a cornucopia of knowledge, when all things were considered, and as a quiet place to study it seemed like an appropriate place to start reviewing things.

As soon as I had settled in front of a computer, I started seeing what I could dig up. I tried to find records of 50 Thousand Consulting, or anything even tangentially related to the company, by looking through public records of Hamilton County. At first, I found nothing: every satellite image, every photo, every single construction permit and tax audit showed that the lot where the emerald building stood was nothing more than a simple parking lot.

I moved away from the computer and found a desk in a far corner of the library where I spread out my study material and went to work. The Employee Handbook had become my closest friend in the last 48 hours, and I was determined to have a better understanding of the world I was now inhabiting. I took copious notes.

The phrase "I'll explain later" had become my biggest pet peeve, but the Handbook, in its generosity, was always full of answers. Things that had been nagging at my mind were explained in short, plain paragraphs, such as the reason why I was not allowed to say I worked *for* 50 Thousand: As Killian had mentioned in Casting, only a few head honchos worked *for* the firm because their debts and ownerships were inexplicably tied to the firm. This was important when dealing with goblins, for example, who might try to call the whole company on a debt owed by one person if everyone worked for the company.

I also looked up the Vaultkeeper position. The Employee Handbook only mentioned it once, and the description of the job was a very brief sentence: "The Vaultkeeper oversees the removal and return of any of the valuables in the 50 Thousand Vault."

I was thumbing through the index for more useful keywords when I heard someone approaching and I looked up to see a mousy-haired young woman holding a piece of paper. A library employee ID hung from around her neck bearing the name Nanette. "Hello," I said politely, sliding the Handbook closed.

"Hello," she said, offering me the paper. It had a long list of books on it. "I saw you were reading that

Handbook. And I know it has a long 'additional reading' section, but you won't find any of those books here. There's a bookstore across the river that has some of them, but a lot of them are actually available online, link I wrote there at the bottom."

I looked down at the list and then back up at her. "So…so you're…?" I gestured with my hand, wondering if it would be rude to ask "what are you?" but she seemed to read my mind and gestured to a gold *Vulnerabl* bracelet on her wrist. "I spotted your tattoos when you took off your hoodie earlier. Hope I didn't bother. You just looked a little…lost."

"No, not at all. I mean, yes, I'm lost, but no, you didn't bother." I folded up the paper. "I really appreciate your help."

She waved good-bye and headed back among the bookshelves with a quiet smile on her face. I didn't have much time to contemplate, however, as I checked my watch and saw that my lunch date with Apollo and Killian was coming up. Grabbing my book and papers, I headed for the door.

"OK. So I don't get it." I looked down at my plate dubiously.

"What's not to get?" Apollo looked particularly offended at my response to what had been ordered and placed before me. A "Three-way", it was called, and despite getting over the initial shock of Apollo's proposal to get them in order to sample local Cincinnati fare ("Who wants a three-way?", Killian explained, was a poor choice of words in ordering such a dish, coming from an Incubus, which had led to a brief argument about stereotyping and language) I continued to be cautious.

"It's chili on spaghetti." And not just any chili, mind you, but a thin, soupy substance Cincinnatians seemed to call "chili"— with cheese. "It just seems weird." I picked up my fork and pirouetted the noodles around my fork.

"It's classic," Apollo retorted, and gestured to my fork. "Also, you're not supposed to do that. You're supposed to cut it with a knife and shovel it in your mouth with the fork." He demonstrated this with a scoop of off his plate of nonsense.

I resisted the urge to gag and reached for a cheese fry from the shared plate. "So different subject here. What do magical people do in their spare time? Where do they go?"

"Depends," Killian interjected. She had shown up for our lunch plans a little late, but looking completely different than I had ever seen her. I'd done a full double-take as she had approached, her conservative business attire replaced with a loose black Led Zeppelin t-shirt, torn but form-fitting jeans, and motorcycle boots. I hardly believed she was the same person as she had walked up to join us, and Apollo had politely reminded me not to stare.

"Mostly on what society you're a part of," Killian was saying. "*Sorcera* tend to end up doing your normal mundane stuff—shopping, socializing, all that stuff. *Vulnerabl*—correct me if I'm wrong, Apollo—do that a lot too if they can, but there's also a couple magical-friendly places around the city that attract traffic. The coffee shop, for example."

Apollo nodded. "Yeah, and *Vulnerabl* like our high-class joints, too. Restaurants, parlor parties.

We're uh, sort of…" He searched for a tactful word

"Bitchy?" Killian offered.

"No—"

"Yeah, we'll go with that. Then of course with the internet people can connect with each other more, and I think that's led to a lot more people just staying in. The *Kobolda* don't have a way to really blend in easily so they tend to keep to themselves and spend time connecting online. When they do get together it's usually coordinated through social media. It's pretty wild."

Apollo took another bite of his chili spaghetti and nodded eagerly. "And *Kobolda* parties are friggin awesome—they rent out abandoned factories and such on the north side of Cincinnati and throw huge things with lots of drinking, dancing, all that stuff. Like werewolves! They love throwing barbecues, for example—I highly recommend you go to one, by the way. The local pack has, like, an industrial smoker. It's out of this world. Pork that just melts in your mouth." He turned to Killian. "Remember that one time we went to—"

"Yes," she interrupted apathetically.

"—and you got so drunk that you—"

"I know."

"—and you got in a fight with that—"

"I *remember*, Apollo." She shot him an icy glare and he resumed his spaghetti consumption.

I looked back and forth between the two, my suspicions about them all but confirmed at this point but swallowed my curious questions as Killian moved to change the subject. "So. What's next on your investigation route? Figured out what you're going to do with that coin?"

I swirled my spaghetti around my fork (eliciting an irritated glare from Apollo) and contemplated my answer. "I don't know. I've been trying to figure out why it was hidden under the floor in the first place." I took the coin out of my pocket, now sitting comfortably inside a tiny plastic bag. "Is there some kind of magical forensic testing I can do? Please tell me there's a wizard's version of CSI."

Killian shook her head. "Not really. The Dragon has a police force of his own appointment—they work for a city office called the Constabulary. But you never want to get involved with them: they can screw your life up hardcore and have a license to do basically anything they need to do. The last thing you want is for them to know your name."

"Do you think they are investigating my dad's death?" I pressed.

"Didn't you say," Apollo interrupted, "That you were going to let your investigating chill for a bit so you could get some foundation? Yeah, we did some scrying and found a clue, but the clue's not going away and getting the Constabulary involved is definitely not the best way to go. Don't get me wrong: I want to help you however I can, but that also means telling you, as your friend-you-met-only-a-week-ago, that you need to chill."

Kilian took a sip of her coffee. "I literally told Andy the same thing about a half-hour after we met."

I deflated slightly as I put the fork down. "Alright, alright. So what are we doing today, then? Anyone have plans?"

"Actually, I do," Apollo said poignantly, rising from his seat. "Not that you two aren't just lovely company, but I've got errands, and not everyone works a Monday-Friday. Coffee to make, customers to flirt with. See ya, kids." He flashed a characteristic smile and headed up to the register to pay for all the food.

I looked over to Killian, trying not to look desperate. "And you?"

She fixed me with a gaze as she sipped her coffee, and I couldn't tell whether she was trying to decide whether or not continuing to spend any time with me at all was worth it. Finally she set her cup down. "You don't know anything at all about Hedging, do you?" I shook my head. "Do you know how to throw a punch?" I nodded. "OK, that's a start. See, I have this feeling that you're going to continue to get yourself in oodles of trouble and I only have so many hours in the day I can stand between you and somebody dangerous. So I don't do this often, but if you want I'll give you some pointers."

I shrunk slightly in my seat. "You're going to teach me how to fight?"

"No." Her eyebrows punctuated the finality of that statement. "I'm going to *try* to teach you how to *avoid* getting *hurt*." I had a feeling that in her head Killian was mentally adding a string of irritated condescending statements. "Most wizards don't bother with hedging because they don't go out in the field and interact with things, or people…because they're insular, exclusionist, self-important windbags. You, on the other hand, seem like the kind of person who knocked over mailboxes in middle school and spent half your high school years in detention. No offense."

I balked. "How is that *not* supposed to be an offense?" It had really been more like six months in detention, and like, one mailbox. Maybe two.

"Hush." Killian drained her coffee cup. "Finish your spa-ghetto and then we're going shopping."

I looked down at my plate of chili-spaghetti. "I think I'll pass. Shopping it is." We headed out of the restaurant, with me following Killian to her ride. "Hey…is that *your* Harley?"

She threw a leg over the bike and started it. "You bet your ass. Get on."

I furrowed my brow. "I don't have a helmet."

Killian finished strapping hers on and reached into her jacket. A moment later she was holding another helmet and I just stared, unsure of what just happened. She explained as I put the helmet on tentatively: "Pocket space. It's a pretty simple enchantment and one we'll work on later. For the moment, *get on the bike*."

I obeyed and a moment later we were zipping down Vine Street toward the Ohio River. Across the water, I could see the flashy buildings that formed the Kentucky town of Newport. I held onto Killian for dear life, probably making it very clear that I had never ridden on the back of a motorcycle before. She didn't comment, however, as we rode across the bridge into Kentucky, nor after we had stopped and parked down near the water. "We're not going to the Market?" I asked.

"No."

I followed behind Killian as we strolled under the bridge we had just driven across. There, painted in the concrete wall, was a grey patch of paint on the otherwise plain concrete wall. I watched, curiously, as the redhead took out a piece of red chalk and drew a small circle on the side of the painted patch. Before my eyes, the circle began to protrude from the wall until it had turned into a cement doorknob, which Killian turned. The door swung inward, revealing a set of brightly-lit stairs.

Killian caught me with my jaw dropped and gave me an exceptionally judgmental look. "Oh come on, if you keep gasping at every bit of magic you see you'll end up hyperventilating. You would think, eventually, you'd just stop…being surprised or something."

"Sorry."

We descended the single flight of stairs and emerged into a small tiled landing: several store fronts were labeled and had large, glass windows with clothes and various survival gear behind them. Around, here and there, people moved about—no one appeared to be the slightest bit magical, but I glimpsed the dark marks of *Sorcera* tattoos on a few bare arms. The entire place gave the impression of a small shopping mall very much, save for the air of secrecy and lack of a Cinnabon.

Killian pointed to a few of the stores. "Bookstore. Great for research because it doubles as a library. Potions are that way—good place to start until you brew your own. That place sells magical protective gear, which we'll probably go to…and then there's the clothes place." She shot me a sidelong grin. "Because kicking ass and looking good aren't mutually exclusive."

I looked down at my clothes, which looked okay, I suppose, but certainly weren't good for anything but lazing around or getting weird food at a Cincinnati restaurant. "OK, where first?"

An hour or so and a couple hundred dollars later,

we walked out of the underground shopping mall, with me carrying the fruits of our shopping catharsis. "That should do you for a while," Killian remarked, kickstarting her bike, "Next weekend we'll actually do some training. For the moment though, I gotta jet."

I looked around. "You're leaving me here?"

"Take the bus back across to Cincinnati," she replied, starting to pull her bike away and onto the road. "Just be careful. See ya."

Mildly irked, I trudged up to the bus stop and waited, my bags of stuff under my arm. I took a seat and poked through the bags. I had picked up some defensive one-time-use trinkets, like potions to help me escape or hide. The first step in fighting Dark Magic, Killian had remarked, was avoiding fights at all in the first place.

The bus pulled up to my stop and I boarded, feeling increasingly irritated at having been abandoned in Northern Kentucky of all places, even if it was right across the river from my condo. I shifted uneasily into a seat, wondering why I didn't call for a cab or a car by app. That regret increased even more as a bulbous man that resembled a living couch cushion took his place in the seat next to me, filling the air with a sour smell like German sausage.

I felt a tap on my shoulder and swung my head around. No one was behind me. I returned my attention forward, hoping I didn't get touched again—but there it was. Another tap. I looked again—no one there. I heard a slight giggle and looked up.

A tiny creature hovered in the air above me: no larger than my own palm, nude, and with tiny gossamer wings that flittered excitedly. It seemed very amused at its prank. "Hey! Hey wizard! Hey wizard!"

"I'm not a wizard," I hissed and looked around. No one else seemed to be able to see the creature.

"You work for wizards?" The creature was doing mid-air somersaults.

I didn't answer the question, thinking it was another kind of trap. Instead, I busied myself with my phone's headphones and pretended to make a call with the ear bud in my ear, so I would look just slightly less crazy. "What are you?" I asked quietly.

"Pixie!" the thing chittered, dropping down into my lap.

"What do you want from me?"

It crawled around in my lap making me mildly uncomfortable. "You have something that's not yours!"

I gulped. "No I don't."

The pixie dove into my pocket in an instant, and before I could even react it had yanked the Drachma free of my jeans. "Ha! Here tis!"

I tried to grab at the pixie, but it dodged me effortlessly. I looked around again to see if anyone had noticed me acting strangely, and then swatted again. The pixie only moved higher and further out of my reach. Gently, I set my bags down and stood up, gripping the bus's silver handrail as I eyed the pixie cautiously. I reached out, very slowly, only to have the pixie swoop down and rank something sharp, like a pin, across my knuckles. "Dammit!" I hissed. "You asshole!"

The pixie only laughed again. I wondered why it

hadn't yet escaped and continued playing with me. I glanced around to see the bus's windows were all closed; perhaps it had to wait for the next bus stop like the rest of us. Keeping this in the back of my mind, I took a tentative step closer. At that moment, the bus jerked as it came to a rather abrupt stop at a red light. I lost my balance, and fell forward in a heap, catching the pixie off guard.

As I tried to recover from my daze, I found a lump in my throat and I sputtered. In my fall, I had caught the pixie—right in my mouth. I felt tiny legs kicking at my teeth and tongue, and as a reflex I spat forward onto the metal grate of the bus floor. The pixie fell to the ground in a wet heap, and the coin rolled off to the side. The bus, having stopped, now opened its doors.

I only had a moment. Grabbing my shopping bag, I dashed for the coin and snatched it from the floor before the pixie had a moment to get up. I hopped off the bus and took off, hoping the doors would close before the creature could manage to fly again. My lungs began to burn as I hustled down the street in the direction of Central Avenue, not even thinking to stop until the bus was long out of sight and I was sure the pixie hadn't caught up.

I leaned against a stone wall and sat down, shaking from the unexpected exercise. I coughed slightly, still trying to get the nasty pixie taste out of my mouth.

Someone knew about the coin. And worse, it was important enough that someone was trying to recover it. I opened my hand to see I had been gripping it tight, and it had left an impression on my hand. The smooth and shiny surface glittered in the afternoon light, and I felt a strange sense of familiarity as my thumb stroked over its surface.

Get up, Andy, I told myself. *Get up. Now.* I pocketed the coin securely back in my pocket and stood up. My lungs still burned, but I felt rested enough to at least get home. I fought the urge to just curl up and stay here, though; my anxiety was stinging my head like a wasp between my ears, and the idea that someone had attacked me over this tiny piece of metal made my heart race in the worst kind of way. I started to shake and had to force my legs to start moving.

I took out my phone and debated on who, if anyone I should text. Apollo? No, he was probably working. Killian was off doing whatever she was doing. No, this afternoon I was on my own and I'd have to deal with it.

I kept looking around over my shoulder as I made my way down Central Avenue as quickly as I could speedwalk. The sight of my building made me speed up as I drew closer, to the point where I was nearly back to running. I don't know if it was some kind of unseen sense or just my anxiety kicked up into high gear, but I felt like I was being watched or followed and all I wanted at that moment was to be safe behind the brass and glass doors of the condo building. I hammered my card key against the lock and as soon as I heard its telltale click I slipped inside, slamming the door behind me and squeezing my eyes shut as I tried to catch my breath.

"Andy?"

I popped open my eyes and was met with a familiar pair of deep mocha-colored ones right in front of me? "Apollo?"

He pulled me away from the door and looked out the glass. "I saw you coming down the street. Looked like you were being followed."

I sputtered. "I...I don't know, I think I might have been. Th-there was a p-pixie on the bus and it almost got my d-dad's coin—"

"Breathe." He looked so determined as he gazed out the door. He had spotted something. I crept up and looked through the glass at what he had seen. Across the road, on the opposite sidewalk, a goblin was pacing up and down the pavement. It looked like it was searching the ground for something.

Apollo tore his eyes away from the window and started looking at the floor and walls as if he was searching for something. "Do you still have that scry stone?"

I nodded and pulled it out of my back pocket. It was still glowing lightly with the magic from the previous night's activities. I passed it to Apollo, who began to sweep up and down the walls and floor. Finally, he stopped, the light from the crystal finally having revealed something: a glowing sigil directly above the door. It was circular, and I could make out a stylized D and some other sorcerous-looking symbols. "What is that?" I asked.

"That's a mark of secrecy—a protection spell. It repels intruders and hides you from being found by anybody who wants to hurt you." He looked at me. "Really well done, too. I'm guessing this was put here by your dad."

I took in a deep breath and looked again out at the waiting goblin. It appeared to get frustrated and then took off down the street. "They must be after the coin."

"Maybe. In which case, maybe you should leave it here when you go out. It must be undetectable as long as it's in here, which is why they only started looking for it now."

I took the tiny silver thing from my pocket again. "But what *is* it? Why is it so important?"

"No idea. But until we find out, you should probably just leave it here. Hide it somewhere."

I nodded and tried to catch my breath again, looking up at Apollo curiously. "Wait…why are you here?"

He relaxed a little and gave me a grin that instantly made me feel a little safer. "I…uh…I have a surprise for you. Come on." He started up the stairs and I followed, dropping the coin back in my pocket and picking up my bags again.

At the top of the stairs, I found my suite door open. "What the f—"

Apollo hushed me up with a wave of his hand. "OK, so your apartment being empty is super depressing and probably bad for your mental health so…" He gestured inside, and I crossed over the threshold into the condo.

In the living room, which had previously been completely bare, now sat a large plush couch, loveseat, and a coffee table. There was an end table against a far wall, decorated with tasteful accoutrements and a small music player that was currently plugged into Apollo's phone and was softly playing Frank Sinatra's *Pennies from Heaven*. The air smelled like vanilla and cinnamon, and the simple but contemporary lamps that lit the room cast it in a warm and inviting glow.

Apollo shooed me into the kitchen, where

implements of deliciousness-creation hung from hooks near the stove, and a set of "WHO's cooking?" oven mitts (complete with winking owls) hung over the top of the burner. The oven seemed to be the source of the vanilla and cinnamon smell, where a pan of toasted almonds was currently cooking.

I spun on Apollo, completely at a loss for words. I tried to formulate some kind of grateful-sounding noise, but I think it came out unintelligibly. Apollo leaned against the kitchen archway. "Had a feeling you'd like it. And really, don't worry about it. You have bigger things to worry about than basic decoration."

"I can't…I don't have the money to—"

He shook his head and grinned mischievously. "I got a major deal by seducing the furniture salesman. So don't even worry about it."

I dropped my shoulders, feeling a wash of emotions filling my stressed and jumbled head. "I don't know what to say. I'm just…I don't know. Thank you."

Again he waved a hand dismissively. "Really. No trouble. And if you want to swap something out because it's not your taste that's fine. But then again, I'm an incubus, so I think I have a little handle on what is your taste, hm? One of the perks of my species, I think. We're good at making others comfortable." But I wasn't comfortable. I was downright uncomfortable with this huge show of kindness and I swallowed another gulp of overflowing emotions. Apollo seemed to sense it, and he took a step forward and hugged me. I sighed then, relaxing into a feeling of sudden security, and a moment later my friend's arms were gone but I still felt their warmth. "Get some rest and relax. I'll see ya on Monday, ok?" He grabbed his phone, ending the sound of Sinatra, and retired from the room, closing the door behind him with a click.

Feeling dazed and with a ball of feels tangled up in my stomach, I headed up the small set of stairs to my bedroom, which I found to be furnished with a large, comfortable-looking bed. A wooden dresser and escritoire were against the far wall, and my boxes of clothes I had brought from the East coast were stacked neatly in my closet. I sat down on the bed, part of me wanting to collapse immediately into a fit of panic, but another feeling was creeping up my limbs toward my chest that I could not push away. I got up and headed across the hall to the other room. The other room was unfurnished. I wondered briefly if Apollo had left this room alone on purpose, and I again felt some gratitude for having the foresight to do so. I pulled the scrying stone from my pocket and held it aloft, once again watching the shape of my father's desk-bound form materialize. I took the coin out as well, holding it up. "What is this? What the hell did you get me into, dad?" I demanded of the shadow, knowing not to expect an answer from the silent image.

It didn't move or respond. How much like my living father this shade was! "Argh!" I swept my arms and legs through the shade but still no response came. It ignored me just like the living one had. It didn't recognize my existence any more than the living Tom LaFayette had recognized his child's life. With as dedicated as this shade was, having blocked out the world in lieu of whatever important matter was on its desk, it might as well have been the genuine article.

I stopped as I heard something move behind me, and I spun on my heel, nearly losing my balance and falling through my dad's shimmering image. At the door, barely visible in the low light, was the Moddey Dhoo.

"Have ya ever considered," the Moddey Dhoo said in a surprisingly neutral tone, "that puttin' out yer anger at shadows idn't the best way ta handle yer feelin's?"

I froze, unable to reply. I hadn't thought much about my Silencer since our brief meeting earlier in the week. The glowing eyes, the matted fur…I wasn't sure why it was here, but the sight of it made the blood in my veins positively freeze.

"Furthermore," the Moddey Dhoo said, taking what seemed to be a threatening step closer, "Shadows can't really reply to ya, now can they? Can't be too cathartic, ya know, yelling at somethin' that you know ain't gonna talk back."

I took a shuddering breath. "I just…I want answers…" I slowly lowered myself to the floor against the wall, my eyes never leaving the piercing glare of the mangy black dog.

The Moddey Dhoo nodded. "I know ya do, but this ain't gonna get ya any, now is it? I told ya to be careful in yer investigatin', now didn't I?"

I nodded, feeling warm tears welling up at the corners of my eyes. "I got some…some things to protect myself—"

"Sure ya did, and that's good. But yer biggest weakness is that ya keep jumping into trouble at the slightest chance ya might get some kinda answer and a half." I said nothing in reply, knowing that as much as I didn't want to admit it the Moddey Dhoo was right.

The dog took another step to put himself in front of me, and then sat back on its haunches, fixing me with a gaze that I could not meet. "Yer looking too hard, and yer not thinkin. Yer not thinkin about who ya might be puttin' in danger. Apollo? Killian? They're supportin' you for whatever reason, and now that ya've dragged them into this mess, ye have to be all the more careful. But most importantly," he growled, and I felt myself genuinely recoil, "Ya have to stop chasing *shadows*!"

The Moddey Dhoo swiped its tail, slamming it through the father-shaped cloud of sparkles and causing them to suddenly disperse into nothingness. I thrust out my hands as if to try and gather the sparkles as they flickered out of existence. My hand just moved through them, and a small, helpless sound escaped my throat as the image of my dad vanished forever.

The Moddey Dhoo reached out and touched me with a paw. It was cold, and wet, and sent a chill through my skin but it got my attention and I swiveled to look the creature in the eye. "I don't…I feel like I'm…"

"Drowning? Over yer head? Lost in the woods? Stumbling in the dark?" I nodded to all of these. "Of course ya do. Yer adjusting. And yer exploring a brand-new world full of dangers ya don't even know *while* dealing with the fact that yer damn dad is dead. That ain't an easy bucket to carry, kid. Yer gonna wear yerself out."

The Moddey Dhoo was right in every sense of the word. The last few days had been a major roller coaster of emotions that had started to feel like it was leaving me with whiplash. I swallowed hard, finding my mouth and throat dry. "What do I do?"

He pointed to the door with his tail. "Bed. Rest. Get ready for Monday."

I groaned in protest but slowly pulled myself up the wall to a standing position. My head felt fuzzy as I trudged across the room toward the bedroom, my muscles sore like the stress in my body had manifested as a sack of bricks hung across my back. I numbly made it to the bed and dropped into it, curling up against the pillow with my eyes closed tightly and leaking warm tears.

I didn't hear the Moddey Dhoo leave, but I felt its breath briefly over me while I laid there, and I swear I felt the blanket get pulled over me by a set of powerful jaws. I did drift off into sleep eventually, and when I awakened the black dog was gone.

SHAPES

Ugthak was destined to be strong. It was part of his blood, and his father's blood, and his father's blood, and so on as far back as Troll's records allowed. Ugthak was the fourth son of the eldest brother of the strongest Troll in the den, Chief Bogbug. Ugthak had lost his father early in life and had become the Chief's ward.

Ugthak learned to use a club when he was young. He learned to run fast. He learned to hit hard. But what confused the den elders the most was that Ugthak also learned to think and consider the strategy of a fight. He was one of those "thinkers", who used their mind along with their body.

Troll society was not about the mind. It was about the body. Once, they had been creatures of war, but now they focused on strength in its many forms: the body, the community, the soul. One needed to be strong not just for his own well-being but for the well-being of the den.

Ugthak grew into a fine young troll, muscled and dignified, and though he held no claim to even be chieftain of the den, he held his family's name and reputation in high esteem and he did well by his legacy. He was strong, both in body and in mind.

Until, one day, Ugthak met with Chief Bogbug for midtime meal, and spoke something very unusual. "Chief," he addressed his uncle with respect, "I wish to go out into the world and gain knowledge. I wish to bring this knowledge back to my people and make them stronger. Then, maybe I will have pleased my people and my chief, and I will receive the Mark of Glory. Not for fighting, or blood, or strength, but for service to the world beyond."

"The Mark of Glory is not for the world beyond the den," Bogbug snarled. Ugthak protested but Bogbug quieted him with a slam of his fist on the table. "The Mark of Glory is for strength given in service to *your* people!" Bogbug was unhappy. Leaving the den was not forbidden, but those who did rarely returned. They would pick up those shiny things and take homes in big buildings and find other, different lives that Bogbug did not want to think about. If Ugthak were to leave, it would likely be for good.

But Bogbug was also not a harsh troll. He was strong and powerful, but he saw in his nephew's eyes a yearning. He knew that forbidding this course of action would do one of two things: it would either drive him to leave of his own accord, or it would break the young troll's spirit. And then, the Mark of Glory would never be granted—and what a dishonor that would be!

In times long ago, before Bogbug, chiefs forbade

leaving. But the den suffered and grew restless over time. It wasn't long before some snarky young troll ran away and went on a huge adventure, complete with a talking animal companion, before returning having learned some valuable lesson about family. It was not the best solution to this problem.

"If you must go, you will go!" Bogbug said, with as much kindness as he could muster, "But you will return and devote yourself to strength, and service to your people. Then, maybe, you will receive the Mark of Glory."

Ugthak was overjoyed and swore on all the stones and ancestors and elders and the Earth itself that he would return and devote himself to strength and service. Ugthak said goodbye to the elders the very next day and disappeared into the world in search of his place.

It was many moons before Ugthak returned. Bogbug had borne five more sons before he saw Ugthak again crossing over the hill toward the cave that marked the entrance to the den. Ugthak was dressed strangely, like one of the mundane human creatures that sometimes camped in the Den's woods for days and listened to loud music and sprayed foul things on his trees. How Bogbug hated those humans! He often watched them near the river and considered breaking his den's rules by killing them…but Bogbug was wise and believed in his den's strength and unity, so he left them alone.

Ugthak met with the elders at once and shared his stories with them: he had met an apothecary who taught Ugthak how to brew a potion that would let him disguise himself as a human. He went to a school and posed as a student; he earned high marks and learned quickly with the help of a magical force called "internet". Ugthak had been accepted at a job where he could put his knowledge to work and accomplish many things.

Bogbug was quiet as he listened, silently overjoyed at Ugthak's success, but at these last words he stiffened. "You come back now, but you leave again? You promised you would devote yourself to strength, and service to your people."

Ugthak looked taken aback. "And I will. I simply must gain more knowledge and strengthen my mind first. Then, with my mind, I can serve my people."

Bogbug was angered then. "You have deceived me! You will receive no Mark of Glory ever! You will go!" Bogbug slammed his table and retired from the cavern without another word. Ugthak departed at first light, and Bogbug felt a sunkenness in his heart. He had not meant to lose his temper. But he was angry that Ugthak had forgotten his duties to others. Ugthak was so selfish, strengthening his mind and forgetting about service to his people. This was dishonorable. This was action unworthy of the Mark of Glory.

It was many more moons later that Bogbug awoke late in the night to the crisp and unpleasant smell of burning leaves. As he left the cave he could see that the blaze was growing quickly. Soon the humans would be here with their big boxes full of water and would put it out. Fires were not uncommon, and they posed no danger for the Troll's sanctuary—

—but he heard a pained scream, carried along the breeze in the trees and knew something else was wrong.

Tearing through the forest, he located the source of the blaze—one of the foul human camps had not put their campfire out, and while they slept it had caught the trees above them. Now the humans cowered near the running river, trapped between the dangerous rushing water and the creeping orange death.

Bogbug was quick, and strong, and not heartless. The humans had made a dumb mistake because humans are dumb and make dumb mistakes. But that was not a reason to leave them to die. Bogbug invoked ancient magics, and seemed to pull at the air itself, twisting it to move the fire away from the people. Next he slammed his fists into the ground and picked up large rocks, throwing them into the river near the terrified people, making a small bridge. Finally, he swept the three of them up in his arms and dashed across the rocks, clearing the river and barreling through the trees.

Bogbug did not stop, and the humans did not know what was going on. Two of them had collapsed, from the smoke and their fear—how weak. The other, a young girl, was staring up and him in awe as he carried them to the edge of the den forest, near swirling red and blue lights in the distance. He set them down near the road, just out of sight of the lights, and pointed toward the human's metal cars. "Cry," he growled at the child, and she immediately obeyed, letting out an ear-piercing screech that hurt the old troll's ears.

Bogbug retreated into the tree line and watched as the dumb humans came up and started to help the people. "Three more!" one shouted, and some people in red coats came out of nowhere, it seemed, to wrap the people in blankets and put strange clear devices to their mouths talking about air and smoke inhalation. They were human medicine men with magic medicine boxes and tubes.

Bogbug was going to leave until one of them caught his eye. He was big, and muscular, and moved with a gait that carried a man filled with inner strength. Bogbug rubbed his eyes and he could sense that this human image was an illusion over a much more powerful creature beneath.

He watched as Ugthak helped load the child onto a moving bed, asking how they had gotten out here and if there were any others. "The big man carried me!" she squeaked through tears. The young troll looked up and his eyes swept the trees searchingly. He finally spotted Bogbug, hidden near the tree, and nodded to him respectfully before resuming his work tending to the sick people.

Bogbug thought a long time as he watched his nephew expertly caring for the people as they loaded them into a big human metal box and took them away. He considered the Mark of Glory that Ugthak had sought, and likely would never receive. What dishonor! And yet…It was clear that this dishonor was not a burden on his nephew's heart. Perhaps he had found something more important. Perhaps Ugthak had discovered his own Mark of Glory somewhere in the knowledge of the human people as one of their medicine men. Bogbug was not sure, but he had a feeling that what Ugthak was doing was important for many people beyond the den. He grumbled to himself as he trekked back through the trees, the sounds of the human boxes slowly disappearing in the woods behind him.

CHAPTER 11

There was a significant difference in the way I walked through the doors at 50 Thousand on my second Monday, compared to the first. For one, I was not so awestruck by the massive green-glassed building this time. I think it's one of those things, when something awesome and amazing is under your nose for a long time, even it becomes commonplace. I'm reminded of my first time visiting the Statue of Liberty. Seeing it overlooking the New York skyline I was struck with a sense of complete awe and wonder, but some resident New Yorker friends who were there with me shrugged and rolled their eyes, having grown up with the huge green lady always *there*.

Second, of course, I was prepared and confident. The 50 Thousand Employee Handbook tucked neatly under one arm—I had begun to get in the habit of carrying it with me most places I went[13] at this point—and a cup of Apollo's most caffeinated brew ("You aren't allowed to have more than one of these in a day," he explained, "Or you may literally explode. Yeah, you think I'm kidding, just watch"), I strode across the 50 Thousand Lobby, my shoes clicking neatly on the marble floor, and passed through the security gate with a smile plastered on my face.

I made it to my cubicle and took a seat, taking out my PC and booting up my computer. As soon as the desktop showed up on my screen I saw the blip of new notifications in the bottom right telling me I had an email. I took a gulp of my coffee (holy mother of God, if I wasn't awake before I certainly was now) and clicked it.

---

[13] "50 Thousand Consulting provides excellent carrying bags, folders, and other travel-friendly accoutrements for your copy of the 50 Thousand Employee Handbook. Employees found to be abusing, misusing, or vandalizing a copy of the Handbook may be faced with severe disciplinary action up to and including Termination. And you know what? Maybe more than termination. Maybe you might have charges pressed against you. Or, like, maybe you'll just get set on fire. Do you want that? Huh?" - 50 Thousand Employee Handbook, Page 611 (Caring for your 50 Thousand Employee Handbook)

From: Hampstead, David
To: LaFayette, Andy
CC: Warner, Carrie
Subject: URGENT

VERY URGENT![14]
Please come to my office as soon as you clock in. Bring a notebook and pen. Please do not delay. Room 115-B

VTY,
Lord David Hampstead
Senior Associate Wizard
50 Thousand Consulting

I reread the email quickly before shutting the computer and grabbing my notebook and a pen. I dashed down the hall and around the corner to the rows of Wizarding offices with their glass office doors, counting as I went. I slowed right before I hit 115-B, taking just a second to compose myself and catch my breath before knocking and letting myself

---

[14] "Before marking an email as urgent, ask yourself three important questions: If it turns out to not be as urgent as I think it is, do I feel secure in my job? Is there a more efficient way of relaying the information? If I received this email wrapped around a brick and lobbed through my office window, would I still thank the person who threw the brick for informing me of such important information? The answers to these questions should guide you as to whether or not an email is really urgent or not." - 50 Thousand Employee Handbook, Page 840 (Email etiquette)

in.

The office was very conservatively decorated; the same greyish and green tones of the rest of the building made up the little neo-contemporary furniture in the room. Behind the glass desk sat the Wizard I had met last week who had assigned me the task of going to the Market and later paid me a compliment. His back was to me, typing away on his laptop on the side part of the desk. I glimpsed a photo of what looked like a wife, children, and grandchildren before he turned around and I met his gaze.

"LaFayette," Hampstead said approvingly, picking up a folder. "Thank you for being on time. Now, I have something rather important coming up tomorrow and I am going to need you to be present. Here, have a seat. Got coffee? Good." I sat down. "I have received a summons from Most Venerable to attend his office tomorrow afternoon. Todd, the Dragon," he added for clarification upon seeing me tilt my head in slight confusion. I nodded in understanding. "Usually this is also an opportunity to show off some of the more standout new hires. So I have a few of those. But the Dragon has also asked for you, specifically, to attend and I would like some understanding why, if you would not mind."

My eyes went wide and I tried to think of an answer. "Maybe because of my father, Tom? I know he, um...worked for the Dragon or something like that, right?"

Hampstead leaned back, considering me for a moment—and perhaps considering his words. Of all of the people who I had met who knew of my dad, this man might have more information than all of the rest combined, it occurred to me, and I immediately had to suppress the urge to bombard him with questions. "That's right. He was the Vaultkeeper here. Your dad was somewhat of an expert on magical artifacts, and had quite the reputation for it. I know he was one of the few people ever allowed to see the Cincinnati Dragon's Hoard—to identify some baubles of some kind, no doubt." He shrugged. "But yes, you're probably right. It's likely that The Dragon wants to offer respects. Yes, that's it." Hampstead sounded more to me like he was trying to convince himself.

My resolve to keep myself form blurting questions failed. "What was he like? My dad, I mean? Did you get to know him?"

Hampstead tilted his head at my question, and I could almost see cogs turning in his head. "He really...he really kept to himself. I saw him once a week at Casting, but that's all. I'm...sorry to disappoint." He could see that I was desperate for a crumb of information and he adjusted his glasses while he formulated the words. "I remember once, I caught him at the espresso machine and he mentioned, sort of in passing, how he...*regretted* that he didn't have a good relationship with his family, but he didn't really expand on that. So for what it's worth, I'm sorry about that. For all of it. So. Anyway." He shuffled some papers and turned away.

"Thanks. I appreciate it." I took a breath while Hampstead was awkwardly collecting himself. He regretted not having a good relationship with his family? Alright, Andy, get a hold of yourself. There is work to be done. "Is there anything I need to know about meeting the Dragon? Like...protocol or something?"

"Not as much as you'd expect, given how important he is," Hampstead said, and his voice sounded a bit more clear and decisive. "But so long as you're polite then you should be fine. Also, if the Dragon or one of his deputies tells you to do something, you *do it* without question. The office of the Dragon answers to no one, so if he decided to kill you, that'd be the end of it."

"Do what he says or he eats me?" I gave a promising smile, recalling the Dragon-related pamphlet I had read earlier.

"Exactly." It wasn't a joke. "Now, here's the address—you'll meet us there at the Lair. Note the specific time on the page, right? The Lair moves, for security, so be sure that you're there on time. The doorway only manifests on the ground for short periods of time; the rest of the time it's floating high up in the sky, invisible. So do *not* be late. OK?"

I nodded emphatically. "I won't let you down."

Hampstead seemed convinced. "Alright, good. Now back to work with you." He made a 'shoo' motion to the door—which really would have annoyed me if I wasn't so excited— and I headed out and back toward my desk.

I was going to meet the Dragon. I hadn't said what I was really thinking when Hampstead asked: that the Dragon wanted to talk to me about Dad's death. I recalled Apollo saying that the office of the Dragon was investigating it, and the idea that they might have answers—and better yet, that they might *willingly* be given to me—was an utterly unfathomable but exciting concept. I texted Apollo. *I have an appointment with the Dragon tomorrow.*

His reply came uncomfortably fast. *oh my god what happened what did you do*

No. I'm going there with some of the new hires from 50K.

so youre not in trouble?????

No. But I think the Dragon might want to talk to me about Dad.

ok that doesnt sound bad. holy crap though, don't scare a brother like that ok?

I dropped a thumbs-up emoji and put my phone away as I returned to the storeroom. I found the door open, and curiously I poked my head inside.

A young man and woman stood inside, both looking over a very thick folder and talking in quiet voices. They weren't dressed like wizards. They had knocked over several stacks of files—my *files!*—in order to get to it, and did not appear to notice me in the doorway.

"This is insane," she said, flipping a page over. "He's immune to just…everything."

"That's what happens when you're in charge," the man replied. "You get the best protections. Magical immunity is really expensive. But with protections like this, well…he'd shrug off every spell we could throw at him. We're talking death spells, master jinxes, everything."

"What about…you know…"

"Chartreuse?"

The woman made a sound like an audible cringe. "Y-yeah."

"Honestly, I think so. Look at this. I've never seen an anti-hex web set up so strong. I bet it would stop anything."

"Well, let's get this back to the—"

I cleared my throat. "Can I help you both? I'm…in charge of this storeroom." Sort of.

They spun quickly, slamming the folder shut. I glanced at the cover label, and spotted the title "The Dragon of Cincinnati". I hadn't recalled seeing that one while sorting, but then again there were a lot of folders I hadn't gone through yet.

"Yes, of course," the man said with a puff of his chest. "We were asked to collect this file for…" He tried to think of a name.

"…Lord wizard Caliburn," the woman continued. "For research. The symposium. You know. Wizard stuff."

I narrowed my eyes as the two of them very quickly swept past me with the folder and left me, confused, to clean up the mess they had left behind.

"Thank you all for joining me here this evening."

The other five people at the table nodded cordially and took their seats. Red wine was poured into glasses as each settled into their chairs. Even in the dim light that illuminated the glossy wooden table, they could not hide the creeping nervousness in their expressions. The man at the head of the table finally spoke. "Greetings, Black Magisters. Lord Rathnul, give us an update on our timeline."

Rathnul, a svelte but sweaty man, pulled out his cell phone and pulled up a document. "Well, with the loss of Magister LaFayette, we are looking at some delays. We are going to need to find a new recruit to fill the hole he left. People with his advantage are few and far between—"

"I hear nothing but excuses," the leader said, a growing growl of threat in his throat.

Another Magister spoke up while Rathnul took a sip of his wine embarrassedly. "Lord Grimsbane, we also have the slight problem of having not recovered everything we needed from Magister LaFayette's Estate. Our agents cleaned out his condo completely but the coin was not there. So now we are on the lookout for it. The Goblins have already been informed and they are on our side in this matter."

Grimsbane knotted his fingers together. "Then everything is going to plan."

Rathnul looked up, his face in shocked confusion. "Um…I don't mean to upset you, but I feel like this is not going according to plan. Like…it's strayed pretty far off the plan, if you ask me. If Cory hadn't screwed up the budget in the first place—"

"You will address Magister Thorne by his proper title," Grimsbane said, his teeth nearly bared like a wolf preparing to pounce. "And expect that your lack of confidence in the way your Lord and Master conducts the execution of these plans—"

"Would you like parmesan on your salad?" the server—a pleasant-looking redhead with a badge that read "Rosie"—asked, setting the huge bowl of greenery down on the table. "And can I get you more breadsticks?"

Grimsbane gave her a polite smile. "Oh yes, please. Thank you." He watched with hungry, vicious eyes as the spiraling strands of cheese poured out of the grater onto the Italian-spiced salad. "Yess…gooood," he growled under his breath, making the other people at the table rather uncomfortable.

Rosie left and Grimsbane resumed his threats. "As I was saying, when Lord Grimsbane commands, it is expected that—"

"Oh, get off it, Manny," Rathnul retorted. "And can you quit this 'grimsbane' stuff? We were all here when you pulled every single one of our 'code names' off an Evil Name Generator. None of us take it seriously." The other people at the table nodded in agreement. "What we really need is to *modify* the plan in case we don't get the coin back. We can still do it, but we need to prepare reasonable countermeasures in case whoever has it gets some silly ideas."

Grimsbane took a large gulp of his red wine, his face flushing a deep red. "We will do that when *I* say we do it, Magister Rathnul, and not a moment earlier. Or have you so forgotten who it is that holds your debts?"

Rathnul's shoulders dropped immediately. "Right, of course, Lord Grimsbane."

Grimsbane turned to the woman at his right. "Has His Magnificence been informed of the situation, Magister La Rouge?"

La Rouge nodded politely. "I spoke to him yesterday, and he is distressed, but he had faith that we will be able to, at the least, complete the first part of the plan."

"And we shall," Grimsbane said with confidence. "Let us not forget who it is who empowers the authority of this Circle—oh here's breadsticks." Rosie laid down the basket and asked if anyone wanted additional drinks. After taking her order and disappearing again, Grimsbane continued. "We will prepare the ceremony at next full moon."

"Actually," La Rouge piped up, checking her

calendar on her phone, "The next full moon is actually the weekend I'm out of town for that leadership conference I signed up for."

Grimsbane looked irritated. "Alright, we shall instead meet at dusk on the thirteenth day—"

"The thirteenth is no good for me," another Magister added, "My daughter has a dance thing."

"How about the…last Thursday?" Rathnul offered. There was a general agreement around the table.

Grimsbane pulled out his phone and checked it. "No, no, that won't work. I have dental surgery in the afternoon and I'll probably be on pain meds." The others grumbled in frustration and began comparing calendars. "How about Tuesday, the 21st?" he suggested, glancing at some of the phones around him. Everyone seemed to find that acceptable.

Grimsbane grinned menacingly and resumed his dramatic posturing. "Yes. On the 21st, we shall perform the ritual, and His Magnificence will rise again and take over this city." He began a guttural, deep laugh in the back of his throat but it turned into a cough. La Rouge patted him on the back as he took a drink of water to make the coughing fit subside. At this moment Rosie made another appearance. "Is this all on one check?"

"Separate," Grimsbane choked out. The others at the table made frustrated noises. One of the Magisters piped up. "Can we stop meeting at Olive Garden every week if you're not even going to pay for our dinner, Manny?"

"Lord *Grimsbane*," he shot back, "and if you can't *afford* it, Magister Bloodstone, you don't have to *order* anything."

Bloodstone closed his menu. "OK, then I'm good." The other Magisters agreed.

Rosie made a clicking noise with her tongue. "If you don't order over $50 in food, then you can't have this private section and you'll have to eat in the main dining area," she reminded, "How about I let you all decide and I'll come back?" She excused herself from the room.

Grimsbane looked quite put out, and stroked his goatee impatiently. "Fine, fine," he said to the group, "But don't go over ten dollars." they made more frustrated noises and started looking for the lowest-priced items on the menu. "We wouldn't have these restrictions if Cory—I'm sorry, Magister Thorne—hadn't made mistakes with our budget."

"It was a simple math error!" Thorne protested. "And now that LaFayette is gone we can hide the errors and get the budget back on track, OK? Can we let it go?"

"Your 'math error' almost got us caught," Rathnul said sternly, closing his menu, "But you're right—we can blame LaFayette for any discrepancies in the ledger. Lucky you."

Grimsbane nodded. "We all can learn from LaFayette's mistakes. And I expect nothing like it will happen again. Now decide on what you want to eat before the waitress gets back."

"They're *servers*, Manny," Thorne interjected, "Waitress is such an outdated term."

Grimsbane silenced him with a glare. "Choose...your...food," he said slowly, and Thorne resumed looking at his menu.

La Rouge stood up very quickly, making Grimsbane jump slightly in surprise. "You know what? If we're all agreed on plans and the meeting is over, I think I will just get my food to go. I'll just…I'll go place my order directly with the *server*." She gave Grimsbane an irritated glare and left the room. The other Magisters, seeing no reaction from their leader, slowly packed up and excused themselves as well.

Finally, only Grimsbane was left, to sulk at an empty table with a half bottle of wine that he pulled close to him. "Yes, very well," he said to the empty room. "It is just as well that Lord Grimsbane dines alone. Yes. Grimsbane dines…alone." He sniffled slightly, feeling quite deflated, and poured himself another glass of wine.

CHAPTER 12

I had mentioned the weird people in the storeroom to Killian the next time I'd seen her. Her eyebrows knitted together for a moment and then she rolled her eyes. "I wouldn't even worry about it," she had said. "People cause trouble all the time, but it rarely goes anywhere. And they might actually be working for a wizard."

"But why would they be interested in Todd's file?"

"Who knows? 50 Thousand is the steward of Todd's protective spells, for obvious reasons. They might be checking to make sure they're all still up and running in time for the Symposium."

That did make sense. At Killian's urging, I put the weird file-stealing people out of my mind and focused on the task at hand.

I was downtown and ready to go an hour and a half before my scheduled appointment with the

Dragon. My first stop had been to the coffee shop, where I had tried to garner some useful knowledge about what to expect from this visit into the City's powerful leader.

It occurred to me that I had never even seen or met the mayor of a town I had lived in before learning The Secret. So many machinations of the normal, mundane world were controlled far above my head even outside of the realm of magical influence. How often had I personally bitched about local or national officials on facebook? And with jurisdictions of countless people the idea of being able to meet any of those lawmakers was a foreign concept to me. Now, of course, the stakes were higher and the jurisdiction stranger, but the same sense of talking to giants was lingering over me.

"So I know the rule is 'don't get eaten,'" I told Apollo, "But what exactly is the Dragon like?"

Apollo shrugged. "I've met him a…couple times. There's a Dragon Symposium every year where all the dragons get together, and at the last one, which was in Louisville, he gave a great address to the Societies…but I don't know how much of that is PR. He seems like a nice enough guy." Apollo pulled another shot of espresso into the cup waiting below, and then moved on to steaming some milk. I watched him do his coffee dance as I had many times before. He looked up and smiled as he handed over my latte. "You promise to be careful right? And you left the you-know-what at home?"

I nodded and shuddered internally, for a moment thinking about the evil pixie on the bus. "Well, I've got to be off. I have to get to this address…" I pulled out my phone. "It's not too far but I don't want to be late—"

As if on cue, my phone rang in my hand. I glanced at the unknown number and answered. "Andy LaFayette."

"Andy!" It was Hampstead. "Meeting's been pushed up. I'm texting you the new address. You're over at the coffee shop, right? It's about two blocks from where you're at right now. But you have to get over there fast." The call ended and my phone buzzed with a new text. "Oh no…" I looked up at Apollo. "I'll text you see you later bye!" I was out the door.

I dashed down the street, coffee still in hand, trying to navigate the numbered streets of Cincinnati as best I could. According to the text, I had about 4 minutes before the lair moved on. I stopped at 8th street and waited, bringing up my map on my phone and trying to discern which direction I was headed. The 8th street traffic finally slowed and the light changed; I dashed across, ignoring the painful burning in my lungs as I tore down the sidewalk toward 7th. I dodged an old lady carrying a grocery bag and two potential drug dealers outside the library, glancing down the street to be sure there was no traffic before dashing to the opposite sidewalk leaving me just one crosswalk away from where the entrance to the Dragon's lair was supposed to be. I got a glimpse of a decorated archway that had come up inexplicably in the center of the opposing sidewalk. I checked my phone to see that I had literally less than a minute to cross through those double doors into the space beyond.

How did I let it get this bad? Last minute change of plans were a major frustration of mine. I wasn't even sure what the procedure was if I missed the building before it vanished for the morning. The final light change was too slow for me, and I took my chances, jaywalking—jay*running*—and dashing across corner toward the archway. I was going to make it. Just barely, but I was going to—

I was easily a foot and a half from the door when the archway, and the doors, simply ceased to be there. I stumbled in surprise, landing in a heap on the asphalt and ripping my knees up across the rough surface. I clutched my leg with a frustrated cry, and desperately tried to catch my breath.

My heart was sinking. What would I do? Was there a number somewhere I would have to call? Surely Hampstead would be upset. Would I lose my job? Would the Dragon be mad at me? Would I get eaten?[15]

"You ok?" I heard a voice behind me. Dammit, I must look like a spectacular sight for sure, what with having just taken a nasty fall after dashing across a Cincinnati sidewalk for absolutely no reason.

"Yeah…I'm fine," I said, pulling myself to my feet as quickly as my bruised legs and scraped hands would allow me. "I just, uh…" I turned around to face the bystander who has just witnessed my embarrassing wipeout and stopped.

Magnificent and pale, before me stood a beautiful winged horse. I stood silently, my mouth agape and

---

[15] "Associates who inadvertently raise the ire of the Dragon of Cincinnati are immediately considered withdrawn from, and become ineligible for, the company's Term Life Insurance plan. If you're not sure if you raised the ire of the Dragon, then you probably did. Sorry, bud." - 50 Thousand Employee Handbook, Page 608 (Insurance Benefits)

no words to fill them whatsoever. The noble beast shook its head with a pitiful look at my bloodied knee, his mane shimmering as it moved in waves of silk around its face. Around its neck was a jeweled charm *Vulnerabl* necklace.

The Pegasus gave me a curious look. "You okay, kid?"

I composed myself. "Yeah, I just...um...I was...uh..." I couldn't properly string words in the presence of such an intimidating and beautiful creature. I could never imagine a sight. It was even saddled! A tawny leather saddle, lined with gold, which it opened gently with its muzzle and delicately removed a...uh...

The Pegasus closed its saddlebags and looked at me, the menthol cigarette hanging from its mouth like a little stiff worm. "You got a light?"

I blinked as the Pegasus took a step toward me, and the smell of cigarette smoke—and something else—was that gin?—was noticeable. "Uh....yeah." I pulled a lighter from my pocket and lit it. The creature smiled with its rather yellow teeth and moved close enough to light the cigarette. It took a long draw and I recomposed myself. "I missed the...the door—"

"You work for 50 K?" The horse had now sat back on its haunches and I vaguely considered the fact that I probably appeared to passerby as someone talking to myself.

"Yeah. Wait, no—I work *at* 50 K. Do you? I mean, is there a way to—"

"You trying to get to the Dragon's Lair?" The Pegasus was now fiddling with a second cigarette and trying to chain-light it to the best of its ability while hindered by hooves. "And no. 50 K doesn't hire felons, didn't you hear?"

Trying to ignore the logistics of how a Pegasus might end up with a criminal record, I pressed. "Do you know how to get in once the building's flown off?"

The Pegasus nodded. "Oh yeah, for sure. I can give you a lift. I can track the Lair. It's a Pegasus thing."

I breathed a sigh of relief. "Oh thank goodness. I thought I was toast."

The Pegasus gave me an apathetic look. "Yeah, no worries. Also, it'll be forty bucks."

I blinked. "What?"

"Ffrty bcksh," the Pegasus repeated, his mouth now holding two cigarettes, which he adjusted to be able to talk properly again, "and a pack of Newport lights." He gestured with his wing down the block. "Garfield Mini Mart is around the corner. Get me some cash and some smokes and I'll get you there in a flash."

I looked around. My gut told me this was an awful, awful idea…but there was nothing else to be done. It was either this or potentially not having a job tomorrow. "Alright, alright, deal." Remembering what I had learned about *Vulnerabl*, I offered my hand and hoped that Pegasi adhered to the whole Promise Code thing like the *Kobolda*.

He look at my hand and offered his hoof, shaking it. "Get to it. I got places to be. You got any weed?"

A quick jaunt to the mini mart later, I was climbing on the back of the winged horse. I had ditched my coffee; the idea of accidentally dropping a hot coffee onto someone from a hundred feet up was terrible. In a moment, with a loud belch from the Pegasus, we were up in the air. I gasped and held tighter to the reins as the ground slipped away below me, and the Cincinnati buildings become very visible beside the roaring Ohio River.

"So my cousin," the Pegasus was saying, "he decides to get involved in this whole black market deals thing. Starts selling something that looks like love potions, right? Because they're banned in Cincinnati. Problem is, it's not a love potion at all, and it's like…orange soda or something. Then he acts *surprised* when a bunch of angry customers come back and say it didn't work and they didn't find their one true love…and then he tries to get *me* to defend him. Can you even believe the nerve of that—" I stopped listening.

Above us, in the clouds, a building began to materialize. It was a castle: Gothic towers and buttresses swept upwards toward other castle-specific architectural words that surrounded the massive keep in the center.

The Pegasus led me over the wall and into the courtyard, where he landed and bent a knee to allow me to dismount. "Thank you," I said politely to the Pegasus as I waved good-bye.

"Next time it's fifty bucks," he snorted and flew away. What an asshole.

I looked around the courtyard, which was empty, in search of where I was supposed to go. There were several doors leading from the courtyard that might potentially be the right ones, but it was impossible to tell without any kind of map or building directory which I had half-expected to be plastered somewhere nearby. In front of me, I could see the massive keep on the other side of one of the interior walls, so I headed in that direction, hoping luck would be on my side at least in the short-term.

It was. I hadn't gotten thirty feet before the door swung open and a well-dressed butler gestured me forward. His face was long and his eyes were sunken and for a moment I was reminded of a living version of a cartoon villain. "Apprentice LaFayette?" he inquired. I nodded. "You will head through that door, up the first flight of stairs, and then take the elevator to the tenth floor. I would advise that you not be late. He *so* hates lateness."

I thanked the butler and dashed off toward the doors, and then though them, to arrive in a massive front hall with a sweeping staircase. I had only a moment to admire all the marble and brass before I forced myself to take the stairs two at a time. I reached the elevator and headed upward, finally catching my breath in the few moments of silence between floors. My anxiety steadied and my breath caught up, I straightened my jacket as the door opened.

The tenth floor was one large office. A massive desk was the centerpiece of the door, flanked by a clock on one side and a row of paintings on the other. A comfy-looking couch was pressed against one of the walls next to a coffee table, and I spied a small mini-bar in one of the far corners. To the left, two gigantic wooden doors filled nearly the whole wall, easily twenty feet high and just as wide. I had never seen an office so spacious and grand, and I couldn't help myself letting out a soft whistle at the sight.

"Aha. You're here." It was Hampstead who rose from the couch and gestured me over. "Let's all get acquainted before he arrives. These are Lord Wizards Columbia, Kilwinning, and Blake…and apprentices LaFayette, Mariemont, and Birch. This is going to be a short meeting for the apprentices, and a long one for the Wizards."

My heart sunk a little. This wasn't about my dad at all; it was some kind of group thing. I hate group things in general. In fact, I might just go on record and say I dislike people as a whole. Has that been obvious?

Case in point: to my left, I heard a familiar voice sneering. "Oh, it's you." I looked to see Devin, dressed in an impeccable suit, standing up and looking me up and down. "I didn't expect to see you. I figured you'd be in a filing room somewhere."

I returned his derisive look with one of my own, silently mouthing *WTF is your problem* at him before shaking hands with everyone else politely. I immediately recognized Blake. "You're one of the managing partners, right? You led Casting last week?"

Blake nodded. "That's right. Was that your first casting? I'm made to understand you're new." I was taken aback by how immediately personable Blake was; he seemed to lack the air of haughtiness I had come to expect from the other wizards. Perhaps, I mused, he was more modest given his junior standing among the managing partners of the firm. "I knew your Dad. Heck of a guy. I guarantee he would be proud to know you're here with us."

*I'm not so sure…*I thought to myself as I smiled, hiding my gritted teeth. I didn't have a moment to think too deeply on that thought, however, as that moment the main doors to the room opened wide.

I honestly can't say that I know exactly what I

expected to see walking through those doors, from a huge scaly beast to a smooth eastern creature, but I did not expect the Dragon of Cincinnati to look so utterly *normal*. He was tall, and lean, with thinning but distinguishedly-cut hair and a neat dark suit accented with silver jewelry. As he neared closer, I spied a fancy gilt jewel hanging from his breast pocket featuring a scaly reptilian beast curled around a red gem in the center. He extended a hand to Blake first and then introductions were made.

"Lord Wizards," Todd said, shaking hands and giving quite familiar smiles to them. "And these must be…?"

"Apprentices Andy LaFayette," Hampstead said, "Nannette Mariemont and—"

"Devin Birch," the slimy jerkward interrupted, offering his hand to the Dragon. Todd shook it and gave Devin a polite smile. "It's a distinct honor to meet you, Most Venerable Sir, here at your most magnificent Lair." Oh god. Every word Devin said made me hate him more. He was like that brown-nosing older brother that always sucked up to the family members who had money so he could badger them later for cash.

Todd, for his part, made no point to acknowledge the slight breach in decorum, but I could see on Hampstead's face that Devin had likely erred. He stepped in to steer any perceived faux pas in a good direction. "Apprentice Birch is a rising star here in 50 Thousand. He's definitely going places." I saw a bead of sweat slipping down Hampstead's face and I could only imagine that he was like an overworked secretary here, trying to balance the whole situation for fear that any calamity might be blamed on him personally.

And given the insistence at every corner that angering the Dragon of Cincinnati even slightly would end in disaster, I hardly blamed him.

The Dragon shook my hand and then moved on, and I actually felt quite relieved to not hear the words "I knew your dad" because it was honestly starting to grate on my nerves that everyone and their brother seems to have known about my dad and what he did except *me*. This did, however, leave the question open about why exactly the Dragon of Cincinnati wanted me there personally. I gulped down the rising lump in my throat and kept on politely smiling. I watched Devin for a moment as he sort of butted into the conversation Todd was having with the Wizard I had been introduced to as Columbia.

"So now that we're all here, let's have a seat." He gingerly took his place in the leather chair and gestured for us all to sit on the couches. "This was meant to be sort of an informal meeting with you three," he gestured to the wizards, "over my upcoming symposium for this year. And we'll get to that. But I also thought it would be a good opportunity to also meet you three," he gestured to Devin, Nannette and I, "and congratulate you on your Sorcery permits. The three of you scored the highest of the candidates this year on the *Sorcera* Permit Application Exam. so…well done." He applauded quietly.

I blinked. There was no way that I had gotten a high score on that multiple-choice test. I had guessed in over half the answers. I had been surprised I'd succeeded enough to get a permit in the first place.

"I make it a habit to know who is doing what in my city, so I thought it might be a good idea to do a little meet-and-greet. You meet me, I learn a bit about you." He turned to Nannette. "Let's start with you, Miss Mariemont, was it? Please."

Nannette looked momentarily taken aback but recovered. "Well, my name is Nannette Mariemont and I work in research. I have degrees in English Folklore and European Linguistics. I shared a class with the Espresso Machine from the break room," she added to the Wizards on the opposite couch, eliciting knowing chuckles. I briefly wondered how exactly an espresso machine might take notes. "I was really lucky that the exam focused so much on identities and descriptions as well as folklore…it was really far up my alley."

It suddenly hit me that I had met this girl before. She had given me that list of books in the Cincinnati Library, which I still had not had a chance to thumb through.

Todd nodded with a smile and then looked over to me. "And…Andy, right?"

I nodded. "Yes, sir. I'm Andy LaFayette. I'm a casting technical analyst. I have an associates in liberal arts and uh…" I felt so thoroughly inadequate. I also didn't want to add in anything about dad because unlike the smarmy jerk next to me I was proud of getting here without prior networking, even if it had been sheer luck. "And I am learning a lot and hope I can really…uh…be an asset to the company and contribute positively to your city."

Todd nodded his approval. "I'm sure you will. And Devin?"

Devin stood up and gave a low bow. "Most Venerable Sir, I am thoroughly humbled to be in your presence and I thank you for the opportunity you have presented. My name is Devin Allen Birch, and I am a senior Apprentice…but I don't have business cards yet because I'll be a Wizard soon enough." He gave finger guns. *Finger guns.* If I had been one of the wizards I'd have been mortified, but they stayed rather stony-faced on the other couch, watching Devin like he might catch fire any moment.[16] Todd was similarly unreadable, even with his bright and optimistic smile, and I wondered if he was eating up all of Devin's sycophantism or was just getting ready to eat Devin himself. Devin thankfully took a seat before he could ruin his own image further.

"I really appreciate you three being here. Every year there is a hiring season and permits get made and I get to see name after name cross my desk, and the opportunity to put name to face for rising stars like yourselves is a great boon to an old dragon's memory." He stood up. "One thing I want to emphasize is that this city and its people are deeply ingrained with a culture and beauty all their own, and that we—which is to say, all of the societies, not just *Sorcera*—have a duty to protect them and live among them in peace. You are part of an ancient and honorable craft that spans lengths of time nearly to the limits of Human record. You have the opportunity to be the example. Be like these fine wizards before you who have time and time again proven their invaluable nature protecting people from the forces of darkness. Be like the many Apprentices

---

[16] "It is worth noting that setting an employee on fire with magic is not an appropriate response to insubordination in most cases." - 50 Thousand Employee Handbook, Page 1034 (Conflict Resolution)

who walked before you and took up a mantle of right in the face of wrong, and proved the work was…worth doing." These last few words rung with a great emphasis, and I felt uplifted hearing them, like my heart had become lighter.

Todd thanked us again and then excused us to return to work, so we rose and headed out the door. Devin fell in far behind as he had stopped to shake the Dragon's hand vigorously once more, but we all boarded the elevator together and rode to the bottom in silence. We strolled across the courtyard and, at the direction of the sunken-faced butler, were led to a stone arch at the far end. On the other side of the arch lay a Cincinnati street that looked a lot like Race Street. We passed through and began the trudge several blocks toward the towering green 50 Thousand building.

Devin ignored Nannette and I completely, tapping away excitedly on his phone as we walked. I imagined him updating his social media with his adventure meeting someone as awesome and influential as The Dragon, and wondered whether wizards used any social media with hashtags that might be appropriate. I vaguely envisioned a wizarding version of twitter, and Devin rolling out updates like *just got done chilling with the Dragon of Cincy, #tight #friendsinhighplaces.*

Nannette was quiet as well, but her nose was deeply in a book. I caught her glancing at me a few times on our walk and wondered if she was wanting to say something but couldn't get the courage. I know I've felt that way more than a few times, so I tried to strike up some conversation.

"Research sounds like a fun department."

"Yep." She continued reading.

"You uh…I met you at the library, right? Thanks for that book list."

"Sure." She didn't even look up.

"I uh… I thought you were *Vulnerabl*. From the bracelet. How did you end up being part of *Sorcera* stuff?"

She gave me sidelong glare and I realized that might have been a bit too much of a personal question. So much for dispelling the awkward silence.

Not wanting to bother her further, I kept walking along to 9th and then all the way down to Walnut, where we crossed the parking lot and stepped into the comfortable and spacious lobby of 50 Thousand. We boarded the elevator and waited. Devin was the first to get off, on the 2nd floor, and I pulled out my phone as the doors closed—

But my hand was suddenly grabbed. Nannette was looking at me, and she suddenly looked terrified. "Did you say your name was LaFayette?"

"Y-yeah—" I tried to pull away.

"Was your dad Tom? Tom LaFayette?" She seemed desperate and on the verge of tears.

"Yeah—!"

"I need to tell someone but I don't know who. I found out something down in research. There's a plot to kill the Dragon of Cincinnati. Someone needs to know. Your dad found out about it and was investigating. He came to talk to me about a month ago and asked for all my notes; he said it was important that it get in the right hands. And then he was killed like the next day." By now Nannette was gripping my lapel with her other hand. "Someone needs to know, but you have to be careful. They might already be looking at you. They might already know. They might try to kill me. You need to get out of here. Like really."

I wasn't really sure how to respond. "Why would someone want to *kill*—?"

"If the Dragon dies then another Dragon takes its place. Makes its own rules. There's a group called the Black Magisters. They have a replacement dragon, like…somewhere, and they want to kill Todd and replace him with the other dragon. They're going to do it at the Symposium. Please, you have to believe me—"

The door opened and Nannette released her hold on me, looking quite normal again as she exited the elevator onto the 10th floor. The door closed, and I stood there shaking, my brain trying to parse the information I had just heard into something manageable. I didn't know what to do…but I knew who would.

CHAPTER 13

I punched the button for the 14th floor and stepped off, rounding the corner to the glass-windowed office and dashing up to the counter to ring the bell.

A muscular man (honestly, like, a sack of muscles shaped like a man) stepped out of the back office and glowered at me. "Can I help you?"

I was taken aback slightly but recovered. "Killian Fletcher, please?" I said as steadily as I could.

"Yeah, yeah," I heard her voice from the back and the tower of muscles retreated as she appeared. "Got another shopping list or some—" she stopped when she saw me practically quivering. "What happened, and who do I gotta beat up?"

I steadied myself on the counter and spilled what I had just been told by Nannette in the elevator. By the time I was done I was practically in hysterics and Killian took a step closer to put her hand on mine as I talked. "Breathe, Andy."

I breathed. "So what do we do?"

She shook her head. "*We* aren't doing anything. *I* will file a report and see what *I* can do. You will take some meds and calm down. I've got this."

I grabbed her hand. "No, you can't. I can't let you get involved in this. I'm a new hire but you're not and I can't risk your job if something is—"

"What was that I literally just told you about breathing?" She was looking particularly annoyed. "As for whether or not people know you associate with me or something…" She paused, her tongue touching her top lip thoughtfully as though she was trying to figure out how to word something important. "It's fine. I know people. Let's talk about it later, *okay?*"

I took another few steadying breaths. "Alright, fine. I'll let you handle it."

Killian nodded sagely and patted me on the shoulder. "Seriously now, go back to work, don't worry, everything will be fine. I promise."

I looked at Killian with searching eyes, trying to read her expression. I had to remind my anxious brain that Killian had been here far longer than I, and that she seemed to have a lot more expertise in this kind of thing than I did. "I'm just… I'm not sure."

"It's my job, literally. Look in your Employee handbook," Killian said with what sounded like a mildly-irritated tone. Killian waited with growing impatience as I stood there and steadied myself with more deep, anti-anxiety breaths. "Andy, please just go back to work. We'll talk about all this later, I promise."

"But what if—"

"No. Stop. Back to work, drink some tea, put

your mind back to *work*. If you keep going down this road you're going to end up with heart problems." She gave me a very stern look and I dropped my gaze to my feet. I didn't say goodbye as I slipped out of the security office and out into the elevator bank, where I pushed the button for the 19th. The elevator seemed to take an inordinate amount of time to get there, and when the mechanical brakes finally slid to a stop and the doors opened I felt slightly lightheaded, like my head was rubber band that had been stretched out and then relaxed, leaving it all wrinkly and less stretchy.

I pulled out the thick 50 Thousand Employee Handbook out of my drawer and opened it in quietly on my desk. There had to be something else I could do. I pulled the thick book out of my bag and flipped it open stubbornly, finally spotting a section on "Internal Security". I scanned the relevant section[17] twice, noting that it seemed maybe slightly *too* relevant, and I had to push to the back of my mind the idea that the book was somehow able to understand my current situation. I flipped to another random page which made me sick to my stomach to read it[18] and then closed the book. There was no way

---

[17] "If, during work, you stumble upon a conspiracy or other highly dangerous internal matter, it is advised that you seek out the Security office for an internal investigation to be started. Under no circumstances should you attempt to investigate it yourself, have an anxiety attack, or break down into a sobbing mass in the security office." - 50 Thousand Employee Handbook, Page 678 (Internal security).

[18] "The 50 Thousand Employee Handbook is the guide to the best career of your life! This guide is helpful, inclusive, and *definitely* doesn't understand your current situation at all times.

to know if I was being watched like Nannette had suggested.

The rest of the day was almost unbearable. I kept looking at my phone in between piles of sorting, hoping for a text or email from Killian, but none came. I worked through my lunch, trying to keep my mind occupied and preventing it from drifting too far into the realm of a massive panic attack, and with the help of mid-day medication I was able to make it through to the end of my shift. I felt like I had aged twenty years while doing so.

I finally decided to text Killian on my way up the elevator of my condo. I hadn't reached out to Apollo yet, trying not to scare my sassy black mom-friend.

What happened?

No response. I put my phone away and calmed my nerves with a breath as the doors to my floor slid open.

There stood Killian, hand on her hip and looking royally pissed. I just stood there, not sure what to do or say, and feeling somewhat afraid to make sudden movements. She just stood there and surveyed me for a moment. "What did she tell you?" I stuttered and the elevator door started to close. Killian slammed her hand against the door's side, making it retreat back inside, and her demeanor got, if possible, more irate. "What did she *tell* you, Andy?"

I took a slow, and deliberate, sidestep around Killian and off the elevator. "S-she said my dad had

---

That would just be absurd, Andy. Get back to work." - 50 Thousand Employee Handbook, Page 309 (Learning to love your 50 Thousand Employee Handbook)

come to her and asked f-for her notes. And she handed them over, and Dad said he'd investigate…and that he ended up dead the next day." I felt hot, anxious tears welling up in my face and I did my best to hold them back. "I d-don't know what's going on. She didn't say anything else." I gasped a breath. "And she said something about a group called the Black Magisters. I think they might be behind it."

Killian didn't react at all to this. I might have thought that she'd turned into a pissed-off, redheaded mannequin with as silent and still as she had suddenly become. Finally, she seemed to relax a little. "OK, this isn't working. You need to get the coin."

I nodded and started toward the condo. "Yeah, ok. I put it inside, come on. What are we going to do with it?" I unlocked my condo door and stepped inside. In the kitchen, under a jar of marmite on my shelf, was the coin. I had hoped that any home invader wouldn't want to touch the jar of marmite and thus the coin would be safer.

"*We* are not going to do anything." she replied, closing the door behind me. "Here, give it to me. I'll keep it safe."

I stopped and turned, slowly. "What…you know something, don't you?"

Killian glowered and held out her hand. "I am not playing with you, Andy. Give it here. Please."

I didn't move. "Killian. Please tell me what's going on."

She slowly lowered her hand, fixing me with a gaze I did not very much like being the target of. "You really don't know what the coin is, do you? I thought you were just playing stupid. But you really don't know."

"Killian, you're freaking me out."

"See, 50 Thousand was founded a long time ago when someone paid a group of sorcerers 50 Thousand Drachmas for protection.[19] They still have those coins, and the story goes that as long as those 50 thousand drachmas stay owned by the firm, all of the company's magic stays strong and its luck continues to hold."

I nodded slowly, still gripping the silver coin in my hand.

"If one of those drachmas was to somehow change ownership, then I'd guess they'd become the luckiest person around. And 50 thousand, meanwhile, would slowly see its spells unravel. So you see, Andy, I need you to give me the coin." She held out her hand again.

I still hesitated. "So...all this stuff that's been happening to me has been...luck?"

"I heard you got a really high mark on the *Sorcera* exam. People who have been living around wizards their whole lives didn't get scores like you. I'm guessing you guessed a lot on the answers and they just happened to be correct? That kind of thing happens with multiple-choice tests but I guess

---

[19] "The original 50 Thousand Drachmas were given to sorcerers in the employ of Charax Macarius in return for protection enchantments places upon a traveling merchant's fleet of caravans which the merchant believed were cursed since very few ever reached their destinations. The protection spells were effective enough to keep all of the caravans safe, and the traveling merchant shared his success story with the towns he came across." Page 101, (History of 50 Thousand Consulting)

nobody noticed."

It was like my heart had been suddenly dipped in cold water. All this time it had just been luck. And not just any old luck, but artificial luck. It somehow made my cheap success even cheaper.

Killian shook her head. "Someone got to her before I did. I went down to see her, to try and hush her up before she got hurt, but it was too late. Looks like someone set it up to look like she fell off a bookshelf, too."

I took a step back, leaning against the kitchen counter. "Oh god. So she was right, then? About—" I paused, all of Killian's words sinking in. "Why were you trying to 'hush her up'? Did you report the plot? If she's dead...that's evidence, right?"

Killian leaned against my kitchen doorway, her eyes fixed irritatedly upon me. "Do you think it was luck that you ran into me last week? Or that I keep being the one to run into you for company security stuff? No, I was *assigned* to you. Because the rest of us didn't know how much *you* knew about your Dad's involvement."

I took a few long breaths, refusing to tear my eyes away from Killian's gaze. "What do you mean by 'the rest of us'?" I already knew the answer before it was said.

"The Black Magisters," Killian said casually, "Your dad was one. And so am I."

I stood there for what seemed to be an inconveniently long second before I bolted for the door, but Killian was far too fast and exceptionally too prepared for my slow, inexperienced ass; I saw her touch a runed metal ring on her finger and a moment later the windows had grown inexplicably dark and the door clicked shut. I ran to the front door and tried to unlock it but the lock was stuck and the door was jammed. I pulled fruitlessly at it for a long moment, trying to get out as quickly as I could, but it was to no avail.

I finally gave up, turning around and edging past Killian, who was admiring the ring apathetically—perhaps even smugly. "Useful thing—it's called a Secrecy Ring. When you activate it, you can't enter or exit. Very useful for a Hedge Magician."

I got back to the kitchen and considered grabbing a knife off the block, but for all I knew Killian was one more magic rune away from taking me down with Dark Magic. She continued, now looking at me with a determined rigidity to her features. "The coin. Now." I looked down at the coin in my fingers, swallowing my nerves as Killian wrenched it forcefully from my grasp before I could hand it over. I slid down the side of the counter, crouched on the floor as my legs could no longer support me. "Are you…going to kill me?" I whispered to the redhead I had thought was my friend.

Killian snorted. "No, you idiot, I'm not going to kill you. I've been trying to *protect* you. I'm not doing this for kicks, you know. The head of the group…he's got blackmail on most of us. Now I thought you might be the key to getting out of this mess, but apparently you're not. In fact…you're pretty much useless. And that's why I'm taking this coin and fixing this problem myself and I'm not having you get in the way."

I looked up to argue, but she had already turned and walked out of the condo. I heard the distinct snap of my door's lock clicking shut, and her heels clicking on the tile floor outside. I didn't move for a very long time, my brain feeling foggy and numb in the silence of the empty condo.

CHAPTER 14

Knock knock.

I jolted awake, feeling sore and stiff all over. My head was pressed against the tile floor of the kitchen, and one arm had fallen asleep under my own weight. Had I passed out from the stress? It was certainly possible…

Knock knock knock. It was the door. I tried to pull myself to my feet but my legs didn't want to cooperate. Around the corner I heard my door open—Killian must have left it unlocked. I wasn't sure if it was Killian returning for some reason or what…but I took a wild guess. "Apollo?"

It was. He dropped onto his knees the moment he entered the kitchen. "Oh my god—Andy, what's going on, are you okay?"

I nodded, trying to formulate words. I had had a dream. It was terribly prophetic, and full of massive, colorful descriptions, but now I couldn't even remember. "Killian was here. She...She took the coin from me."

Apollo looked confused. "Killian? Red hair, sour demeanor, paladin-in-business-causal Killian?" The idea seemed utterly foreign. I spilled the details of what had happened, from Nannette to Killian to now. Apollo shook his head when I had finished relaying the story. "That makes no sense. Killian doesn't...she doesn't really work that way."

I felt the need to clear something up here. If my suspicions were right then I couldn't be entirely sure Apollo was on my side either. "Are you guys dating? Or did you used to? I mean...you seem to bicker like an old couple. And I just want to be sure that—"

He nodded. "Yeah, we did, a while back. But she has some issues and they were, ah, too much to deal with. But we're still friends. At least...I thought we were?" He took a breath and met my eyes. "I'm on your side. I promise. You said she said she was being blackmailed, right? I can't imagine what this Black Magisters group must have on her. And...I mean, I don't want to sound like I'm backing up a friend who did something pretty crappy, but if she's in trouble I feel like I want to help her. If you don't want to, though, I understand..."

I tried to build a response but I couldn't think of one. It was becoming perfectly clear to me, now, that I was just completely over my head in this one, and that I was treading into dangerous and potentially-lethal territory. I studied Apollo for a moment while he busied himself in cleaning up some of the things on the counter that had been knocked over. "I don't know. I mean, if I can help somehow let me know, but right now I'm not...I don't—"

"I understand." He offered a hand and pulled me off the floor. "It's going to be alright. You just relax. Get to bed, get some more sleep, and get ready for work tomorrow. I'll deal with Killian, okay? Don't stress."

I gave Apollo a deep look of appreciation before he left, and as I dragged myself up the steps to my room I tried to take deep and relaxing breaths. Even so, my stomach wouldn't stop doing weird flips and I eventually had to run back down to the bathroom and get sick in the toilet.

"They might try and kill you, ya know," An awful, wretched stench hit my nose as I heard the familiar voice from behind me and I twisted around to see the Moddey Dhoo, reclined in my bathtub which was filled with slowly-darkening water.

"Oh my god, why are you here? Why didn't you help me with—?"

"Silencers only get involved if ya might start giving away secrets," the dog interrupted, and it turned slightly in the tub to wet more of its fur and release more wet-dog smell into the air. "We ain't gettin' involved in quarrels, or break up fights, or stop ya from gettin' killed. That's not our job."

I felt another wretch in my stomach and I turned to cough up more emptiness from the bottom of my intestines. When I stopped, I flushed the toilet and slowly turned back to the creature. An idea had suddenly stuck me. "So…here's a question. If my dad was a wizard…then he'd have had a silencer, right?"

The Moddey Dhoo grinned with a smile full of wicked teeth. "Now yer thinkin'. Go on."

"So that silencer would have been there when he died, right?"

"Almost fer certainly."

"So that silencer is a witness, right?"

"An' there's the rub. Ya see, we witness all kinds o' nonsense, but we only share it at the order of the Dragon."

I frowned in frustration. "You know something, don't you? Why don't you tell me?"

"Because if I *did* know something," it growled threateningly, "then I couldn't share it neither. But ya need to pull the gunk outta yer ears and listen. We only share secrets at the order o' the Dragon, but I'm *not* saying not to ask around. There's more'n a few answers ya can find if ya look for what *can't* be found."

I let out a frustrated groan. "Can't you just be straight with me here? Where would I even look? I—" I stopped, remembering the pristine *Sorcera* building where I had taken my exam. The glass lasered door was etched into my mind from the anxiety it had caused. "Moddey Dhoo, all of the silencers are part of the Empyrean society, right?"

It nodded slowly, its grin becoming even wider.

"Where exactly is the Empyrean Society office? I was told every city has one."

"I can't give ya answers, kid." I deflated. Another dead end, then. "But who told ya there's an office in every city?"

"A guy I work with. Devin. Huge slimeball. He said that—" I jolted upright in realization. "He said he knew where all the offices are. I mean, he might have just been bragging, but if he wasn't then—oh, oh!" I clambered up into a standing position. "I need to see Devin. Like…right no—" I pulled out my phone to look at the time and was disappointed to see it was still in the middle of the night. "...first thing in the morning."

"There ya go," The Moddey Dhoo said, turning over in the water, which by now was an inky black, "Tha' wasn't so hard, now was it?"

I scowled and leaned against the sink. "You never said why you were here," I added.

"Needed a bath. I like yer bathtub. Very roomy. Speakin' o which..." it pulled the shower curtain closed with its jaws. "Can a pup get a little privacy?"

I closed the bathroom door to keep the smell from escaping and returned to bed to try and get some sleep, but my mind wouldn't stop working. It was trying to devise a plan on the best way to extract information from Devin's stupid face.

The next day I arrived at work early, a hot cup of coffee in my hand. The coffee shop had been entirely devoid of my favorite barista, which was mildly concerning, but I had to focus on the task at hand. I was ready to start my search when my phone buzzed and I checked it. It was an email from Carrie. *Conference room as soon as you get in.* I took in a sharp breath as I read it, and hammered the button for my floor. Hopefully I wasn't getting assigned another different task to handle. The storeroom was nearly clear, to be sure, so maybe I could manage it. I was feeling pretty confident in my abilities as I dropped my bag off at my cubicle and headed along the edge of the cubicle farm toward the conference room office.

I rapped gently on the glass door and then went

in. At the far end of the table sat Carrie, along with the sour-faced Baba Yaga from the coffee shop and two other people I didn't recognize. On the desk there were a few papers and two copies of the 50 Thousand Employee Handbook. My elation dissipated and I suddenly felt a chill, as though an ice cube had slipped down my throat and landed somewhere in the depths of my stomach.

Carrie gave me a half-encouraging grimace. "Please take a seat."

I slowly made my way to a chair and sat down, trying hard not to start shaking. "Hi, how is everybody this morning?" I said as jauntily as I could muster.

One of the people I didn't recognize sat a folder in front of himself and then opened it. "LaFayette. I appreciate the time you've taken out of your morning to meet with us. My name is Stan, and I'm with Human Resources. This is Carol, our HR employee advocate."[20]

I nodded politely.

"I've had some discussions with the partners upstairs and it looks like you're not quite the fit we had hoped for here at the company. While we appreciate and respect the short time you've been with us, it's in the best interests of everyone involved that we sever our relationship at this time."

I blinked. "Wait...hang on. You're firing me?

---

[20] "Carol, the Employee Advocate, is very difficult to work with and should be avoided at all costs. Did you know that she just *throws away* unused copies of the 50 Thousand Employee Handbook? Unbelievable." - 50 Thousand Employee Handbook, Page 1184 (Avoiding Horrible Employees)

After a week and a half?" I looked over at Carrie. "You're my supervisor—have I done something wrong?"

"Of course not," Carrie protested, glancing at Stan. "But I don't make these decisions...you understand, right?"

I shook my head in protest. "No, I don't understand, actually. What prompted this? Yesterday, I was being congratulated by the Dragon of Cincinnati for being a 'rising star' and 'the future of sorcery in Cincinnati'. Today I'm losing my job? This makes no sense." I glared across the table at Stan, but his face was completely unreadable. "What is really going on? I haven't done anything wrong."

Stan shifted a piece of paper toward me that had a check embedded at the bottom. "It is fortunate that Fifty Thousand Consulting has such a...*robust* severance program, however, which hopefully will make this situation all the more palatable..."

I looked down at the check and my eyes went wide. For a moment I actually almost gave into the urge to just pick up the check and walk out, but I caught myself. "This is...*hush* money? Are you trying to quiet what I know about Nannette?"

Stan looked mildly irritated. "I don't know who that is or to what you're referring." he picked up another piece of paper. "This is your official termination letter, which you will notice bears a shell company letterhead and is a registered company with Hamilton County—"

I wasn't listening at this point. I had been found out and I was losing everything. My luck had officially ran out, and I considered whether or not the fact I had lasted this long was attributed to the coin and its magical luck powers. I had to get to Devin and I had to get out of here...but causing a scene wasn't helping anything.

I made a very visible effort to take a calming breath. "OK, I understand. I—I'm sorry. I'm just going to take this, get my things from my desk, and go. Is that OK?"

"Actually," Stan said with what seemed to be mock sympathy, "We have Security on their way to— *Hey!*"

I grabbed the check and a copy of the Handbook, and headed out the door. Security meant Killian and Killian potentially meant *death*. I couldn't take the chance on whatever the betraying witch had in store. I ran to the elevator and threw my hand into the closing doors to stop it and jutting myself between them. I didn't know how much time I had before I was caught, but I was ready to comb the whole blasted building for the cubicle of the "Senior Apprentice", which I could only assume was adorned with executive ball clickers and probably a brass engraved nameplate or two. I remembered Devin had gotten off on the 2nd level, so that was my first stop. This floor was laid out almost exactly like my own, with minor differences, and the search for the mucosal man-child was not a very tedious one; I found him hunched over his cubicle desk with an open notebook and a pen. "Devin," I hissed.

He startled and looked up at me as though he had never been interrupted at his desk before. It occurred to me that he probably hadn't. "Oh. It's you. Sorry, I thought it was someone *important...*"

I glared at him with the utmost contempt. "I don't need your crap, I need some answers and you're—" I stopped and I glanced down at the notebook, where Devin was apparently writing "Devin A. Birch, Senior Wizard" over and over. "Are you *kidding* me? What is *wrong* with you?"

He covered the notebook with his hands. "*What* do you *want?*"

I took a breath. "I need to know where the Empyrean office is in Cincinnati. You *said* you knew where they were and I hope to god you weren't just trying to make yourself sound cooler."

He looked highly affronted at having his fragile ego pecked at. "I will have you know that I—"

"I really don't care, I don't care," I interrupted, waving my hand to dismiss him in the way one dismisses an annoying app notification, "I need an answer."

Devin leaned way far back in his chair, a smug grin spilling across his face and his arms moving behind his head in a way I thought people only did in bad workplace comedies. "And what exactly are *you* going to do for *me* if I give you this information?"

I heard a shout and looked over the cubicle farm to see one of the walking bags of muscle from the security office starting toward me and I knew I didn't have time to lose. I don't recall exactly how Devin's monogrammed brass letter opener (utterly unused, probably) had ended up in my hand, but now it was pointed at him and I was seething. "What I'm going to do for you is not *stab* you in your *slimy*—" I released a string of profanity that included intertwined insults about his hair, his mother, and the fact that he enjoyed the pleasant company of multiple kinds of animals—"*if you don't tell me right now!*"

Devin moved to roll back from the brandished

letter opener and ended up only losing his balance, tumbling over backwards and landing in an exceptionally undignified heap, sputtering something that sounded vaguely accusatory. Grabbing Devin by the front of his monogrammed shirt, I jabbed the point of the letter opener right at his throat. He coughed and squirmed but I think he did believe me that this crazy random Casting Technical Assistant might just do exactly what was promised and stab him, which would not only hurt but also have the very unfortunate side effect of spilling blood on his nice shirt. "The Betts House!" he squeaked. "Under the front porch!" The words had barely left his mouth when I had dropped him and took off down the hallway, digging in my pocket. I nabbed one of the one-time-use defensive reagents Killian had bought for me and threw it behind me as I headed for the stairs, glancing back to see it explode in a cloud of shiny green glitter which had, as Killian had described, "sufficiently stopped them and stripped them of their dignity all at once."[21]

I hit the door to the stairs a little harder than I had intended, leaving a tingling feeling in my shoulder as I skipped down them, two at a time, hoping that another pair of security guards wasn't waiting for me at the bottom. Once I reached the bottom landing I

---

[21] "Glitter in all of its forms is entirely prohibited on the premises of 50 Thousand Consulting. It has been determined that the manner in which glitter particles stick to everything, and the way that they seem to eternally infest a carpet or clothing item onto which they are applied, is a form of Dark Magic and should be avoided." - 50 Thousand Employee Handbook, Page 992 (Prohibited Paraphernalia)

barreled through the exit door and out onto the street. Where could I go? My first stop would need to be Apollo. I had completely forgotten my bag upstairs, so I wouldn't be able to text him. I started off in a run, dashing down the sidewalk toward the coffee shop.

I pulled the door open and quickly stepped inside, out of breath and sweating. "Apollo," I croaked.

He looked up from where he was cleaning the bar and immediately hopped the counter to come over to me, seeing my distress. "What's going on? What happened?"

I opened my mouth to speak but a sudden jolt of pain in my arm made me yelp and drop the employee handbook to the floor.[22] I watched in horror as the mark that signified my employment to 50 thousand began to darken and wrinkle as though my skin was being seared off. I gasped out a painful squeak as the symbol completely disappeared, leaving unmarred skin beneath.

Apollo watched with growing horror. "Oh no. You...you..."

"I got fired, yeah," I said, trying to catch my breath and calm my anxiety at once. "I have no idea what to do but I need to get to the Empyrean offices at The Betts House right now."

Apollo's face drained, making him look more like a cheap hot chocolate than a mocha, and he swallowed his fear in a somewhat visible manner. I recalled his previous reactions to discussions about

---

[22] "Ow." - 50 Thousand Employee Handbook, Page 1290 (That Hurt)

Silencers and for a moment I was sure he would bail on me and tell me I was on my own. But then I saw something cross his face—at the time I thought it was some kind of anger but looking back on it now I realize that it was a kind of determined sense of loss—the kind felt by someone who knows they're too involved to go back now.

He grabbed a broom that was leaning against the wall near the door. "Alright, coffee shop's closed. Everybody gulp down your lattes, time to go. You—hipster kid. You can wax your mustache later. Come on." He started ushering people out of their chairs and to the door while I watched, rubbing the skin where the 50 Thousand marks had once been.

APOLLO AND KILLIAN

They met in June. She had been working at 50 Thousand for a few months and had really honed her Hedging skills. She was happy to be in a new place, but less so that it was Cincinnati of all places. The city bored her. It was too quiet, too orderly, too overlooked. Nothing interested her.

Except Apollo.

It's hard to tell if the source of her attraction was influenced by his power, or if it was her own, but either way she suddenly started drinking coffee in the mornings for the first time since her university days. She liked his smile, his hair, and his sculpted arms. She liked the way the t-shirt he wore seemed to cling tightly to his shape, displaying the ripples of muscle. She liked the way he hummed lightly while steaming milk and pouring the velvety froth into her cup. She liked the way, sometimes, when he handed her the cup, their fingers brushed together.

But she was not the passive type. Their flirting—it was hard to tell if he was actively flirting with her, to be honest—was not satisfying. So she planned out her first move carefully. Perhaps slightly obsessively. She knew his schedule well enough to know he worked late on Wednesdays and opened the store alone on Thursdays. She watched, and cataloged, the volume of customers week after week to determine the best time to make her move. She had notes—detailed notes, the kind only a trained Hedge Magician like her could produce—on behavior and statistics and angles and architecture and sometimes she had to stop herself from describing Apollo's calf muscles when writing her analyses of the environment.

And so it was, on a September Wednesday evening near to 8:30, when Killian came into the shop with a smile. Apollo greeted her in the otherwise-empty store and asked if she was working late and would she like a latte. She said no, and made a cheesy comment about how she was in the mood for some caramel.

Apollo leaned over the counter with a smile. That damned smile that made her stomach do a flip. Her eyes were tracing the shape of his jawline and she almost missed his retort about considering himself to be more of a mocha than a caramel. In the meantime she fumbled with her ring on her finger, tracing the rune there and waiting for an opportune moment. But she wasn't as patient as she wanted to be that moment, and all of her academy training about self-control seemed to vanish. Triggering the rune, she hardly acknowledged the sound of all of the doors locking and the windows darkening before she had leapt the counter in a single bound and landed in the barista's arms.

Apollo had to open the store the next day, and in her lightheaded state she could barely make out correct words, let alone goodbyes as she headed out the door. At work she couldn't concentrate, her head still foggy and her body sore, easily explained by the significant amounts of physical exertion several hours before. For the first time in her career she left work sick, excusing it as some kind of passing bug.

But she didn't go home. Instead she went to the coffee shop and sat inside, sipping a coffee and staring at Apollo. He looked at her a few times throughout the day, giving her a smile, but there was something odd behind his smile. Was it apathy? It hurt to think that might be the case. She stayed until the coffee shop was ready to close, and asked Apollo if he might want company for the evening. He agreed.

It was November when things changed. She was distraught one evening, coming home very aggravated. Home being Apollo's, since halfway through October she broke her lease and moved in with him.

They argued that night. She held in her hand a formal warning about missing too many days, and that if her performance did not improve she might lose her contract with the company. There had been inquiries about substance abuse, and reports that her peers and superiors were concerned that she was no longer on top of her game.

Apollo wasn't angry. He was reserved when he told her he was worried about her. Their conversation turned to addiction, and he explained, carefully, that he had never been with someone who had been so affected by his innate charm and abilities. He asked if maybe they should have some space.

She got angry. Angrier than he had ever seen, and she screamed foul words at him, denigrated him and his species, and when he tried to calm her down, she struck him and broke his lip before storming to the bedroom and locking the door. In the morning she apologized before leaving for work.

Apollo left a note before he took a bag of clothes, explaining that he cared for her and just wanted a little space.

For her credit, she gave him space for a few days, but they were tortuous days. Her skin crawled and she couldn't concentrate. A trip to the Market was in order, to find a calming tonic of some kind. A goblin spotted her at once and sold her a box of some kind of enchanted chocolates that at least helped her focus, but the desire grew.

It was the first week of December that she returned to the shop. It was a quiet evening, with only one other patron in the dingy café. She talked to Apollo softly, soothingly, and he all but forgot the feeling of her fist across his face. She asked if he would come home.

He said he would, but under certain circumstances. She had to promise that her behavior would change, and that she would get some help for her addiction. She agreed.

It was near to Christmas that year when he told her he was going on a retreat with some friends in January. He'd be gone two weeks, and he was excited. She had gotten a lot better at managing her anger and her desires, and they had fallen back into a better routine that felt healthier. But this conversation seemed to frustrate her. The idea of being denied the things she desired lit a spark in her, and they argued again. She told him the addiction was his fault. He told her no, it wasn't. Giving in to the addiction of his species was a conscious choice on her part, and that the point at which he might be considered to blame for her predicament had passed.

She didn't strike him, but foul words poured from her mouth again and she left to go for a walk, slamming the door behind her hard enough to break it. When she came back, she was apologetic, and spoke so sweetly. She had also brought a small box of candy he liked and said that it was her fault all along. She encouraged him to take his two week retreat and he was happy again.

In January, he took his retreat. Out into the mountains of Colorado, he and several friends camped and hiked and had a good time. But a few days in, he caught her scent and knew that he wasn't taking this retreat alone. Leaving the others behind, he doubled back and found her.

He confronted her and asked why she had followed him all the way out here. She said she was doing it to surprise him and it was meant as a romantic gesture. He wasn't so sure; he asked her if she was jealous. She said no—why would she be jealous of Apollo's other friends, who were *clearly* more gorgeous and talented and personable than she was? She laid the passive-aggression on thick, saying that if he didn't want to spend time with her after she'd gone through *all this trouble* to be romantic, then that was his choice. Apollo got angry and Killian could see it, but he stifled his anger and said he would make it up to her by taking her on her own retreat, with just the two of them, another time. He left then, and rejoined his friends.

But she did not go home. She spied them, and now that she knew Apollo could track her she took extra steps to mask her presence. She watched from the trees as he laughed and joked with his friends. She felt a fire in her stomach that hurt her beyond measure.

One night he awoke in his tent. His other friends were gone and instead the tent had her in it, speaking softly and sweetly and tempting him with things. Apollo didn't like this and asked where his friends were. She tried to dodge the question, but Apollo got angry and compelled her against her will—something he had never done before. She confessed that she had enchanted Apollo's friends and sent them home.

Apollo became exceedingly angry, and he screamed at her for the first time ever. As the incubus within him grew to a great rage, she felt afraid for the first time in his presence. He seemed to grow in stature, and behind his beautiful façade she saw the demonic force below, whose presence had been so well-hidden. Apollo then fled, and she was left all alone in the mountains.

Snow was covering the coffee shop when she returned to Cincinnati, and she had in her hand more candy, and a love letter, and flowers. She went to the door with a smile on her face, and her hair newly done, and a calm, upbeat outfit. She reached for the handle and stopped.

She trembled. A powerful force held her hand back and she withdrew it. She tried again, but the handle seemed just out of her reach. She groaned in frustration and took a seat on the patio outside. Night fell, and she waited. Finally, Apollo met her at the door and told her that she couldn't come in. He had taken precautions to ensure this. He gave her the keys to his apartment, because he would not be returning. She could keep all his things.

She started to scream and curse at him, but he sighed and closed the door. She tried to break the glass on the window, but it, too, was just out of her reach. She screamed out, collapsing in the snow and crying for what seemed like hours. Then she picked herself up and walked away.

She tried to text, but the messages always failed to send. She tried to call but the service always dropped. She tried to mail a letter, but they were always returned. Whatever incubus magic he had put on himself and the store, it was powerful enough to make all communication impossible.

She took a vacation from work, using all of her accrued time. She tried to plan and analyze, but inside she knew it was wrong. She had become an addict and an abuser. There was no answer. She fell into a deep depression and shut herself away from the world for as long as she could.

It was June of the following year that she got a text. The withdrawal of her addiction had cleared her, and she felt like her world was beginning to make sense again. The text was short, and succinct: *I have an answer. Cafe, 8pm*. Her heart began to race and the addiction surged, and she nearly lost her balance, steadying herself on the counter.

The next 8 hours seemed like days as she paced, sweating, in the apartment. Finally, able to take no more, she left and walked toward the café, staring at the sidewalk to focus herself. In what seemed only a moment she was there, standing on the stoop of the shop, her hand outstretched to the brass handle on the door. She still could not grab it.

Apollo was then at the door, opening it and stepping outside. He told her not to speak as soon as she opened her mouth. He told her that he had called in some favors, and that things would be different. He told her that there was a program to manage her addiction. It would take time. It would take a support group for people like her. He admitted he didn't know such things existed, but he had done research while they had been apart. He offered her some paperwork and told her that he had made arrangements. He told her that he would be willing to see her again, as friends only, if she agreed to go to these meetings. He told her that, if she stopped going to the meetings, he would stop seeing her. He told her there was no argument to be had. She either accepted the terms or their interactions would end. Then, without another word, he disappeared into the shop.

She stood there a long time with the papers in her hand. The Cincinnati heat beat down on her shoulders and sweat beaded across her face, mingling with tears that already stung her eyes. But she was strong. With a trembling finger, she dialed the number on the pamphlet and walked away.

CHAPTER 15

The Betts House, I was told, was the oldest structure still existing in the Cincinnati area. Built in 1804, it was originally a farmhouse on a huge hundred-or-so acre farm and peach orchard. Now, it was a building nestled between others on the busy Central Avenue street.

Wherever the entrance to the *Empyrean* Society offices might be, however, was not immediately apparent. There wasn't really a "porch" so to speak—there was a stoop in front of the white front door and a small path that led to the black wrought-iron fence that bordered the property. Apollo and I searched up and down the sidewalk, back up to the door, and all around the front of the property that we possibly could.

"You know of any spells that find hidden entrances? Like…'detect secret doors'?"

"What is this, D&D?" Apollo said through

slightly gritted teeth, "want me to make a spot check?"

I rolled my eyes. "Oh great, you're a D&D nerd, too."

"Geeks dig me, Andy, that's all you need to...hey." I looked over to see him tilting his head at the welcome mat in front of the door. Curiously, I moved around the mat to get a look at what he was seeing from his perspective. "This mat looks like it's secured to the ground. It might be a trap door. And...OK, tell me that that—" he indicated a brown stain on the edge of the mat, "—doesn't look like dried blood."

It did. "Maybe we have to, like, put a drop of blood on the mat before it'll let us in." Apollo looked at me quite worriedly, and I dug in my pockets for a penknife. Finding one, I unfolded it and held the blade over my palm.

Apollo stopped me. "No, no, Andy. This isn't the movies. You don't have to friggin' slice your palm open to get blood. Like, prick the back of your finger or something, jeez." I obeyed and got ready to jab the knife into the back of my ring finger. I trembled slightly, and just I lowered the tip of the knife to my skin—

"Excuse me," a polite voice said, and I looked over to see a woman poking her head out the window. "If you're trying to get into the Empyrean offices, you might have considered knocking and asking, you know."

I didn't actually have a response to that. Before I could formulate one, the woman ducked back inside, and the trapdoor lifted upward to reveal an entrance to a tunnel and a staircase. The stairs went down in a twisted, spiral mess that was quite dark, and as I took out my cell phone to light a flashlight, I took a glance at Apollo and saw that he had become slightly pale again. "You alright?"

"Never been here," he remarked. "I've been a lot of places, but never here. I, uh…"

"Scared?"

He bristled. "I…have no way to confirm that without undermining my really cool façade."

"So I guess you want me to lead, huh?"

"Yes. Wait—I mean—if you want to. I mean—it's whatever."

I headed down the stairs by the light of my cell phone, my fingers feeling along the wall for a light switch. There was none to be found, and I quickly pulled my hand back as I brushed the moist concrete. The stairway twisted and turned, going ever and ever downward, until finally we arrived at the bottom and at a green metal door emblazoned with a faded metal plaque: EMPYREAN SANCTUM #433, CINCINNATI, OHIO. ESTABLISHED 1803.

I reached out and pulled the antique doorbell. I heard it ring somewhere beyond the door, and a loud click announced that it was now unlocked. I shrugged at Apollo and went inside.

Within, the underground chamber opened up into a massive lobby, with checkered tile floors and a dusty old secretary desk in the very center. From the ceiling, brass chandeliers, each with dozens of candles, hung from the ceiling and illuminated the spiderweb-covered ceiling. All around the room, sweeping staircases went up to dozens of doors, none of which were labeled in any way.

I stopped at a dusty corkboard near the door,

covered in employment regulations and announcements. *"New Haunting Journeyman Courses Available." "Sanctum President Carson to celebrate 120 years of Service." "Do you or a family member suffer from ectoplasmidosis? You might be entitled to compensation."*

"Apollo, look at this. I think Empyrean is like…a union."

"It is." It wasn't Apollo speaking to me. I spun and found myself face to face with the Moddey Dhoo. The black dog's face when it was standing at full height was able to be level with mine, and the glowing eyes made my skin shiver like I had just dove into a bucket of ice water. To top it off, the dog smelled foul and was dripping water from its thick, shadowy fur.

Apollo stiffened quite suddenly, from what I assumed was because of the Black Dog's sudden appearance. "Apollo, I told you about the Moddey Dhoo. Here he is, in the fur—" I furrowed my brow at the state of its fur, "—which is sopping wet. Why are you wet? Were you in my bathtub again?"

The dog gave me what I assumed was the glowing-eyes equivalent of a sideways glare. Apollo also did not reply, and I realized that his sudden discomfort was not from the dog at all: a long, hairy and bony appendage slipped quietly over his shoulder. Something was crawling up his back.

"And…um…this is Iktomi." He slowly pivoted so I could see the red, yellow, and white spider that was clamped onto Apollo's shirt, nibbling on his dreadlocks.

"What is that thing?" I asked before I could stop myself, and as soon as the words had escaped my mouth I knew I had probably offended the creature. I seemed to just be unable to stop myself from being offensive every time I turned around.

"Trickster spirit," The Moddey Dhoo interjected. "Yer incubus friend's silencer. Makes sense, though, since Iktomi can see the webs that connect folks an' such. See things before they happen. Useful if ya have a Lilin that might want to avoid, uh…*messin' around* with the wrong kind o' folk."

Apollo looked rather embarrassed to have his situation laid out so plainly, and he looked away. I tried to diffuse the awkwardness. "What's with all the spooky décor?"

"Hall'ween decorations," Moddey Dhoo said indifferently.

"But Halloween's not for another—"

"Some of us just like thinks a bit spooky 'round here, ok?"

"Fine, fine," I relented. "Why are our silencers hanging out here, anyway?"

"Because you are, stupid," The dog growled, "An' ya didn't even warn us. We're supposed to be here if'n ya ever need something with the Empyrean. Did ya miss that part in yer handbook?"

"It's a big Handbook![23]" I protested. "I have gotten through a lot of it but it keeps, like, expanding."

"Fine, fine," The Moddey Dhoo held up a paw. "Jus' do what yer here to do. I'm not helpin' ya neither, so don't even ask. I'm just yer escort."

"Fine," I said in a mock defiant tone, "Someone's

---

[23] "The Handbook considers itself to be quite happy with its size, thank you very much." – 50 Thousand Ex-Employee Handbook, Page 488

not getting a biscuit for being a good boy."

"Now hold up," The dog stepped in my way. "I dunno what yer playin' at, but I know you di'nt just say that I'm not a good boy. I'm the goodest boy. The bestest, ya hear?"

I crossed my arms; I was undeterred. In one day I had lost all my leads, my job, and one of my only friends. I had come to the rather firm conclusion that I was taking absolutely no more nonsense. "Well you're not being very helpful. You've been following me around this whole time, keeping secrets, and washing yourself in my tub…I mean, I've never owned a dog before but a part of me wants to swat you across the nose with a newspaper."

It snarled, baring its teeth. I heard Apollo off to my left responding in whisper to the chittering sound coming from the spider that had now climbed its way onto his head. "Alright, *human*," the dog snarled at me with its vicious teeth gnashing, "First off, you don' *own* me. *I* own *you* and what yer doin' is pissin' me off. I been givin' ya hints, keepin' a closer eye on ya than I normally do with yer kind, an' maybe a little show o' gratitude might be in order, but no, ya stand there with yer stupid human face and yer stupid human hair and yer stupid human stupidity, and ye have the audacity to act like I'm some common house mutt? I ain't havin' it. You want me to help you? I'll help you, but you will offish'ly *owe me one*." It presented its paw.

I glanced over to Apollo. He was standing in a very frightened stillness, and his expression was entirely obscured by Iktomi, who had decided to crawl across his face. I turned back to the dog and shook its grimy wet paw. The Moddey Dhoo then stood up and raised itself up to full height.

"Stay," the dog said, and I obeyed.

The dog vanished, and I was left in the awkward silence with Apollo and his spider. "So. Um. Iktomi, huh?"

Apollo nodded slowly, the spider still covering his face.

"And you've known each other since you were born?"

Another nod.

"That must be...nice."

The silence went on for another long and nigh-unbearable minute while I waited for whatever was coming. It was finally broken, however, by the sudden return of the wet and smelly dog and a companion.

I was taken, momentarily, by surprise at the creature's height: nearly a foot taller than me and robed in a silky black cloak. Emerging from the collar of the cloak was a goat's head with large, spiraling black horns that twisted sinisterly and glittered in the dim light of the lobby. I heard a chittering squeak and out of the corner of my eye I saw Iktomi retreating into a dark corner and Apollo scooting back against the wall.

"Greetings, child, and fear not." the creature said, looking me up and down as though cataloguing my appearance, "I am Eratosthenes, the Master of the Archives of the Dead. The Master Dhoo has...let us say...called in a favor and as a result I am here to answer your questions. But pray, be wary, for I shall answer no more than three."

The Moddey Dhoo stared at me to fiercely that I could almost feel my face beginning to burn. I forced myself to meet its gaze while it waited expectantly. I sighed and held out my hands in defeat. "Fine, fine. You're a good boy."

It puffed out its chest smugly. "Damn right I am."

Apollo crept up to my side, the initial shock of the creature's appearance apparently having worn off. Iktomi now rested comfortably in the back of Apollo's shirt. "You're a Phooka," he said. It wasn't a question.

"I am," it replied simply.

Apollo saw my confused expression and explained. "Phooka are powerful creatures of mischief. Really old, and really smart, and almost never helpful. But when it *is* helpful…and willingly…oh man…" He put up his hands in surrender, shaking his head.

The Phooka didn't seem particularly offended by being talked about in front of its face. "Indeed," Eratosthenes said. "You will follow me to the archives. Do not tarry." It turned and quickly started off toward one of the staircases, gliding up the marble without making the slightest sound. I hurried behind, not wanting to disobey directions or get lost somewhere in a secret facility underground. The stairs became a long hallway, lined on both sides with rusty filing cabinets, and lit with an unearthly glow that seemed to have no immediately recognizable source. We stopped about thirty feet into the corridor, which seemed to stretch on as far as I could see.

"The archives contain all information that was, that is, and that could be." It paused, and turned to look at me with those fiery, glowing eyes. "And no, I cannot tell you who killed your father or about the circumstances of his death. Those records are sealed—"

"—by the Dragon. Yeah, yeah…" I said the words before I could stop myself. Clapping a hand to my mouth I glanced up at the Phooka. "I'm sorry…that was really rude of me…"

"Yes, it was." The simplicity of the statement shook me to my core and I instantly felt ashamed to even exist. I looked down at the floor and tried to steel my resolve with a deep, lung-piercing breath that turned into a cough as I inhaled the dust. I shook the cough off and heard a yelp behind me; Apollo's spider Silencer was now trying to force its way past his belt and into his pants while Apollo pulled it back. "No, stop! Just behave!" He hissed through gritted teeth.

I gave my attention back to the Phooka. "OK. If you're still willing to answer the three questions…" It nodded. I paced back and forth a short distance in the hallway, thinking of potential sources of information. "OK. Question one: Who was my dad's silencer when he was killed?"

The Phooka reached out a hand from its cloak. The hand was wrapped in bandages but otherwise looked perfectly human. He stroked the file cabinet with his finger, making a scraping sound with his fingernail that echoed down the chamber. The file cabinet began to shudder, the contents within making a sound like an electric card sorter, and then it stopped. The top drawer opened and the Phooka took out a single sheet of paper and read it. "Thomas LaFayette was at the time of his death *Pro Veritate*."

"Pro Veritate?"

"I told you about that," Apollo said. He had succeeded in keeping the skeletal spider out of his pants and it was now clamped tightly to his left leg.

"It's when you do something really big and the Dragon honors you by calling off your silencer."

"So my dad didn't have any witnesses to his death. Dammit, another dead end."

Apollo patted me lightly on the back. "Well maybe we can find out why he was killed. Ask about the coin, maybe."

I nodded slowly and formulated a question. "OK. So I found a coin—a silver drachma. My dad owned it. How did he get it?"

The file cabinet shuddered again the Phooka retrieved a second paper. "Thomas LaFayette was the Vaultkeeper of 50 Thousand Consulting and had access to the vaults. He stole it."

Alright. That wasn't exactly the answer I had expected, but it at least gave me an understanding of how my dad had slipped past the massive vault security of 50 Thousand's underground chambers.[24]

"OK," I said, standing up straight as I determined my last question, "What will happen if the silver drachma isn't returned?"

The file cabinet shook for much longer this time, and the paper that was pulled from it looked slightly thicker for some reason, but I may have been

---

[24] "The vaults of 50 Thousand Consulting are well-known to house secret, powerful, and downright legendary items. These are rumored to include the Blackbeard's treasure, Oliver Cromwell's head, the entire lost city of Atlantis, a copy of the unreleased third installment of a popular video game, and the Ark of the Covenant. Note that the vaults of 50 Thousand Consulting are not a dungeon that you and your well-equipped friends can 'raid' under any circumstances. For this reason, the phrase 'looking for group' is banned on company property." - 50 Thousand Ex-Employee Handbook, Page 893 (Assets)

imagining it. "If the Silver Drachma is not returned to either the vault or one of the managing partners of 50 Thousand, then their protective spells over The Most Venerable Todd will fail, and then the Dragon called The Harrow will become the new Dragon of Cincinnati and impose a new iron rule upon the Queen City."

"Who is 'The Harrow'?" I yelped in surprise.

The Phooka put the paper back. "Your questions have been answered to the satisfaction of our agreement. If you've no further business to attend at Empyrean, perhaps you should leave."

I sighed in defeat and thanked Erasthenes for his help, staring my way back down the hall toward the Exit. Apollo moved quickly ahead of me, a new spring in his step having manifested at the notion of us leaving the union hall. Before long, we were back out into the daylight of Cincinnati, the noontime sun beating down on the brilliant sidewalks around the Betts House.

"Come on," Apollo insisted, taking my arm and leading me away, "Before you start getting all caught up in your own head about your dad again. Let's go get some food and I'll help you find a new job. I know some people who are always hiring. Also, do you need some money to tide you over for a bit?"

I followed, trying to think of a response and contemplated the young incubus who was being so undeservedly generous. "Dammit Apollo, why are you being so nice to me? You've already said you're not trying to get in my pants. So I feel like there's some motive—"

He stopped walking and put up a hand to stop me. "Don't even go there, ok? You're feeling that way because *Killian* had an ulterior motive for being your friend. I'm not like that. See," He reached out and brushed a cobweb off my shoulder. "I see two kinds of humans come through my coffee shop—the ones who have grown up surrounded by magic and the ones who haven't. And the ones who have, get everything—the have the knowledge, the leg up, the connections. Like that guy you were talking about, Assbag Johnson—"

"—Oh, Devin?—"

"Yeah, that's what I said. He's one of those guys. They don't even need to be wealthy or influential. They just have more to start with. Then there's humans like you: don't know about all of it. They find out somehow—a friend, or an accident, or something—it happens. Sometimes people get hired for specific skills. But whatever. Those folks are struggling just to get onto even ground."

He rounded on me, and for the first time, I could see something that looked like anger behind his eyes. "Then, there's your old man. He knew about it. He was probably born into it. He then chose, for whatever reason, to deprive you of that better opportunity. So now you're double-screwed, because you not only don't have the knowledge, but people expect you do. It's a mess and it's not right."

I furrowed my brow. "If you're right, then maybe he...maybe he wanted me to appreciate it more."

"Why are you defending him?" I don't know if Apollo had meant to raise his voice, but he immediately corrected himself. "I'm sorry. I'm just...I don't understand this. And I'm not trying to stress you out. But from here, it looks like your dad wasn't a nice guy. And I hope that I'm wrong, but you ought to hear it outright. Maybe you'll stop trying to get yourself into the middle of it if you stop putting your old man on a pedestal. Maybe, you will finally start taking other people's advice and focus on *yourself* for a bit, huh?"

I glowered. I honestly wanted to just last out…scream, yell, maybe even hit him—but I knew that wouldn't accomplish anything and, the more I thought about it, he was right. All signs pointed to a person who abused the system and tried to hurt everyone with the benefits of his station. My dad wasn't a good guy, and the longer I kept waiting on a third-act redemption plot, the more disappointed and frustrated I was going to make myself.

"OK," I sighed finally after a few steady breaths. "Where can I start looking for a job?"

CHAPTER 16

I found The Cornucopia online, just like I had found 50 Thousand. It had solid reviews, too—people complimenting the "diverse" and "accommodating" menu, and the fact that they helped serve people with "alternative palates". These phrases, Apollo had explained, were code phrases used by restaurants that had special selections for magical creatures, particularly *Vulnerabl* who might want to go out and get a bite but were, for example, actually a Clurichaun and unable to imbibe anything that wasn't made of sheep or alcohol.

The most popular of these restaurants was The Cornucopia. Not only did it offer dining room seating exclusive to the magical populous, it also offered a rare bonus: delivery service. To the often-intelligent but monstrous members of the *Kobolda*, this was a distinct luxury, or so I was told. A good delivery driver at a non-magical place could make decent money if they were fast and polite, so it seemed logical to me that if I was at a more exclusive joint I would have an even better chance of staying afloat.

That was particularly important given that my mail had now started to pile up in my condo's entrance hall. My severance package I had gotten from 50 Thousand would have been fine to ride out on for a little while, but I discovered the hard way that *Sorcera* society does not like rogue wizards running around without jobs. The first letter had been a polite reminder that I had thirty days to find new magically-inclined employment, and included several places to look for a job as a matter of "convenience". The second letter, which had arrived the next day, had escalated so fast it would have made a fine Ron Burgundy meme—it let me know that at the end of 30 days *Sorcera* would be revoking my license and tracking me down to wipe my memory.

So it was then that I went to The Cornucopia, dolled up in a nice polo and slacks with my best fake smile and my short hair done all up in a spiky thing that used far too much hair product. I walked in the door with confidence that I could get a job here, which would at the least get the Silencers off my back for a while.

"I would like a job," I announced to the host, a tired-looking young man who had to be under 25. I spotted one of those *Vulnerabl* bracelets on his wrist and felt assured that I was, in fact, in the right place. He looked at me for a moment, as though trying to figure out what I had just said, and then reached up to pull the earbuds I hadn't noticed before out of his ears. "I said 'I would like a job.'"

He nodded and grabbed a plain generic job

application from under the host table and passed it over to me. I reached into my pocket for a pen, but before I could find one, I glanced at the paper and watched as it began to fill itself out. I took in a deep breath, trying to stifle another gasp (really, I should have been over this stuff by now), as my name, address, telephone number, and a dozen other fields started to auto-populate in the sheet as if being typed by an invisible typewriter. I frowned at a few of the fields (Next to the box which asked if I had ever committed a felony, it populated with "Yes, but I didn't get caught, so it's OK") but handed it back, fully completed. The teenage host took the application and pointed to a staircase nearby. He then put his earbuds back in and continued to stand there looking rather stoned.

I headed up the stairs, confident and excited. I took them two at a time to start, but then changed back to one-at-a-time as I made my way up the third and fourth flights. Around and around I kept going up this staircase, quickly feeling my legs turning to jelly then then to hot, sweaty jelly. I stopped climbing for a few minutes, immediately reconsidering my chosen course of action, but the thought of some *Sorcera* suit stealing everything I had known about the Secret world drove me onward and upward until I arrived at a single wooden office door with a nameplate: *Brenda Michaels, Proprietor*. I lightly rapped on the door and heard it unlock.

Pushing the door open, I immediately thought I must have been teleported to a countryside cabin: the floor was covered in mismatched rugs, the walls with stained but vintage wallpaper, and the entire room was filled with cushiony and plush chairs. I took a moment to stand there and catch my breath, looking around the room from the empty birdcage to the shelf full of fine china. And the cats! I spotted the first one basking in the sun that streamed in through the cottage-style window, and I quickly saw them all around the room—under and behind furniture, resting on shelves, and even one sitting relaxing inside the bowl of the lamp hanging from the ceiling. I coughed, trying to clear my lungs of the gunk it had accumulated on my way upward. "H-hello?" I choked out

"Oh 'ello dearie!" I heard a voice from the other room, and a moment later an old woman emerged in the adjacent doorway, clutching a knobbly wooden cane and dressed head to toe in black robes trimmed with white lace. She beamed a great old-lady-smile and gestured to one of the couches. "Please, please, have ya self a seat. Want a spot of tea?"

I carefully made my way to the couch and took a seat. "Um...no thank you. I'm really just here for a job."

She handed me a cup of hot tea that I'm sure she didn't have in her hand a moment ago. "Oh nonsense. Everyone could use a spot of tea. Now what are you 'ere for?"

"A job," I repeated. "I am looking for a job."

"A job?" She took a seat across from me, causing two of her cats to scatter.

"Yes ma'am."

"Where?"

"Here." I took a tentative sip of my tea. It tasted like mint and licorice and, to be honest, was kinda awful.

"Oh, a job here? Oh maybe, maybe..." She

seemed to be suddenly holding my resume in her hand and looked it over. "Oh, look at that. You worked over at 50 T'ousand. But only for a week? Still, still…shows you've got potential or a lot of luck."

I tried to keep myself from looking suspicious and wondered if the old lady could read minds. I had kept my little piece of onyx on me just in case.

"What else can you do? Know any magic? Be honest now, be honest now…"

"I cast a spell once," I said proudly. "And I have some…hedge magician training?"

Her eyes went wide in surprise. "Oh a Hedge Mage! Why didn't you say so? That makes this much, much easier." She picked at her chin for a moment in thought. "I suppose I'll have to call Empyrean and check with your silencer—"

"No need," came the black dog's voice from behind me. "I'm here, mad'm." The Moddey Dhoo stalked across the floor, did a few circles, and then flopped down at the old lady's feet.

"Moddey!" She seemed genuinely excited and reached down to scratch behind its ears. "Well well, that's a nicety, now ain't it? I haven't seen you since I retired. Hope ya have been well, eh?"

"Quite well, Most Ven'rable," it said with a sort of catlike purr in the back of its throat.

I glanced from the Moddey Dhoo to the old lady. For one, it was good to see that the Moddey Dhoo was, in fact, not a figment of my imagination since up til now it had only appeared when I was alone. Secondly, I recognized the title. "Most Venerable?" I inquired. "That's the Dragon's title, isn't it?"

The Moddey Dhoo nuzzled against the old

woman's leathery hand. "Tha' it is. But Todd wasn't always in charge of the city, ya see. This old bat was in charge til tha…what was it? The 30's?"

"1937," she said with a grin. "But that flood pretty much took the last I had, and I figured I'd move it along. Todd was an up-and-comer and seemed like a nice bloke, so…yeah. He took over and I opened this place."

I felt a crushing feeling in my chest and tried to banish it: this woman was a dragon. And I was in her lair. The implications of this fact suddenly hit me and I might have physically jolted upright in the chair as my heart jumped a beat or two in my chest. "Miss Michaels, can I ask you a sort of off-the-wall question?"

The Moddey Dhoo looked over at me and narrowed its eyes. "Aren't you trying to get a job here? Don't you think…other matters should wait or are you being impulsive again?"

The old woman patted the dog's head. "No, no, the child has good intentions, I can tell. Ask me your question then."

"What happened to the dragon called The Harrow?"

Her face became twisted in a thoughtful, curious look as she stirred her tea with a long fingernail. She glanced down at the Moddey Dhoo, who shrugged, and gingerly set the cup of tea down. She reached over to a side table which had a shallow porcelain bowl and stroked it with a fingernail. "The tale of The Harrow is a tragic one, I'm afraid," she said with a melodramatic amount of somberness to her voice, "and it's one I could tell you if you want…" she looked at me with a depth that indicated centuries—

maybe millennia—of wisdom. "Or if you would like, I could *show you.*"

The bowl shimmered with magic, and I felt a pull against my heart to move closer. I shifted uneasily in my seat, leaning forward to look into the surface of the water and gaze into the depths of whatever she was offering, and then—

I held up a hand. "Actually, I'm not really interested in magical flashbacks right now, sorry. So…can you just tell me?"

She looked disappointed and set the bowl aside while I heard a stifled chuckle from the shadowy dog on the floor. "Well, it's sort of a long story. You think you still have time?" She looked up at the big grandfather clock that rested patiently against the wall. "Your shift starts in ten minutes."

I sputtered, parsing what she had said as quickly as my mind could compute. "My shift? Like, a job shift? As in, I got the job?"

She looked me sternly. "Nine minutes."

"OK, OK, please…" I'm sure I sounded like a whiny child. "*Please* just tell me."

"Wound up tight, this one," the old dragon-lady said to the Moddey Dhoo with a half-smirk.

"I know, righ'? Humans are so entertainin'."

The old woman sipped her tea for a moment. "So back in the day," she began, "There used to be dragons all over in countrysides and such. Long before towns and cities. They had their own plots of land and whatnot, and a lot of the ones that weren't too good at managing cities went out and claimed mountains and rivers as territory. One o' them was a feller named The Harrow. Now Harrow was a bright one, fer sure, and had a knack for the magical arts—

the same ones you humans use, ya know—and folks used to come from far and wide to get taught by the legendary magic-teaching dragon out in the State of Illinois."

I nodded and took a sip of my tea, which seemed to have changed flavors to something resembling blackberries and garlic. "But he wasn't so good at actually *running* things, ya see, but he liked ordering people around like dogs… an' so then in comes Chicago. Early 1800's, I think, and there that town started to get bigger. It expanded into his plot o'land, it wasn't a surprise to anybody that he wanted to jump at the chance to call it his own. Now, the Dragons are pretty particular about who they let run cities. Dragons have some rules about it—nothing I'll get into now—but basically if a Dragon claims a city, it's theirs until they get beaten in a challenge from another dragon, or if he does something so awful the rest of the Dragons step in."

"The Harrow was a fool," The Moddey Dhoo snorted.

"Maybe, maybe, but The Harrow was strong and probably one of the more learned dragons when it comes to magic. So when a few o' the other, more…um…*competent* dragons tried to claim Chicago, they lost their challenges. Especially since The Harrow allowed wizards and witches in Chicago to cast Dark Magic…dark times, dark times," she added and a sigh.

I glanced at the clock. My shift started in six minutes. "Then what happened?"

"Well, The Harrow, like I said, was still a brute. He used to get drunk and angry, and one night he let his temper get a hold of him, and he started a fire.

Maybe you heard of it, eh?"

My jaw dropped. "The Great Chicago fire?"

"The very same. So after hundreds of dead people, hundreds of thousands homeless, and massive damage to the city itself, the Academy of Dragons stepped in and removed The Harrow. But he wasn't going down without a fight, and the group that showed up to claim the city couldn't convince him to leave peacefully…so we banished him as far as we could…" She grinned. "The moon."

I rubbed my head where it seemed a headache was beginning to rise. "So wait…there's a dragon trapped on the moon? Just…sitting up there? Doesn't he need food or air?"

"Has no one explained the whole 'magic' thing ta you yet?" The Moddey Dhoo said, looking at me incredulously.

I felt dumb and glanced at the clock. "OK, I *really* appreciate the information. And the job. I…" I mentally reordered my next words, much in the way a mad scientist combs his hair to make it orderly. "What is my job exactly anyway?"

"You'll be delivering food. Go downstairs and talk to Codwell, he's the Puck downstairs."

I mumbled another "thank you" and darted down the stairs without even asking what a Puck is. After a single flight of stairs down, I arrived at the bottom landing. I blinked, looking back; they apparently had become significantly shorter. I didn't have time to gawk, though, and I dashed past the host's stand toward the kitchen and the back of the restaurant.

CHAPTER 17

I wasn't really sure what to expect from Codwell—for all I knew he could be literally anything—but I was still taken aback by him as soon as I spotted his nametag. Not more than 4 feet high and supported by greyish-brown cloven hooves, the creature was covered in soft-looking, tan fur with dark spots. His tail swished back and forth as he moved, and even the monstrous horns protruding from the space between his fawn-like ears could not detract from the fact that Codwell was absolutely, and utterly, adorable.

"Hello," I said as soon as I had caught my breath, "Are you Codwell? Just got hired as a delivery driver—"

Codwell rounded on me and looked me up and down. "Hm, hm…OK then. Ok then sure, sure sure. Let's see, let's see? What's your name, what's your name?" His voice was fast but perfectly coherent, and he appeared to be juggling about ten different managerial tasks at once quite impressively.

"Andy—"

"Andy, Andy Andy. Alright, okay, alright, let's get you an order right now, right now!" He tapped on the counter of the kitchen window. "Order 12, order 12!" I didn't have a chance to even react before a plastic bag filled with something warm was put into my hand.

I tried to get the Puck's attention as he got back to work organizing things. "I don't have a car—" A set of car keys flew through the air at me, hitting me smack-dab in the middle of the forehead. "Ow!"

"Red car, around the corner! Red car!" Codwell had piled a set of plates onto one arm and dashed past me into the busy restaurant. Without any more sources for the answers to my obvious queries, I headed out the front door and around the corner. There, parked at a meter, was a red 1992 Honda Odyssey. Its paint was scratched, and the windows had tint that looked like it was applied by hand—it was dotted with air bubbles and tears. A bumper sticker on the back of the car read *Dole for President*.

Feeling a sinking in my stomach, I unlocked the car and slid into the driver's seat. It wasn't particularly comfortable, to honest, and as I set my bag of food (which had now begun to slightly smoke) on the chair I pulled my 50 Thousand Employee Handbook out of my back pocket to discard it. I stopped, however, when I glanced at the front page. It now read *The Cornucopia Employee Handbook*. I flipped it open to a random page and read a few words[25] before groaning loudly and setting it down next to the food and starting the car.

Or at least, I tried to. I turned the key and it made absolutely no sound. "Oh...come on..." I almost starting cursing right then and these, but I stopped myself as I spotted a used coffee cup in the cup holder that reminded me of another piece of equipment that refused to work. I cleared my throat. "Um...Hello...car..."

"There you go," the car replied politely, the voice seeming to come out of the car's speaker system, "Very polite of you. Are you making a delivery?"

"Yes, please," I said, trying to muster all of the politeness I could and push out my anxious brain. I tried to start the car again and the engine turned over instantly, purring sweetly like a lion under the hood. A coughing, laryngitic lion, but a lion nonetheless.

I pealed out of the parking lot and into the Cincinnati streets, quite thankful that unlike some other cities, Cincinnati was arranged more or less like a grid, with building numbers corresponding neatly to street numbers.

I passed several high-rise company buildings to arrive as a recently-renovated set of condos nestled above a jewelry store. The building façade as adorned with pillars and ledges, and as I parked the sputtering red car on the side of the road, I was taken, briefly, by the lovely architecture of the building. I tried to unlock the door, but it was jammed. "Um...car? Can you unlock this?"

---

[25] "I'm back! Did you miss me?" – The Cornucopia Employee Handbook, Page 45 (The Ride Never Ends)

The car was silent a moment. "Why would I do that? We're having fun, aren't we? Maybe you could just stay here for a while."

I tried the door again. "No, really...I would love to, but I have a delivery to make. Please let me out?"

The voice was very sweet and sultry. "Tell me about yourself, love." I didn't have time to be kidnapped by a car. I picked up my phone and swiped as fast as my fingers could move, dialing Apollo. As I dialed, the car dropped out of park and began to move into traffic again. "Let's go somewhere exciting!"

"Please car, no..." I pleaded. I got Apollo's voicemail. I dialed again.

"See, I'm on the road a lot, but I like to go other places. Like the grass, the beach..." The car was driving down toward one of the riverside parks. It was gaining speed and I was frantically calling and texting Apollo to no avail. I didn't have anyone else who might be useful. Well, except Killian, but she hadn't responded to anything. At this point though, I was about 45 seconds from being in the Ohio River in the most psychotic talking car on earth. My fingers spat out a frantic text to her number. *Tarped in insane talking cat HELP!*

Oh, for the love of—COME ON, Autocorrect. Why do you have to do this to me? I sent a follow up: *trapped* car**

The car had now barreled through an intersection and I tried desperately to yank the steering wheel before it hopped the curb and scraped the side of a sign that read "SMALE RIVERFRONT PARK". I instantly regretted everything I had done that had led up to this point, from taking the job at 50 Thousand to investigating my dad's death to even moving to the stupid Queen City itself, and as the car ramped down the stone steps leading down toward the water, I heard my phone ding and stole a glance at it right before the car hit the freezing and dirty water:

Say NØKKEN

I screamed the word at the top of my lungs as I was thrown violently to the side and nearly into the backseat, all noise drowned out by the sound of the cold water rushing over the door and windshield as the hood of the car crumpled under the weight of the sudden impact.

Everything was suddenly very still. I waited, listening to the water of the river rushing up and lapping at the car slightly, but it no longer moved forward. Only the roof the car remained unsubmerged, and I didn't dare move lest the car be jostled enough to start getting swept away.

The car sighed at me. "Oh…you know my name. Now that's no fun, now is it?" I was about to sputter a reply when the sound of the sunroof motor activating and opening up made me jump to the side in fright. The car seemed to be letting me go. I didn't need any further encouragement, however; I grabbed my bag and the (fortunately) mostly-undisturbed bag of food and climbed out of the car.

I immediately lost my balance, slipping down the side of the crashed car and falling on my back in the foot-high water. Somehow, I managed to keep my food above the waterline and with some difficulty I was able to walk to the shore. I looked around at the people passing by and none of them seemed to notice the car crashed thirty feet away, and I wondered again how they managed to stay so thoroughly unaware of the nonsense occurring around them.

It was a long walk back to the delivery spot, and by the time I got there I was so very certain that I would not have a job when I returned that I hesitated to even deliver it in the first place, but a sense of duty and a bit of pride had dragged my waterlogged ass to this door, and at this point it was difficult for me to imagine how the situation would get more uncomfortable than it was now. I pushed the buzzer.

"Yes." The voice was raspy and deep.

"Delivery from…Cornu—" The door opened and I pushed my way through it to the lobby. The delivery was on the 17th floor, and I groaned loudly as I saw a large "out of order" sign hanging on the elevator door.

Nearly 20 flights of stairs later, I had reached my destination. I was shaking, sore, and questioning my will to live at all as I knocked on the door. It swung open instantly, and I was greeted with the visage of a tall, bipedal rat with twisted front teeth and a pair of spectacles nestled over its nose. "Oh thank you. Must be busy over there for it to take this long, but I'm glad you are here. Please, come in." It stepped back and let me enter. The apartment was nice and decorated in a modern-minimalist thing that was quite pleasant, and but for the giant rat that was now making his way to the kitchen I might have taken it to be a completely normal person's apartment. It occurred to me that at this point the sight of the giant rat man was not particularly alarming to me, and I wondered if I had finally absolved myself of the ability to give a crap anymore.

"Please," The rat said with a polite accent, "If you wouldn't mind setting the food over there on the table with the lids open. Hard for me to open them myself," he added with a chuckle, wiggling his short arms back and forth. I made my way to the table and started unpacking the food, thankful that despite the terrible ordeal I had not spilled any of it. The rat walked over to a computer desk that was facing the other direction and waved at the webcam. "Still here, guys! My food's here." He looked up at me with a smile—at least I think it was a smile—and gestured to the screen. "Would you like to say hi?" I heard a chorus of "Ooh!" and "Say hi!" from the computer speakers, and my curiosity completely took over my better judgment. I walked over to the computer and stood in front of the webcam.

It was a web chatroom. The title of the page read "Monsters Hangout Room 42" and the screen was filled with 9 boxes, each bearing another grotesque or unearthly creature, who were all looking at me with curiosity and excitement. I waved at them awkwardly. "Hi."

They all waved back. A guy who looked sort of like a fish with horns moved close to his camera. "Oooh! Hello delivery person! Hello! What's your name, love?"

I looked at the rat and then back at the camera. "I'm Andy. Nice to meet you...all."

"Oh, aren't you just the most adorable human-thing," A female sphinx said, brushing her hair as she reclined on a fancy chaise, "Don't often see many human-things, do we, folks?" The others agreed. I was instantly awed by these creatures—all of them *Kobolda*, I would assume—because it occurred to me that they all probably hid their existence from the outside world entirely. And yet the internet, in all its glory, had given them the opportunity to figuratively move out of their hovels or homes or apartments wherever they lived, to see the world and communicate with other lonely creatures in the same situation. It was all at once amazing and heartbreaking.

"But you have to get on with your deliveries," the rat said, ushering me back to the table. "Say goodbye, everyone!" The chat room replied with a chorus of short farewells and began excitedly discussing my human appearance in quiet voices. I quickly finished opening the containers, which seemed to be filled with mashed fruits and huge balls of meat and barley, before waving good-bye and heading for the door. "Your tip is just over here on the desk," the rat said as I reached for the doorknob. I looked over and saw small wad of bills, and I thanked the rat for his generosity before heading out and back into the hallway.

I again thought that I might just head home at this point. I was sopping wet, cold, and by the time I would make it back to Cornucopia I would have spent almost two hours delivering one order. I reminded myself, however, that I wasn't doing this for the money; I was just trying to maintain a job to keep the Silencers at bay.

I pushed my way through the back door of Cornucopia, arriving with dripping hair and clothes. As I entered the kitchen, several of the cooks stopped, looking up at me curiously. I tried to play it cool despite the fact that I was shaking internally. "So the car…um…is in the river."

All at once, they all broke into raucous laughter. A hand clapped me on the back and pushed me through the kitchen to the delivery station once again while the staff crowded around. "Chef Babbers Mulligan," a scaly-skinned lady with fangs said, leading me around the steaming kitchen. "The three green guys at the prep table are Bingle, Bangle, and Bungle—plant people. Nice guys. Troll over there is our butcher Ging-Wa. Let's see…" I was driven around the kitchen by clawed hands and I didn't even attempt to resist. "The dishwashers are over there—stay out of their way, though, because they clean the dishes with acid spit. Oh, and the pâtissiere is the one behind you." I turned my head to see that the clawed hands on my shoulder corresponded to an enormous, muscular furry wolf-creature with a wet mouth large enough to swallow my whole head in a single bite. "That's Linda."

I swallowed hard. "W-werewolf?" I asked shakily.

She nodded. I could smell her hot breath on my face. It was strangely minty.

"Did you get the food delivered?" I heard Codwell's cloven hooves clattering across the kitchen tile behind me.

"Yes, of course, but—"

"Next delivery!"

"But the car—"

"Yes, yes, yes," the Puck answered, pushing me a bag of more delivery food, "he does that, yes he does. Go on, go on, no time to lose!" And he was gone again. The kitchen staff turned to get back to work and I was left holding another steaming bag of food.

By the time I had finished my first shift, my legs felt (and smelled) a bit like melted butter as I forced them to move, step by step, to the door of the condo. I closed the door and leaned up against it, my breath coming in shallow heaves in my chest. In the course of four hours, I had—in addition to the adventure with the Nøkken—been the victim of several small calamities: I had gotten lost in a building that turned out to be a stronghold run by dwarfs: short, round people with hair and beards that went down to the hem of their garments and who spoke with very fast Swedish accents. I had accidentally insulted a Tiyanak by asking if its parent was home—I had no idea the Tiyanak all looked like creepy children. Most annoyingly, perhaps, I had gotten about six paper cuts over the course of the day.

I couldn't have gotten as much done, or quite as safely, had it not been for the Employee Handbook, which I had now gotten in the habit of checking each time I stopped the car (the car, which by the way had been mysteriously repaired and now stayed very quiet when I drove it). For example I had delivered a box full of something wriggling to a creature that the Employee Handbook told me was an Afanc, and had I not checked beforehand I might have accidentally looked at the creature and been tempted to take a nap in its lap[26].

---

[26] "In addition to its hypnotic visage, the Afanc's more notable abilities include rapid swimming, invisibility, and the ability to speak a mysterious and incomprehensible language called 'Welsh'." – The Cornucopia Employee Handbook, Page 78

I practically crawled to the bathroom to turn on the shower, freeing myself of my delicious-smelling garments and flopping into the tub under the stream of the showerhead. I let out a toad-like croak and shivered as the water hit my skin but as it warmed and filled the room with steam I started to relax.

I let out a sudden shout as a burning heat scaled its way across my arm, and I thrashed around momentarily while a symbol began to appear painfully in the surface of my skin. I tried to grab onto the side of the tub or the sink, but my fingers slipped and I fell back in the tub, splashing water across the floor. When it had stopped, I had a new tattoo webbed on my skin—signifying my new job at Cornucopia, I would imagine—leaving my arm sore and tingly. I tried to catch my breath, spitting and coughing up water, and finally dragged myself out of the tub into the bathroom floor. I laid there for a few minutes, just breathing heavily, staring up at the ceiling and watching it seem to spin.

One thing I have always admired about humans is that, when we reach a certain point of exhaustion, anywhere becomes a bed. It doesn't matter if you're sleeping on a couch or a gravel driveway or if you're shivering while lying cold, wet, and naked on a bathroom floor; at a certain point it all becomes just another place to sleep.

CHAPTER 18

I think I was having a dream, and it was a good one, but I don't remember what exactly it might have been about. All I do remember is that I was particularly frustrated to be jostled awake to the sound of a doorbell ringing, followed by a swift knock at the front door.

The water wasn't running. I had to have regained consciousness and turned it off in the middle of the night, but I had apparently not regained enough consciousness to actually get out of the bathroom and up to bed. I silently cursed middle-of-the-night-exhausted Andy and the sheer lack of forethought expressed by the performance of this action, because it left currently-on-the-floor Andy sore and wishing for an Aspirin.

I heard the knock at the door again, but this time it was followed by a familiar voice. "Andy? Are you ok?" It was Apollo. I was momentarily relieved until he added, "I'm coming in."

I let out a frustrated noise and pulled my indecent self to my feet. "Wait, hangon! I'm not dressed—" I stumbled through the kitchen toward the bedroom but knew I wouldn't make it. With rising panic in my throat, I grabbed a baking sheet from the top of the refrigerator and clutched it to myself just as he rounded the corner.

I would assume, from understanding the principles of his species, that Apollo had likely seen many different people in various stages of undress. It was terribly amusing, therefore, to watch his eyes go instantly wide and a rosy hue flush the dark skin of his cheeks; mine, I'm sure, were equally red. He spun instantly, putting his back to me. "Oh. Um. Hey."

I coughed awkwardly, sidling across the kitchen toward the bedroom with the pan gripped tightly to my skin. "Yeah. Hey."

"I thought you were—"

"—Yeah, no—"

"—and I got your texts—"

"—right, that's fine—"

"—and I thought you might be—"

"—it's cool—"

"—and I didn't realize—"

"—no problem—"

I finally reached the doorway and threw myself through it, slamming it behind me. I leaned against the wood of the door, catching my breath and trying to dismiss the burning feeling in my face, which I'm sure was a deep crimson by that point. Shaking myself mentally, I put on some clean clothes that didn't smell like food and took my morning anxiety medication before going back to the door, staring at it and trying to will myself to have the courage to open it up again.

On the other side of the door, I heard a distinct sizzling sound and a few seconds later a delicious aroma crept under the door. My stomach immediately began to curse at me, and I pulled the door open.

Apollo looked up at me from the stove. "I'm diffusing the awkwardness with breakfast," he said matter-of-factly, cracking an egg single-handedly into the fryer, "and you tell me about the weird stuff that happened to you yesterday. I'm really sorry, by the way—my phone died and I didn't get to charge it until this morning."

I leaned against the kitchen countertop and recounted my misadventures of the previous day. As I did so, I watched Apollo, with the same graceful movements he used when pulling a shot of coffee, making a full breakfast at the stove that he plated up with the precision of a chef. The utensils danced in his hands, and I even paused my storytelling more than once because I was just transfixed by the grace of his movements.

I got to the part where Killian had replied to my text and he stopped to look at me, looking mildly insulted. "Did she say anything else?"

I shook my head. "No, just that. I texted her later but I didn't get a response back."

Apollo shrugged, but the move looked stilted as though he was forcing himself to not care. "She hasn't talked to me either, so I dunno."

The food was plated and handed over into my still-slightly-numb hands. A single bite of the fluffy, syrup-drenched pancakes was enough to jump-start my tastebuds and, by extension, my brain. I jabbed my fork into a bit of egg and then into a piece of ham before dragging the whole forkful through a glob of syrup and then shoveled it into my mouth. "Ohh my gaaawh. Murry meh, Apowwo." Bits of food dribbled from my lips.

He seemed particularly pleased with himself as he stacked the dishes in the dishwasher. "So onto other news. Are you going today?"

I swallowed the food and tried to reclaim my dignity by wiping my mouth with a napkin. "Going to what?"

He blinked at me. "The Symposium. It's, like…today. Are you going?"

I looked down at my plate of food and moved my eggs around thoughtfully with a fork. "Better not," I said after a few moments, "or I might go chasing after more ghosts and dead ends. The whole *'almost* finding the answer' thing is getting old. Are these *matcha* pancakes? And what is this, lemon curd?"

"And what about The Harrow?"

"Oh jeez, I don't even care. I really just do not even care." I jabbed my fork into some more pancake. "Who cares if there's a new Dragon? Seems like it's not going to affect me anyhow. In a week I've gone from office worker to delivery driver. Who's in charge does not matter.

"I can see why you'd see it that way," he replied with perhaps the slightest bit of frost in his voice. "But the Dragon makes some pretty big decisions that affect everybody, even you. But you're right…you've been through a lot, and you don't need extra worries on your plate." He dried his hands on a hand towel. "I need to go. There's only two Lilin who live in the whole city, and the other one…well, she doesn't like crowds. So I have to go play crowd control."

"*She?*" I was suddenly curious. "The other Lilin is a succubus?"

"Yeah, and before you start getting weird ideas, no we haven't ever *misbehaved*. She's not really my type. She's all into that Anime stuff and spends way too much time writing nerdy erotic fanfiction on tumblr. Honestly," he added with raised eyebrows, "I think she can feed off of shipping characters together."

"Gross. But yeah," I returned to the subject at hand, "I have to work today. And the Symposium is a big event, right? Like Super Bowl big."

"The biggest," Apollo agreed. "The Dragon Symposium happens once a year. The hosting city gets overflowed with magical creatures from all over—a lot of whom are going to be staying in hotels and ordering food." I stifled a groan from deep in my stomach; this was going to be a very long second day on the job. "All the more reason to be fed and rested." Apollo added, sliding another pancake off his plate and onto mine. "You have a crazy car to drive, fancy food to deliver, and some sanity to keep. So don't worry about dragons or conspiracies or anything, alright? I'll come by around lunchtime and say hi."

I was really grateful at that specific moment for Apollo. After all that had happened, I had felt like the entire world and everyone I knew had abandoned me completely. But then, there was Apollo, who for no other reason than wanting to help a falling friend, went out of his way to just be a bro.

✳

The Cornucopia was, if anything, busier than we had anticipated. I got there early, hoping that I might get a couple extra deliveries in as the day started, and Codwell was more than happy to oblige. I actually made my first two deliveries before my shift was scheduled to start, both to the Cincinnatian Hotel down the street. I only caught a glimpse of the other delivery drivers on their way out the door to their respective delivery cars, and both seemed particularly unhappy to be working today despite the extra money from so many deliveries.

As I walked through the kitchen on my return, I had started to feel a little bit more confident in my job. Plus, I didn't have dusty files to sort. I wondered, briefly, if Carrie had reassigned someone else to that job, or if the 50 Thousand File Room was destined to remain chaotically disorganized. Of course, now that my mind was on 50 Thousand, it drifted to my old coworkers, Carma and Jake, and then to Killian. I wondered if she was able to just continue doing whatever she was doing, day after day, without giving me even a second thought. I still hadn't really been able to sort out our brief friendship—or the masquerade of one, as it supposedly was—and figure out how I felt about her as a person. And her text the previous day that saved me from certain doom certainly didn't come from the hands of someone without a little bit of heart.

I dismissed my thoughts of Killian as Chef Mulligan came over and patted my shoulder. "Ah, you. I seen that look. You've got that look. I seen't it sometimes." I was somehow impressed with how her accent was so purely Kentuckian despite her fangs.

"That kind of longing. Got someone on your mind? Boy or girl that's broken your heart?"

Before I could protest, she continued. "Listen, I don't want to hear it. I'm gonna give you some advice my momma told me back in the day and you're gonna listen good. If someone breaks your heart, the best thing to do is to claw theirs out with your bare hands and eat it under a full moon." She winked and gave me a sage smile.

"I…no. No, that sounds like a really bad idea."

"Suit yourself," Mulligan said, shrugging and walking away.

Codwell appeared from nowhere, his hair untidy and his ears flopping. "Andy, Andy, Andy. Got a call about you, yes I did yes I did. Fellow from yesterday, said you were great. Filled out a customer survey, so we sent him a coupon in his email—anyway, anyway, anyway, here's the order. Go on, be quick."[27] He handed over a bag that smelled like the rat food from yesterday.

One short ride in a Nøkken later, I was back at the apartments of the rat man, knocking on his door. He opened it, grinning. "Oooh! You're back! And in record time! Please, please, come in, yes, please come in!"

I gave the rat man a smile, setting the food down

---

[27] "The Cornucopia offers lots of great incentives for Employees to do well. These incentives include things like extra hours (sometimes even paid), taking on other people's responsibilities at no additional compensation, being blamed for other people's mistakes, and being the first person Management demands to come in when another employee calls out." - The Cornucopia Employee Handbook, Page 55 (Benefits)

on the table as before and starting to open the containers. "How is everyone doing?" I said, gesturing to the computer.

"Oh we're great. We're thinking of collaborating and writing a book. Right now we're brainstorming ideas." I considered telling him that I, too had once wanted to write a book, but had determined that writing for a living was a terrible life choice, but I decided to keep that to myself. "You know, most of the delivery people here just leave the food outside, knock, and walk away."

I stopped unpacking. "Wait, really? That's awful."

"Well," the rat man said, plopping down in his computer chair, "*Kobolda* get pretty used to it. We deal with *Vulnerabl* and *Sorcera* who think of us as just monsters. It's gotten better in recent years, but some people just don't want to ruin their day by looking at someone like me." He gave me a very knowing look, or the closest thing to a knowing look that I figure a rat man could give, and gestured me closer. I tiptoed near. "I am not sure if you've noticed, but I am actually a giant rat."

I almost replied by saying something dismissive, like "I never noticed" or "That doesn't matter" but I caught myself. The fact of the matter was, he *was* a giant rat, and pretending he *wasn't* would actually be pretty rude, regardless of whether the rat might be offended by the sentiment. "You are. You're a giant rat, and that's perfectly OK."

The rat looked taken aback. "What do you mean?"

"I mean," I said, unpacking more food, "That the fact that you are a giant rat does not give anybody the right to just ditch you and avoid you. They should just deal with it."

The rat blinked at me for a few moments. "That's just what Todd said! Like a few years ago."

"Really?" I straightened up a little; I hadn't thought I possessed the wisdom of a dragon.

"Yeah. He gathered all the *Kobolda* together and told us that the way we had been treated in the past was going to change. That's how so many of us got these apartments and such—the Dragon pays for it, he makes sure we have food and drink—oh, and then he pays for our internet so we can talk to each other and learn about the outside world without bothering the non-magic people. He gives basically tries to make the world as accessible as possible. Does that make sense? To show our appreciation a lot of us keep the underbellies of the city cleaner and safer and protect the normal people from bad things from below."

I had finished unpacking the rat's food, and now stood with a stone face. I hadn't realized that Todd himself was behind this little setup, and the fact that this rat man seemed…well…*happy* with his life had given me a slightly different perspective on Todd. I had only seen him briefly, in the heat of pomp and circumstance, but it seemed that the Dragon was, at least, compassionate about his subjects.

And The Harrow was a threat to that. The Harrow was a threat to the way of life of not just this Rat but all *Kobolda* society. And other societies, certainly. If the Black Magisters had indeed found a way to overthrow the Dragon of Cincinnati, then the results might be far worse than I had originally considered.

Silently cursing myself for being so selfish, I thanked the rat man for his kindness and excused myself politely before dashing down the hallway and back to the car. *Where is the symposium actually taking place?* I texted Apollo madly as I turned the key.

us bank arena he replied. *am i still meeting you for lunch*
No. Meet me at the arena.

My phone gave the little "..." symbol of Apollo writing a message and I watched it disappear a couple times as he presumably deleted and retyped a response a few times. Finally it popped up: *if your really doing this then im with you but you cant get in without a good reason*

Got that covered I typed. Also: *you're**

CHAPTER 19

I think I mildly frightened the acid-spitting dishwashers on my way through the back door of Cornucopia, on account of how quickly I was moving and the fact that one of them started coughing as I went by. I didn't have time to lose, though, and I skirted past a frustrated looking Mulligan carrying a large stockpot to get over to the delivery desk where Codwell was waiting impatiently. "Do you have any food going to the Symposium?" I stammered through heavy breaths.

"Well yes," he replied, sorting through tickets expertly and his fluffy head bobbing as if to keep all of the orders he had rattling around inside his head from spilling out, "But I wanted to give those to the more experienced drivers who—"

I didn't let the fluffy Puck finish before I lunged. "I'll take one!" I grabbed a ticket before Codwell could protest and dashed out the door with a bag full of something that started making a gurgling noise as I ran back through the kitchen to the car. I practically threw the bag into the passenger seat and before the Nøkken could even say a cheery hello, I had slammed the car into drive and burned out of the parking lot with a horrendous screech from the tires.

"Ow!" The car said with obvious discomfort. "What's the hurry?"

"I have to get to the Symposium," I said, frustratedly slowing down to stop for a red light: it had suddenly become that time of day when downtown Cincinnati became a gridlock of people leaving the office and spilling from dozens of underground garages into the main streets at the same time.

"Oh." There was a pause. "You need to get there fast?"

"Yes, it's very important."

"Very fast?" The light was still red.

"Yes. Very fast."

"Do you want...*me* to drive?"

I shuddered, thinking about yesterday. "I...I'm not sure. You did sort of try and kill me yesterday."

"Maybe a little, but I'm a good Nøkken now. You know my name so I can't hurt you." The voice was so sweet and not at all sociopathic.

"Is that *so*?" I said dubiously, opening up my Employee Handbook and flipped to a section that just happened to be about Nøkken. "*Nøkken, once identified by name,*" I read out loud, "*are quite docile creatures who only want to have fun and go fast. Much like a horse and rider, you can find yourself in a very happy working relationship with your car as it does everything within its power to satisfy your requests—*" I tore my eyes away from the pages[28] and, satisfied, let go of the wheel. "Fine, but I don't want you hurting anyone else, okay? No property damage either. Basically…get there fast but don't break anything. Deal?"

I barely had a moment to register the word "Deal!" blaring out of the car speakers before we had torn around the stopped cars and into oncoming traffic. I screamed and let go of the Handbook, grabbing onto any available handhold as the city of Cincinnati flew past the windshield. I caught a glimpse of a street sign as we turned onto the aptly named "Race Street" and then we were off, the odometer of the car registering a spine-tingling "105" in what was almost certainly a 35 mph zone. It was only a moment before we had cleared three blocks, and, swerving through the 3rd and Race intersection we hit the curb. The instant passed in slow-motion as, to my horror, the car was propelled into the air and left me dangling by my seatbelt.

I would love to say that at that moment my life flashed before my eyes, but it didn't. In fact, I feel that this moment simply became incredibly slow as my brain fired off zillions of neurons all at once. I felt a connection to this moment, and it was almost as if the connection between everything that had happened to me in the last few weeks was the thing unfolding in front of me. The vault, the drachma, my Dad, Killian, Apollo, The Dragon—all of it suddenly

---

[28] "—so long as it can without material injury to itself. It also can be…wait. You stopped reading already? Come on, I got dressed up and organized just for you. Dammit, Andy, you ungrateful little—" - The Cornucopia Employee Handbook, Page 477 (Your Car and You)

seemed like one huge knot: a tangle of lies that was on its way to becoming unsalvageable. I almost felt like I could reach out and feel or even hold the tangle of people and places and things in my hand. It was a moment of clarity and serenity, which seemed to go on and on and on until—

—until I felt the solid thump as the car landed in the right-hand lane of Interstate 75, still moving at an incredible speed. I barely had the ability to glance at the sign for the exit to I-71 before we hopped a second median and flew down an embankment, doing a full 180-degree turn—

—before landing perfectly in a parking space next to the arena's front doors.

I sat there, quite still, as the food bag thrashed around on its own, and I took a few long, steadying breaths, reminding myself that the next time I saw I doctor I would probably need to up my anxiety medication by about six thousand percent.

As soon as my whole body stopped feeling like jelly I reached for the door handle and clambered out. "Th-thank you," I sputtered, and I grabbed both the Handbook and the wriggling bag of food and ambled up toward the doors as the blood started to circulate in my legs once more.

The front gate of the arena was guarded by two very tall, pale-skinned people clad in silver and purple, who were gazing out with hawk-like attentiveness at the people coming in. Many of the people looked completely normal, and I spotted many a *Vulnerabl* bracelet or *Sorcera* tattoo as I weaved my way through the crowd. A few, however, were rather unique in their shapes and sizes, and I assumed that it was only the fact that I was in on the Secret that allowed me to see them walking around at all.

At the gate one of the figures towered over me, looking for a badge.

"I'm delivering food," I said before the guard could question me. He glanced at the bag, which was now softly sobbing, and then back to me. Finally, he looked down my forearm at the tattoos that indicated my entire identity, and he waved me past.

I didn't question further, and disappeared into the crowd, pulling out my phone. Apollo had already texted to ask where I was. *I'm inside* I replied.

me 2. Third floor. Vulnerabl only, tell them you from Italy or something

I ducked out of the throng of people still rushing toward the area seats and hit the button for the elevator, my heart racing. I still needed a plan at this point, because I figured that interrupting the Dragons' symposium was going to be a little more difficult than just popping up and saying, "There's a conspiracy!"

There was a small crowd on the lift to the third floor, and I did my best to not gawk at the others riding along with me. The door of the elevator hadn't even finished opening before I had darted through arms and jackets and out into the hallway—right into another purple-clad guard.

"Hey now, hey now. This area is for *Vulnerabl* only." He pointed at my Society tattoo.

"I'm delivering food," I said, more confidently than I had before.

He crossed his arms. "Unless you're an ambassador's assistant—"

"Italy!" I choked out. "I'm with the Ambassador from Italy! This food's for them."

The guard glowered. "What ambassador from Italy?"

I didn't know what to say but I choked out a response. "Lord…Marinaro." I felt instantly ashamed at my name choice, and feared instantly that any

The guard, however, straightened up. "Lord Marinaro is here? No one told me. Fine, fine, go on then, but be quick about it." I watched, amazed, as he turned and headed back down the hall in the other direction. I shook myself mentally, amazed at my luck, pulling out my phone again to text Apollo. *On the 3rd floor. Where are you?*

"Right here," I heard off to my right as I passed an intersection in the corridor. Apollo was standing by the entrance to what looked like a conference room full of people. "Come on, quickly. And hey," he added as he glanced surreptitiously to the people behind him and then whispered urgently in my ear. "I am about to say some things you might think are insulting, but you *need* to play along, or you *will* get caught. Put your delivery bag down and give me your hand." I did as I was told, and Apollo dragged his index finger across my palm, leaving a red, spiky mark traced there as if it had been tattooed. I didn't have a moment to question it before Apollo took my arm and steered me into the room.

The conference room was filled with the most incredibly beautiful people I had ever seen in my entire life. I had no choice but to feel completely inadequate as I scanned the room, looking from one perfect face to the next—people of all races, shapes and sizes but each and every one of them was sublimely perfect in their construction. It was like walking through a garden of statues crafted by only the most skilled sculptor of all time.

"Apollo!" one voice chimed out from the crowd, and a svelte, braided-haired young woman strode up to greet us at the door. "Good to see you've joined us! We were just talking about you. Your biceps, specifically, if I must be honest. And who's *this* morsel?" She had turned to me. "Have you brought *treats* to share?"

"This one," Apollo indicated the mark on my hand without looking at me, "Is my property, and is to be referred to as 'Andy'. It is not for sharing and it is not to be touched or hassled." My eyes went wide. *Excuse me? Did I just get called 'it'?*

The woman looked disappointed. "Ah, such a shame. You have lovely taste in pleasure dolls." *Pleasure WHAT now?*

Apollo seemed entirely unfazed. "Speaking of that," he said with an icy tone, "I will be excusing myself briefly with my Doll. You understand, right, Carlissa?"

She rolled her eyes. "Of course, Apollo, of course. This one seems far tamer than your last one, at least. What what its name? The redheaded one."

"Killian?" I said before I could stop myself. Apollo glared at me and I fell silent immediately under his fiery gaze.

"That is none of your concern," Apollo addressed Carlissa. "As I said. I will be gone a short while with my Doll. If anyone requires a Cincinnati Lilin, then Agatha is only—"

"Agatha is so...distasteful," Carlissa interrupted with a crinkle of her nose. "Come now Apollo, you can play later. There are people you absolutely *must* meet—"

"I will remind you," Apollo growled through gritted teeth, "That Agatha is the *Princesse de Cincinnati* and is owed your respect. Unless you want to risk her restricting your feeding rights inside the city…"

I found myself staring, almost slack-jawed, at the person standing next to me. I could hardly believe it was Apollo at all with how commanding his presence had suddenly become, and I was both intrigued and terrified by his new fierce glare and intimidating posture.

"Of course not, darling," Carlissa replied, a nervous shudder making her straighten up slightly, "I will find Agatha if I have any need." She turned on her stiletto and gracefully meandered to the next conversation while Apollo dragged me from the room. I grabbed my bag of delivery food as we headed down the hallway.

As soon as we had cleared earshot of the conference room, he spun and let go of my arm. "Okay, I am *so* sorry. Like, terribly. I didn't have any other way to explain your wandering around."

I shrugged. "I get that. Are you, like, important or something? Why does everyone in there know you?"

"Sort of," he said, and we were off down the hallway again. "Remember the succubus I mentioned this morning? Well she's the head of the *Vulnerabl* in Cincinnati, and technically she's my wife, which makes me her second-in-command."

"You're *married?*" The idea was surprising on a deep level I couldn't quite place my finger on. "And if she's the 'Princesse' does that make you—?"

"A Prince, yeah, but only symbolically. Same with the marriage, it's political and I don't like talking about it. Like I said, I'm not really interested in

Agatha, so we keep our distance and don't bother each other. I'm only her default husband because I'm the only Incubus in the city." I didn't reply. I wasn't sure why, but my stomach felt slightly sunken at this revelation, but I had no choice by to push the thoughts aside as Apollo stopped at an elevator and hit the button to go up. "On the other hand," he added as the doors opened, "Being *Prince de Cincinnati* gives me a little bit of privilege during symposiums…" he swiped a card across the electronic keypad and hit the button for the top floor, "…including access to the Dragons' floor."

I grinned as the doors closed and the lift started to rise. "No way! Alright, that should make this really easy. I thought it would be much harder to—" The elevator stopped on the very next floor and the doors opened, revealing one of the last people I wanted to see.

Killian.

Dressed in her finest JNY suit, with her sword glittering at her side, she appeared to keep any surprise she might have hidden and paid us no mind as she joined us on the elevator. As soon as the doors closed, she rounded on me. "What are *you* doing here?" she demanded, as Apollo put out an arm to stop her. I thought she was going to throw a right hook at me.

"I'm d-doing my job!" I choked out, holding up the bag of food and retreating into the corner of the elevator.

"So am I!" She retorted, "I'm working security and I don't need you causing trouble!"

"*Me* causing trouble?" I bristled. "You're the one who joined the bad guys."

Apollo tried to pull Killian back away. "Hey guys—"

"I had good reason!" She spat as Apollo continued to hold her back. "And you kept getting in the way!"

"You pretended to be my friend so you could just *steal* that coin—"

Apollo cleared his throat. "Guys—"

"Well you gave me a fake coin!" Killian shouted, trying to wrestle out of the Incubus' grip.

"The Black Magisters killed my *dad*—" I shouted, dropping the bag of food and grabbing for Killian's collar.

"No, they didn't," A voice interrupted our scuffle, and both Killian and I turned to see why Apollo had been trying to interrupt us. The elevator had reached the top floor, and greeting us at the elevator door was none other than the Dragon of Cincinnati himself. He glanced at the three of us, entangled violently in the small box, and gave us a look of scorn so severe that we all let go of each other almost simultaneously and backed against the wall.

"I killed Tom LaFayette," the dragon announced.

FIRST DAY

It was going to be a good day.

Six years! Six years of schooling and studying and rubbing shoulders. It had been a grueling six years, Tom thought to himself as he walked through the brass doors of his new job. Six years, all for this wonderful opportunity. He was dolled up in his best suit, his briefcase in one hand and a cheap cup of coffee in the other, which he drained in a few gulps and dropped in a trash can.

The opportunities were endless! He thought back to those long hours, filling out formulas and brewing foul-smelling potions. He considered, briefly, the good times spent in a library researching an ancient artifact or an impossibly dangerous creature. And then, of course, it had seemed that every year had ended with a calamity of some massive proportions that was solved within the last few days of the semester and ended with nobody the worse for wear.

Yes, those three million minutes at Sorcery School had been three million minutes of adventures, crammed full of danger and insanity. But now, it was over, and an even bigger adventure was about to begin: The corporate world. Yes, for sure, it was going to be a good day.

"Hello," He cheerfully said at the front desk to a surly-faced security guard, "I'm Tom. I'm your new wizard."

The guard hit a button without changing a single wrinkle of his expression. "Floor 12."

Tom wasn't even fazed by the security guard's demeanor and headed off to the elevator with a spring still firmly planted in his step. This was going to be the newest chapter of his life. A wizard, working in a prestigious wizardry firm, with other wizards. How much better could it get? It was certainly going to be a good day.

The elevator stopped at 12 and he nearly pounced out into the elevator bank, trying to contain all of his sheer happiness that was filling his stomach like a stack of hot pancakes with syrup. Nothing could deflate the balloon of optimism. If only he could run into—

"Blake!" Tom threw out his hand as he ran into the shaggy-haired young man.

Blake beamed a great smile and clasped Tom's hand. "Tom! You got the job. Well you're gonna love it here. They've got a lot of opportunity for bright minds like you and me. I'm glad the referral went through. How's the wife?"

"Great. Got a little one on the way, even. Not sure if you'd heard!"

"That's great, Tom. Just great. I've gotta run to a

meeting, though, your desk should be right around the corner there." He pointed before clapping Tom on the back and walking away the other direction. *My desk!* Tom thought, heading around the corner. How would a wizard even decorate his desk, he wondered? And as he entered the place where his desk should be, his smile faltered for the first time this morning.

Rows and rows of cubicles. Each and every one alike and labeled with names. Feeling suddenly cautious at the quiet, fragmented only by brief sounds of shifting paper, he picked his way along the cubicles looking for a name. And there it was: *LaFayette, T.* The cubicle was bare save for a single huge CRT monitor and a keyboard. He set his briefcase down and looked around.

"Hey there," he heard a voice and spun to see someone standing up from the next cubicle over. "I'm Carl. You must be the new sorcerer."

"Y-yeah!" Tom forced his smile back onto his face and shook hands. "Tom. Is this my—uh…"

"Cube? Yessir. Just for you. The drawer has your cabinet key, UNIX database password and your copy of the Employee Handbook."

Tom tried to keep his smile, but he felt the tips of his lips faltering. "So my j-job is…?"

"Paperwork, mostly. Here we're in Disposal and Containment, but we don't actually do any field work. We fill out the C-738s for the Society, along with entering data into the database for queries and searches. Oh, and sometimes, we get to organize pictures into folders. So that's nice."

Tom swallowed hard. "I don't mean to sound ungrateful, but I thought there would be…you know. Spells and things…"

"As a new hire? Not really. You went to Sorcery school…so they mostly use your book knowledge unless you can get your foot in the door with the Wizards."

"But I *am* a wizard."

Carl cringed. "I mean…yeah? I guess we both have that title. Technically. But you don't really do that job. Not in your first year or two anyway."

Tom nodded, and his smile came back. "So it's just a matter of working up the corporate ladder, then."

Carl raised his eyebrows. "Yeah. Sure. But I mean…don't count on that, eh? I've been here six years and just got my first raise. Anyway, welcome to the job." He disappeared behind his cubicle wall and Tom continued to stand there like a fool. After a few minutes he took a seat in the chair and steadied himself with a few breaths. He reached for the drawer and pulled out his Employee Handbook and HR paperwork with post-its on it to show where he needed to sign and initial. It all seemed so mundane.

"I'm a wizard," he announced to no one in particular.

"Yeah," Carl said from over the wall. "Keep telling yourself that."

It was going to be a good day. It was a shame his cubicle didn't face a window.

CHAPTER 20

The silence left a ringing in my ears, and I could hear my heartbeat clearly over my heavy breaths. Killian and Apollo both looked down to the ground, unsure if this was the moment that the over-arching fear of the Dragon's appetite for people he disliked was about to come to fruition.

I, however, kept my gaze. The way that the Dragon had so matter-of-factly admitted the one answer I had spent to very long seeking was so thoroughly disturbing that it made my heart sink deep in my chest only to get swallowed up somewhere in my stomach. Before I could come up with some kind of witty response to this confession of guilt, or even consider a plan now that the three of us were now backed—quite literally—into a corner, the elevator doors attempted to close.

Todd shifted his foot into the line of the doorway and they sprung back open. "Out," he commanded, and Apollo and Killian scampered past the angry Dragon and into the hall, where several more purple-and-silver guards were waiting. I continued to stand, shaking, in the elevator. Todd looked at me, his eyebrows knitting together deeply as he considered me for moment. "Step out of the elevator, Apprentice LaFayette."

I didn't move. "Or what? You'll kill me, too?"

"No," Todd replied without hesitation. "Or I'll have you arrested. You want answers? I'll give them to you. But you need to follow me, or you'll get nothing." The Dragon then turned on his heel and strode back toward the opposite end of the hall, toward an open doorway.

I looked helplessly to Apollo and Killian, who both stared obediently at the floor. Both of them were breathing very heavily, and they followed behind the Dragon without a word. I still didn't move, and as they walked away I saw Killian glance back at me and mouth the word "please."

I finally stepped off the elevator and, flanked by two more guards, followed the others into the office. Todd had apparently set up a makeshift workspace here for the symposium; a tuxedo hung over a nearby armchair with his fancy jewel hanging off the breast pocket and a desk was covered in papers and forms along with an open briefcase full of what looked like ancient scrolls of parchment.

"Silencers, show yourselves," the Dragon commanded as he took a seat behind the desk. Instantly, the three guides appeared behind the desk obediently: Iktomi sat perched on the Moddey Dhoo's back, while a curvy, wild-haired woman in a toga relaxed against the wall with a cigarette hanging out of her mouth.

"First," the Dragon said, taking a seat behind the desk, "Prince Apollo. I am rather disappointed that you're entangled in all this. So I am temporarily suspending your privileges in the city effective immediately. And do not worry," he added as Apollo looked up and opened his mouth to reply, "the Lilin will not suffer punishment. I will deal with Agatha personally."

He moved on. "Killian Fletcher. There was a time when you were a rising star in this city. And now you stand here, a party to a conspiracy against me and my city. This will…this will *not do*." He took out a smartphone and typed into it. "I will inform 50 Thousand that you are no longer to be employed there. And then you will be turned over to the *Sorcera* Society for further judgement. I expect they will terminate your membership and reimage your memories."

"Please, no…" I heard Killian whisper, but the Dragon turned his attention to me.

"And you. When I had heard that you had not only applied at 50 Thousand, but had aced the *Sorcera* society examination, I must say that I was rather taken aback. Your father was rather insistent that you were not knowledgeable in any of the magical arts, and as his last request asked that my office not contact your family. Curious. But now here you are, trying to get into my private sanctum. For answers? Or to finish what he started?"

"Why did you kill my dad?" I said, my courage rising in my throat. I had given up all hope of having an amazing and wonderful plan stashed in the back of my mind, and at this point I had simply come to the conclusion that I was no longer afraid. Whatever happened to me now, I needed answers.

"Your father," Todd replied calmly, "Betrayed my greatest trust. Five years ago, for his service to the city, I granted Lord LaFayette the right of *Pro Veritate*. He took that gift and used it for his own gain. What he failed to know is that the tradition of *Pro Veritate* is not the right to no longer be accountable…It is the right to be accountable directly to the Dragon of the City." Todd picked up a cigarette from the desk and put it in his mouth. It lit on its own, and he took a drag from it. "When an informant told me that your father entered into a conspiracy to betray me and put another Dragon into power, I knew the score. So I met him, at his home. I talked to him. I gave him the chance to confess and turn on his co-conspirators. He refused, out of whatever misguided loyalty…so I enacted my rights of the city. And I do not regret it."

It was a moment of truth which hung in the air like fog, and I realized that my breathing had suddenly risen to a deep panic, but now it was subsiding on its own. The conflicting feelings in my chest, and the cognitive dissonance in my brain had begun to fall into place as the part of me that had a loyalty to my absent father slipped away down a drain in the back of my head, and I realized then that I had now inserted myself so far into his tangle of betrayal that I had practically implicated myself in his actions. "What are you going to do with me?" I asked after a moment.

"That remains to be seen. From the looks of things you've decided to follow in your father's footsteps, but I don't have any evidence of that yet. So I am going to hold you here until we can discern the truth." There was a knock at the door and he rose from his seat. "I have a Symposium to run and I simply do *not* have time to sort this out right now, so you three will stay here. You will be joined by security shortly. And do *not*—" He addressed Killian and Apollo specifically, "—attempt to escape. It will not end well for you." He turned to address the silencers. "I order you as Dragon of the City: if they attempt to use any magic or flee, kill them." The three *Empyrean* bowed halfheartedly as the Dragon walked past us, picked up his tuxedo, and disappeared out the door with his guards.

I dropped into the armchair, head in my hands. "I'm so stupid," I said through the muffling of my fingers as I squeezed my eyes shut.

Apollo rounded on Killian. "OK, what exactly did you get us into here, Killian? You're joining evil cults and betraying everyone you know? Betraying me—*me*, of all people. What is *wrong* with you? I have always been on your side, even when I shouldn't have."

"I didn't have a choice, OK?" Killian was raising her voice in a way I hadn't quite heard her do thus far. "And I thought *that one*—" I assumed she was gesturing to me "—was in on it the whole time. You know, since Andy ended up getting Tom's condo, which meant Andy got the coin. I thought it was *intentional*."

I looked up, coming to a sudden realization. "Hey Killian—" I lurched back in the chair as Killian spun on me, her face flushed with anger. "Um...you said I gave you a fake coin. What did you mean?"

Killian fished the drachma out of her pocket and brandished it toward me. "This thing. Really friggin' clever, Andy, but when I put it in the vault nothing happened. So I almost got caught, and if I had then the other Magisters would have—" She stopped herself and I could see her formulating her next words, "—done something about it."

I rose defiantly and faced her, eye-to-eye. "What would they have done, Killian? What is so awful and important that you would have betrayed everything…?" I trailed off as my gaze drifted over to the Incubus who was standing there, quietly confused. It clicked into place. "They threatened Apollo, didn't they?"

Killian didn't reply, but as she gritted her teeth and dropped her shoulders I knew I wasn't wrong.

Apollo closed his eyes and leaned back against the desk. "Killian—"

She held a hand up and avoided looking at him. "Don't. Just…don't."

"In any case," I said, pulling the coin from Killian's other hand. "I know why this didn't work. You said the coin became mine when my dad left the Condo to me, right? Well, I didn't *give* the coin to you—"

"I *took* it," Killian finished my sentence in realization. "So the coin was still yours the whole time." She swallowed hard and composed herself. "OK…I'm sorry. I'm sorry for what I did—"

"Later," I said insistently, and gestured to the room. "What are we going to do now?"

Apollo perked up. "Someone is coming," he said, gesturing to the door with his chin. I pocketed the coin as the door opened, and five masked figures dressed in suits walked into the room. Each was armed a standard-issue grey particleboard wand, pointed straight at us. They parted and allowed a sixth through who was dressed more outlandishly, a black and red cape hanging from his shoulders and his body strapped with spiky armor that looked like it must be absolutely uncomfortable to wear. As he moved closer, however, I could see that the spikes, and the rest of the armor, was clearly plastic and might have been purchased as a Halloween store.

"Magister LaRouge," he said with a flourish of his arm and his cape, "So good to see that you have kept the young LaFayette out of trouble. Unfortunately I can't say the same for yourself. *Dormi!*" He raised his wand and pointed it at her; there was a ripple in the air that lasted a moment before Killian's eyes fluttered with sleepiness and she dropped backwards into the armchair, quickly falling asleep. Apollo made a move to go over to her but one of the others held him off with a wand.

Grimsbane erupted into a deep and raucous laugh, and the body language of the other masked people made me think that they were rolling their eyes behind their masks. "But it doesn't matter. The ritual has been done."

"What ritual?" I demanded, taking a step forward, but as two of the others raised their wands I jumped back against the desk.

"The ritual," the leader said, raising his arms, "To bring the Dark Lord back from his imprisonment in that lunar exile of so long ago! That he might rise and cover this land is a darkness do deep that no light can possibly—"

"Lord Grimsbane." Another masked man cleared his throat. "Maybe this isn't the proper time to talk about our plans…?"

"Oh, but it is, Magister Rathnul!" Grimsbane

protested, "And do not *dare* interrupt me again! For now we stand on the precipice of chaos! We, the chosen ones, will serve the Dark Lord in the tasks he has set before us! With the Dragon of Cincinnati's defenses gone, there is nothing to stop us from—"

CLANG. Grimsbane crumpled forward like a ragdoll, hitting the floor with a disgusting crunch. Behind him, Rathnul had picked up a serving platter and struck the leader across the back of the head with it.[29]

"I am *sick*," he said, striking the leader again with the dish, "Of you acting like some kind of stupid—" *CLANK*. "—evil—" *GLANK*. "—overlord—" *FLONG*. "—with no regard for any kind of…of…planning! Or resource management! You wouldn't even give us guns when we all keep telling you that guns are deadlier than curses, you stupid—" *PONG*. "—asshole—"

We watched Rathnul cursing and hitting the poor dude on the floor over and over until, it appeared, he was all out of his bottled rage. None of the other masked men made any move to stop him, and indeed a few of them nodded silently in agreement with the executive decision that had been made.

I watched on in horror as he continued to heave heavy breaths for a few moments before he dropped the platter to the floor, which echoed loudly in off the office walls. "Hey, uh…" one of them piped up, now trying to ignore the slowly pooling blood trailing

---

[29] "The use of serving patters to commit acts of violence is strictly prohibited. Not because violence itself is prohibited, but because people eat off of those. That's nasty. You're nasty." – Cornucopia Handbook, Page 344 (Violence in the Workplace)

across the tile floor, "Can we take these masks off? They're hella hot, make us half-blind, and in twenty minutes it's not going to matter who knows who we are."

The new leader reached up and yanked his headgear off, throwing it to the floor. Instantly I recognized the trimmed beard and professional haircut.

"Blake!" I shouted, gripping the desk with my fingers. "I thought 50 Thousand was on Todd's side! Protecting him?"

The wizarding manager ran a finger through his hair while the other Magisters removed their masks. A few faces looked slightly familiar, but I couldn't attach them to names. I didn't see Hampstead. "Shut up. I'm not answering your questions. Besides, you wouldn't understand. Gerhart, put some silver cuffs on them all. And gag the incubus."

Oh, I understood. Everything was starting to make a lot of sense. "So let me get this story right," I said as two of the guards, wands out, came over to me and clapped handcuffs on my wrists, "50 Thousand casts magical protective spells on Todd because they're all reputable and stuff, right? Powerful enough to repel pretty much anything, I'm guessing. So then someone, I guess that guy—" I gestured to the probably-dead guy on the floor, "—convinces you all that it's a good idea to change the regime. Or blackmails you. I just can't figure out why." Blake ignored me, typing on his phone.

"Money," Apollo replied before another guard threw a rune-decorated rag around his face and gagged him.

I thought of what Carrie told me about Dark

Magic and a light bulb went off in my head. "Oh…of course! Not too many places that practice Dark Magic, but the Dragons of Cincinnati have never made it legal. So…you get my dad involved because he doesn't have a silencer. He's also the Vaultkeeper of 50 Thousand, and you're his boss so he does what you tell him. Or maybe he just does it because he's an asshole, whatever. But he steals one of the drachmas, and that means that 50 Thousand's protection spells lose a lot of their effectiveness. Then all you guys have to do is somehow get the Harrow back to Earth and he goes and challenges Todd. New Dragon, new rules, right? And the company makes a crap-ton of money as it starts offering a brand-new service: dark magic. That's what it's all about, right? Money?"

Blake finally looked up, irritated. "It's always about *money*, LaFayette. And it wouldn't have been possible if it weren't for your old man. So how about you just stay over there and chill?"

"That's right, that's just what you want, isn't it?" I took a defiant step forward, but the guard grabbed my shoulder and pulled me back. "You figured out that my dad left the coin to me when he died but you didn't know where it was. So rather than try and find it, you just tried to scare me into hanging onto it. Bribed the goblins, the pixies…whatever. Because it didn't matter who *had* the coin as long as it never got back to the vault. But here's the thing." I leaned back against the desk and shrugged. "I don't care. I don't work for your stupid company. And now I found out that Todd killed my dad…so I'm not really against you. You can, like, do what you want."

Apollo turned and gave me the most incredulous look I could imagine, but I pretended to not see it.

Blake narrowed his eyes. "So why are you yelling at me? Why are you even *here?*" he asked.

"Because it's my job! I'm here delivering food! I deliver food for a living ever since 50 Thousand fired me! I'm a freaking *delivery driver*!" I shouted, angrily kicking the bag of delivery food over to Blake. "Here! Take it! I'm giving it to you. I'm about an hour late for my delivery anyway so I'm probably going to lose that job too. And if I'm lucky *Sorcera* will wipe my brain and I won't have to worry about your stupid conspiracy and your stupid evil plans. Enjoy your lunch. Enjoy your murder conspiracy. I *just. Do. Not. Care.*"

Blake considered me for a long moment and then put his phone away. "That's fine. Everything is done. Now all we have to do is watch the action." He pointed at the wall with his wand. "Vizio."

The others around him glanced at each other curiously. "What did that spell do?" Someone piped up.

"The TV," Blake grumbled. "Put the Vizio over there so we can watch the beginning of the symposium, so we don't miss our cue." The henchmen set about locating the TV in a cabinet and moving it to the other table.

My pocket buzzed. I looked over to see that Apollo had dug in his pocket and was texting behind the armchair where Killian was still snoozing peacefully. Blake and his men appeared to be fully consumed with setting up the TV and were having an issue with the input cables and figuring out which channel they needed to be on, so it seemed safe to dig out my phone, too. *what are u doing ????*

Trust me, please. I put the phone back into my

pocket as Blake finally got the TV turned on to watch the symposium.

CHAPTER 21

The arena had been a good choice to hold the symposium. Not only did it have eighteen thousand seats and a great accessibility from Downtown Cincinnati, but it had the additional advantage of a covered roof, meaning that the new issues involving drones and spy cameras could be greatly mitigated.

The center of the arena was a raised where dozens of rows of seats were laid out in front of a podium. One hundred and fifty-eight dragons were in attendance at this symposium, from cities all over the world. The rows and rows of dragons waited politely, showing a deep respect to the one whose city hosted this year. To dare interrupt the hosting Dragon would be unthinkably rude at best and considered a challenge for power at worst.

One dragon, however, did not have an invitation. He strode past the guards with his teeth gnashing, the razor claws he bore substituting perfectly for any form of identification needed. He entered the bright lights of the Arena with a puffed chest and his yellow-green scales glittering.

Todd had been at the podium for a few minutes already, the jewel of his office hanging about his tuxedo collar and jangling lightly as he welcomed the visiting dignitaries from around the world. There was much business to be done, and a lot of posturing about how this year had been an exceptional year for Cincinnati, for all of the Societies, and for magical creatures everywhere.

He paused for a moment to indicate an empty chair in the stands, draped with black. "We see here that there is, for the first time in a long time, a complete absence of one of us. The Vampire—who agonized over the protection of mankind and magical being alike—has finally found its eternal rest. These late years the threat of hunters have continued to plague us. But we continue to stand up to them and refute their demonization of us. Many cities—Cincinnati included—have eradicated their kind from our borders. We are strong. Evil has no place here."

The crowd erupted into cheers. Todd was nothing if not a good speaker; he showed, through the way he spoke and the way he seemed to touch the hearts of everyone who heard his voice, a deep concern for the well-being of his city. One might have likened his charisma for some kind of magical force of mind control, but the truth—that his was a respect earned over centuries of selfless dedication—was equally admirable and terrifying.

"What we have to show for our efforts," He said, gazing out not just at the dragons but all of the different creatures in the stands surrounding him, "Is a better unity among our peoples. We stand here with greater strides towards the ideal—that cooperation that all of our societies were founded on. That we might continue to live in harmony, relishing in our differences while bonding over—"

A roar split the highly-recycled air of the stadium and caused a quiet to descend instantly. The air, it seemed, chilled instantly as the creature brought itself back on its hind legs and spread its leathery wings far out wide. "Dragon of Cincinnati!" It roared, fire dripping from its lips and exploding into smoke on the ground, "I have come to challenge you!"

The dragons broke out in whispers among themselves. A moment later, the arena became a madhouse, as every single creature tried to make its way to an exit to get the hell out of dodge. Some ran for the exits, while others phased through walls or simply vanished into thin air. [30]

A dragon challenge! This was quite unusual to do at a symposium, and the hosting Dragon's symposium at that. Surely the scaly usurper was not serious. He was either showing far too much bravado, or his strength was so great that he did not care.

Todd took a long breath and spoke again into the microphone. "I greet you, the one called The Harrow. But there are rules to these things."

"Coward!" The Harrow replied. "I have challenged you rightfully, and you must answer, or

---

[30] "In the unlikely event that you become witness to a challenge of Dragons, then the best thing to do is RUN! RUN FOR YOUR LIFE! GET OUT OF THERE! AND TAKE YOUR EMPLOYEE HANDBOOK WITH YOU!" - The Cornucopia Employee Handbook, Page 846 (Things that will kill you, Part 3)

your city becomes mine!"

"I do answer," Todd replied coolly. "But you return from banishment from this very council of Dragons. If you wish you wish to challenge me, then you *will* follow the laws, or any right you claim to have to legitimacy will be burned away with the flesh from your bones."

The Harrow seemed surprised at this reply. "Do not talk to me of the laws of our people!" The Harrow screamed, "I wrote some of them!"

"As did many of us," Todd sneered. "So will you submit to the laws? I need to know now."

"I will!" The Harrow replied instantly. "Now get on with it! Choose your arbiter!"

Todd nodded. "I yield the microphone to the arbiter. The Most Venerable Brenda, Past Dragon of Cincinnati." Todd took off his jacket as he left the podium, removing his jacket carefully and folding it delicately to pass off to another dragon. Todd stood dignified as he walked to the end of the dais, facing the snarling lizard opposite him. He leapt from the edge then, and in an instant a twenty-foot black lizard landed where a six-foot man should have. Todd raised himself to full height, stretching his purple-and-gold wings as if to warm up the joints, and then curled, waiting.

Michaels took her place at the microphone. "Ello, dearies," she said pleasantly. "Now, let's see…the rules." She took out a small notebook with a plastic cover decorated with images of kittens and thumbed through it. "Ah yes, here we are. 'First: That the fight shall be by claws, magic, or both; Second: That each Dragon should elect his stewards to defend him and offer their aid; Third: That the Dragons shall choose if the fight is to be to first blood, dominion, or death." She waited.

"Death," The Harrow snarled. Todd nodded.

Apollo continued to nudge Killian's chair with his foot, and the redhead began to rouse. She opened her eyes, her pupils fluttering with dilation as she tried to focus on the face of the incubus hovering above her. "Apollo…you're ok."

He nodded, still gagged.

Killian looked down at the silver cuffs on her hands and sighed. "Really? Silver cuffs?" she hissed, "And what's with the sleeping spell? I guess they don't need a veteran hedge witch ruining their plans…"

The Black Magisters were rather enthralled in watching the TV screen and the mess going on down in the arena. "Your stewards?" Michaels was asking, her eyebrows high in curiosity and, just maybe, amusement.

"The Black Magisters," The Harrow announced with a toothy dragon grin.

Killian furrowed her brow. "Todd *does* know that 50 Thousand's defenses are weakened, right? That he's vulnerable to curses and stuff?" she looked up at Apollo, who shrugged.

"50 Thousand Consulting," Todd replied with confidence.

All three of us looked at each other. Apparently not.

"If The Harrow is protected by the Black Magisters," I said quietly, "I bet they'll be casting

Dark Magic at Todd…but he'll think that he's be protected by 50 Thousand's protective spells. And I guess it won't matter that Dark Magic is illegal?"

Apollo shook his head, and I reached up to pull his gag away from his mouth. "Once the challenge has been issued, all of the Dragon's commands and edicts are suspended until it's over."

"Convenient," I grumbled.

We all quieted, and Apollo grabbed the gag back in his teeth as Blake spoke up again. "Alright, ladies and gentlemen, it's showtime. Lock *them* in," he added as they started for the door. In a moment they had headed out into the hallway, leaving the three of us alone without a word.

"We need to follow them, and stop them before they get to Todd," Killian snapped as the door closed and locked. She looked down at her cuffs. "But then there's this. Also, they took my sword."

I raised my eyebrows with a smug look. "Are you telling me that you're completely useless without a sword and magic?"

She bristled. "Of course not, what do you take me for?"

Apollo shook his head. "Even if we had a way out, if we even try—" He gestured to the corner where the Silencers had previous been standing. "—*they'll* kill us."

"You just said all the Dragon's commands are suspended. That includes the death threat, right?"

He blinked at me for a moment, considering it. "That's…true."

Killian didn't need a telling twice; she headed over

to look at the door lock. "Dammit, they put a keyhole on both sides. That's not very OSHA compliant.[31]" Undeterred, she reached down and pulled a knife from her boot.

"How many of those do you have?" I asked.

She glared at me. "A lot. Now shut up for a minute while I get us out of here."

Over on the TV, the dragons were preparing their fight. The other dragons had turned their folding chairs and now watched with great interest to see the fight that was about to unfold.

I gestured in frustration at the TV. "Don't those dragons see what's going on? Didn't they *banish* The Harrow?"

"Old rules, with old loopholes," Apollo replied, "As much wisdom as the dragons are supposed to have, they're really just as fallible as the rest of us. Look at Todd—he doesn't know how much he's screwed himself over."

Killian cleared her throat and he turned to see the office door was now open. "Can we go?"

Apollo was first out the door, with me right on his heels, but Killian put out an arm to stop me. "Hey, wait," she said, in a tone that was uncharacteristically soft. I couldn't help but tense, the memory of our last meeting still fresh on my memory. "I wanted you to know I'm sorry. I made assumptions

---

[31] "OSHA inspectors are often scared by unfamiliar architecture and bright lights. If you encounter one, scream loudly and raise your arms to make yourself appear bigger. If the OSHA employee does not run away, do not engage them further; leave the area quickly." – The Cornucopia Employee Handbook, Page 520 (Dangerous creatures)

about you that weren't true. And I wanted to tell you—"

"I don't care," I said, maybe a little harsher than I'd meant to, "I don't want to hear you're sorry. I want you show me you're sorry by helping me." I ducked under her arm and headed down the hall after Apollo.

We both bumped into him forty feet down the hall, where he was talking rather nonchalantly with one of the Black Magisters.

"I mean, I'm not saying I *wouldn't* go," Apollo was saying, reaching out to dust off the Magister's shoulder with a hand that was inexplicably no longer cuffed, "But let's be real here, I wouldn't be going for the music." He winked at the man, who blushed rather furiously.

"Well, I mean…I dunno if I…um…"

"Make you a deal then," Apollo said, moving in slightly closer and putting a hand on the man's chest just lightly enough to make a point. "If you still feel like you might want my number after you wake up, come hit me up at the coffee shop."

The man nodded slowly. "I…I mean, I…" He seemed to reclaim his sense. "What do you mean by wake—?"

He hit the floor in a heap as Killian slammed his fists into the back of his head. Killian reached down and searched his pockets for keys. "Nice plan," she said lightly, locating the keys and starting to unlock her own cuffs. "He's gonna be one disappointed guy when he wakes up and find out you were just using incubus powers on him."

Apollo held up his arms to indicate his own handcuffs "Still cuffed here, so…no. I'm just that charming."

Killian looked up icily. "Charming enough to turn a bad guy good?"

Apollo winked. "Who said anything about good?"

With our handcuffs opened, Killian picked up the wand and passed it to me as Apollo threw open the arena door and we headed out of the tunnel and into the stands of the Arena, which were now mostly empty. Killian gestured to me. "Do you know any combat spells?" I shook my head. "Jeez, we *need* to work on that. Fine, just stay back here and look threatening."

I looked down at myself and then back at Killian. "Me? Threatening?"

She glared. "Yes. If you're rolling with *me*, you're one threatening motherf—"

Michaels pressed the button on the air horn, which resounded in the open arena for a split second before being drowned out by vicious roars. The two dragons cleared the distance between them in an instant, becoming a blur of claws and wings and teeth that was a spectacle to behold. The magnificence of the creatures in battle was a study in elegance and primal aggression—a balance between the sheer might of the reptilian overlords and the centuries they had spent honing that might into powerful fighting styles that were truly only compatible with the massive reptilian anatomy. It was a style that used flight, ultra-dexterity, and a tough skin that was practically impervious to create some kind of uber fighting style that I could only imagine was made by dragons, for use against dragons.

The challenge had begun.

CHAPTER 22

The Black Magisters were already on their way down the stairs toward the field. Killian shot past me, armed with only her knife, and dove into the crowd. I had not really had the opportunity to see Killian fight until that moment, but the way she moved was a sight so awesome to watch that I actually pulled my eyes away from the reptilian flurry of claws—which was now making its way upward toward the ceiling of the arena—and watched. Apollo, like me, seemed to think that "leave the fighting to Killian" was a great approach, and he stood with his arms crossed, tapping his feet impatiently as if Killian was somehow slacking.

Reaching the back of the group, she grabbed on a Magister's collar and yanked it, flinging him to the ground with a surprised squawk. The noise made the next two closest turn, and Killian's knife split straight down the wand which one of them tried to raise against her; her stylish-yet-conservative heeled boot met the face of the other, and before either of them had a moment to react, the force of her kick made them topple into each other and begin a tumble down the stands of the stadium seating.

The next one was her target, because he was the one who had made the terrible mistake of holding Killian's sword at that moment. He turned just in time to have his scream silenced by one of Killian's hands over his mouth, while her other hand, having sheathed the knife in a split second, now grabbed the hilt of the weapon.

"This is mine, thank you," She said politely. The Magister nodded and let go of it. He then ducked out of his cloak and made a break for it across the row of seats. Killian made no move to stop him.

Blake, to his credit, knew that trouble was rampaging its way down the stairs toward him, and he took the moment to drop something at his feet—a smoke bomb—that went off in an instant; when it had cleared, Blake was making his way across the bottom level of the stands toward the field, his wand out.

Killian turned to face the last Magister within arm's reach. A stocky man with a thick Nordic mustache, he pulled an extendable baton from his pocket and opened it with a snap.

Killian wasn't the slightest bit intimidated; she dove in with a roundhouse kick right to his jaw that, as he staggered back, left him spitting out blood. He swung and caught the redhead in the ribs with his baton, and the resounding *crunch* made both Apollo and I cringe; I made a move to step in and help, but he held me back: "You'll only get in the way. Trust me."

I couldn't fault his logic, I thought, as Killian shrugged off the blow to her ribs and crushed the basket hilt of her sword into the Norseman's face. His impressive mustache was streaked with blood, and as he tried move to make another attack, he found Killian's knife back in her hand and poised at his throat. "Please don't kill me," he spat out.

"I'm not going to kill you, Bob," she said after a second to catch her breath, "Just quit getting in my way." Bob nodded and moved back to clear the route down to the field and the three of us dashed down the stairs as fast as we possibly could toward Blake.

Blake had finally reached the grass of the field and was aiming his wand. High above, Todd was showing a distinct domination of his opponent: The Harrow was suffering a massive gash across his face, and one wing looked like it had been punctured. All considered, Todd looked none the worse for wear, his claws around The Harrow's throat as they tumbled to the ground. "You—will—not—take—my—city—" Todd rasped between exhausted breaths, twisting to put himself atop the wriggling red reptile, and clenched his arms around its throat. He glanced up to see Blake slowly stalking toward him with his wand out. "Blake! Stay back! I've almost got him—!"

I didn't hear the exact words of the terrible curse that was spat from Blake's mouth, but it sounded like an unnatural language. The dragons on the stage, however, seemed to understand exactly what the curse was. Some of them looked highly affronted to have heard it. Blake's wand crackled with lightning and a ray of light, a disgusting shade of lime green, shot from the end of it to strike Todd directly in the heart.

Time seemed to stand still in the stillness that followed. No one spoke or moved; Killian even threw out her arms to stop both Apollo and I. "Chartreuse," she said with a shudder to her voice. "He cast Chartreuse."

"Chartreuse?" I repeated, hoping for some kind of explanation.

"That's the worst curse imaginable, indescribable except by the color of the spell," Apollo said gravely, "It's worse than death."

"But what does it *do*—?"

I was cut off by a deep, raucous laughter that filled my ears. The Harrow, his neck still in Todd's claws, was laughing. "Do you see, you fool? Your own friends have turned against you!"

Todd reached up slowly and patted the spot where the lime-green bolt had hit his chest, his eyes fixed on Blake's wand. "You…cast Chartreuse…at me…?" He sounded utterly horrified to even say the word. Blake puffed himself up but didn't respond.

The Harrow continued to choke out laughter. "Over a hundred years, Todd…all leading up to this moment. You are defeated, Todd. The city is mine—"

There was a sudden sickening sound, like the sound of crunching celery, as Todd returned his claws to the Harrow's neck and wrenched is with all his might. It echoed in the quiet arena and made my stomach flip, and even caused some of the dragons back on the stage to jump back in surprise.

As Todd let go of the Harrow's neck, it was clear that the would-be tyrant was dead.

Blake stumbled backward, his wand raised again. "No! You can't! That was Chartreuse! You can't—"

Todd leapt, his clawed arm outstretched to grab the man, and forced him to the ground, knocking the wand out of his hand and pinning him to the grass. "Explain!" He demanded.

"I can explain it!" I took off toward them in a run, skidding to a halt a short distance from Blake and kicking his wand further away. Todd turned a leery eye on me. "Blake and the Magisters stole one of the Drachmas from 50 Thousand so that all of the protective spells they cast on you would fail and they could kill you with Dark Magic while you were fighting the Harrow because they knew he wasn't powerful enough to defeat you." I had to gasp for breath at the end of my run-on sentence.

Todd looked down at Blake. "Is this true?" he roared.

Blake tried to wriggle away but Todd held him down tighter. "Y-yes!"

Todd looked up again, what looked like realization dawning on his scaled face. "Your father was Vaultkeeper—"

"—and stole the coin, yes, and then he left it to me when he died, but I didn't know until later, I swear."

"B-but you—" Blake had started to panic, the realizations of his plans having completely unraveled very visibly washing over him, "—the coin! Killian—?"

"I never *gave* it to Killian," I explained. "We figured that out earlier. But I *did* give it to you. At the bottom of my delivery bag. I did say I was giving it to you, didn't I? And you're one of the few people who works *for* 50 Thousand, so once you own it, it's effectively back in the company's possession—"

"—and the protections spells come back," Todd finished, turning his eyes back to Blake. "It seems that you underestimated Tom LaFayette's child. Because this young sorcerer has ended your little game."

Blake might have had something to say in response, but whatever it was turned into a scream as the Dragon of Cincinnati enacted a particularly hungry act of justice in a single gulp.

I let out my breath, and it felt like I had been holding it for hours. I watched as Todd returned to the stage and his human form and stood before the arbiter of the fight. Michaels, it appeared, had summoned a rocking chair and was patiently knitting. "It is done," he said softly, but the words still resounded in the stillness of the arena.

Michaels stood up and approached the microphone. "As arbiter of this challenge, I declare—"

"Wait!" Apollo ran over to the edge of the stage and all eyes turned on him. "Can you call off our silencers first? As soon as the challenge is over…we totally escaped the office against your orders and they're going to kill us…"

Todd waved a claw. "Right, right…of course."

Michaels bristled somewhat but recovered from the interruption. "As I was saying, I declare—"

"So who owns the coin now?" Killian asked, perhaps a little too loudly, and she shrunk back as she realized her mistake. "Um…I'll worry about that in a minute…sorry…"

Michaels gave Killian a glare so strong I was afraid the redhead might burst into flames. Clearing her throat, she looked around the room as if to threaten anyone who might dare interrupt her one more time. "I said, I declare the winner of the challenge to be Todd, the Most Venerable Dragon of Cincinnati."

I am not sure what I expected; from cheers to a swelling of heroic background music, to a sudden freeze-frame followed by the ending credits, but I certainly did not expect a chorus of soft golf claps from the dragons on the stage. I glanced at Killian. "Is that it?"

She shrugged. "Dragons are weird."

CHAPTER 23

"Just so we're clear," I asked, "You wouldn't have killed me either way, right?"

The Moddey Dhoo shrugged, the pads of its paws making tiny squeaky sounds on the floor. "Maybe I woulda. Maybe I wouldn't'a."

I patted my bag. "Are you sure? Because if you *wouldn't'a*, then I think I have a chunk of rawhide in here for you..." The Moddey Dhoo shot me a sidelong glare, but I could see the sides of its mouth salivate.

"Oh hush," Killian said, punching the elevator button as we got onboard, and as the doors closed she leaned back against the elevator wall. "I'm going to be really happy once we've got this over with. And a Silencer escort...ugh." She glanced at the Moddey Dhoo. "No offense. I'm sure you're lovely."

"None taken," it replied gruffly, nosing in my bag.

I reached into my pocket, pulling the silver coin

out and running over the details with my thumb. "So weird that all of our problems were caused by something as stupid as a piece of old silver."

"What's that they say about big things?"

The doors of the elevator opened at the lowest sub-level of the building, and ahead of us a short hallway ended in a single beige door. Killian walked up and knocked on it, and a moment later a deep voice responded from the other side. "Who comes here?" it croaked.

"I am Killian Fletcher, the Vaultkeeper!" she announced with pride.

The voice sounded uninterested. "What are you here to do?"

"To deposit a valuable into the vault."

The door clicked and opened slightly. Killian reached out and threw the door wide, revealing nothing but blackness on the other side. A rush of cold air washed over me and made the hairs on the back of my neck stand up on end. Cautiously, I poked my head in, but the whole room seemed to be completely swallowed in blackness. "What—?"

"Explanations later," Killian insisted. "Drop it in."

I took a breath and flicked the coin into the darkness. "Here you go."

The door slammed shut and the voice on the other side let out a sigh. "Have a nice…day."

We turned to go back on the elevator, the Moddey Dhoo having disappeared along with, I suspected, the rawhide from my bag. "If I haven't said it, by the way," I said, hitting the button for the lobby, "Congratulations on the promotion. I didn't think you'd really want to get into taking the job after all that happened."

"It comes with perks," she replied, "And besides, the Wizards didn't want to have one of their own be the Vaultkeeper anymore, which honestly makes sense. Giving the job to security means that you don't end up with one person having too much access to everything."

50 Thousand had indeed gone under some significant changes. There had been a huge change of leadership at the top, along with a massive exodus of all the employees who had not been able to excuse their connection to the Black Magisters. Killian had come out much luckier than most, perhaps with the help of a certain silver coin of which she had taken temporary possession while the Dragon's office conducted its investigation.

"Makes sense." I looked down at my feet.

We stayed in a bit of an awkward silence as the elevator continued to rise. Since the Symposium, Killian and I had been friendly again, but there were still some lingering feelings of hurt that were taking a long time to go away. It wasn't necessarily bad—it was just taking some time to get over and we both had a mutual understanding of that fact.

The elevator doors opened, where Apollo was waiting for us. "Hey hey, what are we doing? We've got a whole weekend to kill, plus I just signed off on a whole week of vacation."

"Is Agatha still mad at you for setting all the high-society *Vulnerabl* on her without notice?"

"Eh, a little. She needs to learn to socialize. So, what about us? What's the plan?"

"Not sure." Killian said, taking out her phone. "I think we're all done here, I just have to clock out on my app…"

Apollo eyed me curiously. "I heard they offered you your job back. Some kind of fast-track to Wizard, right?"

I nodded. "Yeah, but if I'm honest, I was a garbage employee. And Killian's the one who told me that somebody who's good at hedging can make a decent living, right?"

Killian put her phone away. "I suppose so. And Cincinnati's got enough issue that could use a clever hedge mage to shake things up. Keep doing what you're doing, and you might make a name for yourself."

I balked at her as we headed out toward the street. "What do you mean? I saved the whole city from being taken over by an evil dragon!"

She shrugged in response. "Yeah, yeah, that's a start. People don't get famous overnight for killing one big bad guy, you know."

I rolled my eyes and sighed, stepping out into the sunlight. "Well, let's go get something to eat. And no chili-spaghetti," I added to Apollo, who put his hands up in defeat immediately.

"OK, fine. Maybe I can introduce you to goetta…" We started off as a brisk pace, with Apollo naming local places that served breakfast foods.

"If you're going to be a Hedge Magician," Killian said as we stopped for the crossing light, "We're going to need to get you some extra equipment. Maybe a weapon. And," she added with a stern glare, "We need to get you in the habit of staying out of trouble."

"Yeah, right," I replied, and as the light changed I led the way down Walnut Street.

EPILOGUE

Codwell tapped his hoof impatiently, his fluffy ears twitching. "I really hope Andy gets back here, I have a lot of deliveries to go out. Yes I do, yes I do, yes I do."

Acknowledgements

This book began as a National Novel Writing Month project in 2017. It took a lot of planning and the first 50 thousand words were finished by the end of the year. The first draft was completed in January of 2018.

I would like to thank my friends and family, my brothers, and all my fans who supported me and cared enough to encourage my madness.

I want express my deep appreciation for the teachers who encouraged me to be creative, including Moeller, Bounelis, Berard, Brenton, and Palmer.

I would like to thank the Children's Dyslexia Centers of Cincinnati and the Scottish Rite Valley of Cincinnati for the hard work they do.

I want to thank the Fanbuilt Studios community, and especially Lee Tockar, for years of support in my creativity.

I would also like to thank two writers who are far more amazing than I am: M. A. Larson, who taught me that being a writer can be ridiculously awesome, and R. A. Salvatore, who reminded me that "Writing is Life."

About the Author

Sam Swicegood is a native of the Baltimore area now living in Cincinnati, Ohio. He is the son of two US Army veterans who bonded over shared nerdy obsessions.

His prior works include science fiction RPG *Cold Start* and a collection of IT short stories called *The Worst End User*. He has been a freelance writer for over a decade, and founded Elsewhere Media in 2014.

He is an active member of Ohio Free and Accepted Masons, N. C. Harmony Lodge No. 2. He is a community activist, avid podcaster, internet dweeb, and redditor. His hobbies include running D&D games, complaining about Ohio weather, accidentally finding new ways to trigger his own anxiety attacks, and being a general nuisance.

"Expect nothing. Everything else is a sweet surprise."

—Lee Tockar

CPSIA information can be obtained
at www.ICGtesting.com
Printed in the USA
LVHW031833021118
595753LV00001B/40/P